# MAD EILEEN

ANNE STOTTER

Copyright © 2024 by Anne Stotter

ISBN 979-8-882822-09-4

All rights reserved.

No part of this book may be reproduced in any form or by any electronic or mechanical means, including information storage and retrieval systems, without written permission from the author, except for the use of brief quotations in a book review.

## ACKNOWLEDGEMENTS

I am especially grateful to my writing colleagues Susan, Dennis and Wendy, for their advice and patient support.

*For my best friend, Basil*

# PART ONE

# ONE
## SHARON FINDS A PROPER JOB
### 2015

There was that mad woman, Eileen, coming down the road, past the cemetery. Drab, grey mac. She was mumbling. Taking little steps. Pausing for ages before crossing the road. Shifting from foot to foot on the kerb, even though there was no traffic.

Sharon remembered her from as far back as when they first moved here, when she was in junior school. Eileen was always wandering around the village, talking to herself. Scary then. Quite bonkers.

Sat on the bench by the bus stop, Sharon was trying to be calm, trying not to fiddle with the ring she was wearing. She took it off and put it in her pocket. She was far too early for the interview. Clerical assistant to the parish council. Could she really do that?

She had carefully dressed in a not-too-gaudy outfit. Denim skirt, not the ripped jeans she lived in. A white tee-shirt that covered her midriff, with one of her mum's jackets over the top. Convenient that they were the same size. White sneakers. She owned heeled sandals which would make her taller, but the weather wasn't warm enough yet. The chunky necklace of wooden beads that she really liked. Her hair, which she called hamster coloured, was newly trimmed into what she hoped was a cute, pixie cut.

Eileen was coming closer. Sharon hadn't actually listened to her before, but she did now. Random words. Numbers.

'Seven, eight, mmm. Crisp packet. Nine.'

Was she just reciting numbers, or counting things? Sharon paid more attention.

Eileen kept close to the hedge, her head down, looking at the ground. She hesitated when she came to a gatepost. 'Ten. Cracked cigarette lighter, fuchsia plastic. Trodden on. Cigarette ends. Don't count, too many. A conversation,' she whispered.

What did that mean? Maybe nothing.

Eileen scurried across the gateway, twisting her head to look each way but keeping it bowed. More small steps took her along the fence, under an overhanging laburnum, to the next driveway. She paused to stare at the tree, where buds were fattening, the golden-yellow colour starting to show.

Gazing at her feet again, Eileen muttered, 'Pearl button. Dandelion. Chocolate wrapper. Twelve.' She crossed the gap. 'Feathers. Pigeon. Fox had it. Or car then fox. No body.'

What was she saying? That the feathers were from a bird hit by a car and the body taken by a fox? Like in that TV programme about urban foxes? Sharon hadn't really believed this was how they lived, the scavenging in plain sight that most people never saw. But perhaps it was true. She smiled. The old bat might know all about how wild animals lived their lives, might even think of them as friends.

Eileen hugged the next, low wall – 'Torn plastic' – then skirted the bus stop opposite, ignoring Sharon completely. Or was that a tiny glance in her direction?

'Coffee. Celandine. Pretty. Tiny zip-lock bag.'

That'll be drugs, Sharon thought.

Eileen passed the two houses that fronted directly onto the pavement, miniature daffodils blooming from a window box. 'Tin lid. Sardines. Sixteen.' On she went.

Sharon looked at her mobile. Time to shift herself.

. . .

She seemed to be the only candidate. Perhaps they were seeing others another time. Two women interviewed her. None of the questions made her feel small; she was encouraged. Though when Mrs Hilary, who was chairman of the parish council, had asked about her long-term plans, she'd blurted out, 'I can't really make any if I don't get a decent job to start me off.' She wished she'd been able to stop herself. Those sharp comments she came out with often made people wince. But they didn't seem put off. Mrs H had actually smiled at her. They said they'd let her know.

The village hall complex included the library, and, as Sharon came out, there was Eileen again, standing on tiptoe, peering through the rain-spattered window, too small to see in easily.

'Can I help you?' Sharon asked, putting on her waterproof jacket. Might talking to people like Eileen become part of what she did, if she got the job?

Eileen looked wary but asked, 'Library. Is it open?'

Sharon didn't know. She went over to read the noticeboard by the door, wondering why Eileen hadn't done that herself. Maybe she couldn't read.

'Sorry, no, it's not. Actually, that's interesting. It's now only open three half-days a week. That's not much. The next time is Wednesday, ten o'clock.'

Eileen dropped her head again, looking uncomfortable.

Sharon smiled and waited a moment.

Eileen drifted away, mumbling quietly, 'Five zips.'

Sharon fastened her coat then stopped, looking down at herself. 'So there are,' she said aloud.


Two weeks later, Sharon started work with the parish council. It was a more substantial post than the couple of things she'd done since leaving school. Daunting. Almost straightaway, there was a council meeting, and Mrs Broom, the clerk, was on holiday. A long agenda. She'd looked at previous ones. Items that came up repeatedly and others carried over month after month. Decisions seemed to take forever.

'Just concentrate on taking the minutes,' Mrs Broom had said. 'No one will expect more. They know you're new. And I'm Janice, by the way.'

That was reassuring, but, on the day, she felt panicky, certain Janice normally did a lot more than just scribble down notes. And she wasn't at all confident about taking the minutes anyway. How could she write fast enough? They'd see she didn't have a clue. Rats. Should have said she couldn't start until Mrs Broom got back. She gritted her teeth.

At least she'd met three of them before, and those three arrived first. Old Councillor Jenkins had been around for years. He was okay. Ish. He'd helped organise the resurfacing of the jitty by their house, she remembered. The villagers used it a lot, but the land was owned by the publican, who was near to being bankrupt. Mr Jenkins planted his enormous bulk on a chair, which groaned. She'd not seen him close up before. He was sweaty, with out-of-control clothes. Pringle sweater, shirt coming adrift, collar rumpled, worn shoes, trousers concertinaed despite hefty braces. He looked like an old clown. Bifocals that he kept pushing back up his nose. His blotchy scalp showed through his damp-looking, wispy white hair. She looked away.

The chairman, Mrs Hilary, arrived next. A tiny, neat woman, she was dressed in blues, greens and lemon yellow. She talked in little bursts, and bobbed her head as she did so, like a budgerigar.

And then Sharon's ex-teacher, Mr Johns. He looked less fierce than she remembered in class. Others straggled in, chatting, and took their places.

Mrs Hilary looked up from sorting her papers and said loudly, 'Well, we seem to be quorate and it's past seven-thirty, so let's get started.' She turned to Sharon, whom she'd put next to her. 'This is Sharon Weeks, everyone, our new clerical assistant.' She introduced the other councillors. 'Sharon, everyone's names are on the minutes for the last meeting. Which you've got?'

Sharon found them in her pile of papers and gave a thumbs up.

• • •

Not long after they'd got going, a commotion in the corridor outside silenced everyone and they looked at Sharon, so she went to investigate. The caretaker was almost shouting. Eileen again. She had a vacant look and was mumbling to herself, continuing through his protests as if she couldn't see or hear him. What was this about? Sharon hesitated to close the door behind her, worried she might miss something for the minutes, didn't know what to do. Then Eileen turned around and walked out.

The caretaker shrugged and said, 'Mad as a box of frogs, that one.'

Sharon grinned at him. But was that true? She slipped outside for a moment to watch this small, old woman, in her ancient, colourless clothes, work her hesitant way down the street. She'd always avoided and ignored her in the past like everyone else and might have said the exact same thing as the caretaker. Now, she was wondering. She vaguely remembered something awful had happened to Eileen, must remember to ask about her.

Back in the meeting, she wrote herself a note.


Sharon wasn't surprised that Mr Johns talked a lot. She hadn't forgotten his monologues at school.

They eventually reached 'any other business' and he raised his hand to speak. He told them he'd recently walked along the mile of the main street, making notes about the front gardens.

'They're mostly tarmac, paving and gravel, less than half of the area planted, not even lawn or low-maintenance shrubs. There's enough standing for far more cars than are there. We've never been competitive in "Village in Bloom", but now it's dire. What do people think? Might something be done? Anyone have any ideas?'

Several voices responded.

'It's better if cars are parked off the street.'

'There's not a lot we can do if people are too lazy, or don't have time to garden.'

'My neighbour, when he put his house on the market, was

advised by the estate agent to lay some extra hard standing, and they increased the asking price.'

Mr Johns replied, 'And then, when everyone's done that, and it looks grim, the prices drop again. But it's not just about appearances. It affects lots of things. One example – rainwater runs straight into the surface drains from hard standing, causing flooding. Remember what happened on the corner by the pub, last winter?'

'Less messy than refuse and weeds.'

'But weeds are better and healthier. Water drains through earth. Plants circulate water back into the air. Leafy things help settle dust, absorb pollutants. And, of course, we need them to convert carbon dioxide into oxygen.'

Sharon instantly remembered Mr Johns' biology lessons at Chestnut Drive. In class, kids would be rolling their eyes. Here, the councillors were more polite, but some shifted in their seats.

Mrs Hilary actually looked up at the ceiling. She said, 'Another one of your environmental campaigns? To your credit, of course.'

Wry smiles were exchanged, out of Mr Johns' sight.

Mrs Hilary sat up straight and said, 'We have had some discussion about this kind of issue before, and we all know there are no simple answers. I think we'd agree we need to know a bit more if we're to consider any action. Such as – are there systems for recording such things, so we can keep track? What are the back gardens like? Can we find out what's been done elsewhere? You clearly want to take this further, and I think it's worth pursuing, so perhaps, if you've the time, you might write a report, for circulation and more thorough debate at a later date?'

He nodded, half smiling, looking pleased.

Much of the meeting disappeared into a dull blur. Sharon hoped she could decipher her notes afterwards. She needed to read up on planning regulations so she could understand what they were talking about. The process seemed so complicated, and there were so many applications. Also, she wasn't sure she could place them all. She'd thought she knew the large village but in all the years she'd lived there, she now realised, she'd never explored every corner. She'd better get a large-scale OS map and walk the roads she'd never needed to go down, and all the little cul de sacs.

A week later and Sharon had finished typing the minutes, incorporated Mrs Hilary's amendments and additions, and was beginning to feel less overwhelmed. The daily problems were easier to deal with than she expected, since someone, often Mrs Hilary herself, popped in most days.

The money side was baffling, and such large sums were involved. Ten thousand pounds a year from the wind farm. What was that about? Was it a bribe, did it help get planning permission? Was it compensation for harm? Though they claimed the benefits of green power far outweighed the costs – money, materials, the blot on the landscape. And, apparently, the council struggled to find uses for the dosh. It was a fair amount, which you'd think would be great, but it might disappear after a while, couldn't be relied on long term. And there weren't enough worthwhile one-off projects to spend it on. They'd talked about a play area for the proposed country park. Mr Johns was keen on a footpath by the stream, trees, a new lake and a picnic area.

The lake suggestion stirred people up. Between them, the councillors had a whole range of opinions, from 'What a lovely idea!' to 'That just wouldn't be safe. What about children? Wouldn't it need to be completely fenced in?'

In the meeting, Mr Johns had said firmly, 'There have been lakes in parks forever and the risk is really very small. Think of the steep sides and deep water of the canal locks and no one's proposing fencing them off. It could have a shallow edge; we could take school groups for dipping sessions.'

As the meeting disbanded, he asked Sharon if she walked the local footpaths.

'Footpaths?'

He smiled and took her over to the illustrated village map on the wall. 'Here, skirting to the south. There, taking you past the sewage works and over to the canal? Though they're not very obvious on this map.'

'Oh. Right.' How embarrassing she'd never noticed them. And there seemed to be quite a few dashed, green lines.

'I'll take you to explore some time, if you like.'

He wasn't telling her, like he would have done at school. He was asking. It would be rude to refuse. She nodded.

# TWO
## SHARON SETTLES IN

It was a relief when Janice was back. Sharon could quiz her about the council members, what their interests and quirks were, and how best to deal with them.

The worst of them was Mrs Freestone – 'call-me-Jane'. She was a thick-set woman who wore clothes in stone colours – grey, beige, brown – and chose jersey fabrics that stretched unflatteringly over her broad hips. She had such fuddy-duddy ideas, even though she didn't seem that old. She was prejudiced too. In the hubbub before the second council meeting, Sharon heard her say, 'These people who think they're so Christian, but support gay marriage…' Mr Johns grinned when he saw Sharon's 'screwy' gesture behind Jane's back.

That next council meeting, as Mrs Freestone sat down, she put her big ugly bag down on a chair and it fell off, tipping everything across the floor. Sharon helped her scoop things up. A screwdriver, wet-wipes, scissors, a tape measure, tweezers, a sewing kit, all sorts of stuff. It must have weighed a ton. Some of the treasure re-appeared during the meeting. A tissue, when Mr Jenkins had a coughing fit, a paperclip to secure Mr Johns' bundle of papers, despite him trying to stop her. She was obviously aiming to be helpful, but she made Sharon squirm.

She would say things like, 'Don't mind me, I know my opinion can't count for much, but had you considered…?' An odd combination of self-deprecation and domination.

Domination. Sharon had seen Mr Freestone earlier that day, he'd dropped his wife off at the office. He had a thin comb-over, was fat and beige like her. An awful picture of the pair of them in bed loomed up in Sharon's mind, so vivid she had to excuse herself, spluttering.

She escaped to the loos, and sat on the lid of the toilet, suppressing her laughter, mopping her eyes with a wad of toilet tissue. Solid Mrs Freestone was sitting astride her husband, massive, mauve-mottled breasts hanging almost to her thighs, hip bones buried deep underneath thick folds of flesh, her face a picture of triumphant joy. Mr Freestone wore a bra, fitting nicely over flabby man-boobs, a suspender belt pushed high on his hairy belly, the stocking connectors dangling, his face contorted and purple.

Sharon finally got her act back together. She mentally filed the ghastly, hilarious scene. It would help her cope. She assigned Jane Freestone the nickname Domina. She liked nicknames.

'Think of them on the toilet,' her mother had said when Sharon was bullied at school. 'Everyone has to go to the toilet.' Sharon had moved on from toilets.


Sharon eventually remembered to ask her mum: 'Lizzie, did something happen to Eileen, to make her so strange?'

She told her, 'Eileen had a daughter who disappeared. I'm sure I've told you that before.'

Of course. Sharon remembered that time a girl arrived at school all upset because the mad lady had grabbed her, sobbing, 'Alice, my Alice!' and wouldn't let her go. The girl's friends had to shake Eileen off. These days, in the street, kids might snigger at Eileen, but they knew not to go near her. Sharon asked, 'You know any more?'

'Eileen lived with her mum. She was always quiet, kept herself to herself. It was a shock when she cheerfully became pregnant. No one had seen her with a man, and she never talked about one.'

'Wow.'

'Mmm. She had a little girl, Alice, and was lovely with her, would sing to her as she pushed the pram. When Alice could walk and talk, they'd chatter and laugh, swinging down the street together. Mrs Judd, that's the woman lives round the corner from the Mallory's, said they made quite a pretty picture.'

'Wasn't it a really big deal, in those days, to be a single mother?'

'Yes, it was. Though this was the mid-sixties, things were changing. But Eileen seemed oblivious to all that anyway. Then Alice disappeared when she was seven. She was never found. Horrible. Eileen fell apart and got sectioned. She was in hospital for ages. I guess you never recover from something like that.'

It turned out old Mr Jenkins seemed to know Eileen fairly well. He told Sharon, 'Eileen was always rather peculiar, kept to herself. Though she held down a respectable job as a legal secretary once. Really sad, she had a severe breakdown. Yes indeed. She's better now. Comes round to see our Maggie. Alice and she used to play together, around when Maggie was diagnosed.' But he was in a hurry, he turned away, officiously collected his papers, and left Sharon with more to wonder about.

Maggie must be their daughter. She'd not heard the name before. What diagnosis did she have, then? She recalled seeing Mr Jenkins with a stout, learning-impaired woman. Was that Maggie?

Eileen Mallory – no one used her surname, Sharon hadn't even known what it was until her mother told her – was one of the regular visitors at the council office. She would drift in, talking to herself. She was frequently to be found loitering by the library, often there early, before anything was open.

Arriving for work one morning, Sharon said hello.

Eileen blinked at her and replied, 'I wanted to return my book, but I'm too soon.' In her hand was the latest Barbara Kingsolver, *Flight Behaviour*.

'That's about butterflies, isn't it?'

'Being in the wrong place. Climate change,' Eileen volunteered.

Sharon was amazed. And ashamed that she'd thought Eileen illiterate and stupid. Just because she was odd. She conjured up an image of her own mother, how strange she looked these days. She should learn to stop judging by appearances. She should know better.

She looked out for Eileen after that, intrigued. Though the occasions when Eileen actually spoke to her were few and far between.

# THREE
# SHARON WALKS THE FOOTPATHS WITH GEOFFREY

She didn't have much idea what to wear, the day of their first walk. She'd checked the weather forecast, and at least wasn't expecting rain. Mr Johns, Geoffrey – she still didn't know what to call him – had said 'comfortable clothes' and 'walking boots'. Sharon knew that her red patent leather Doc Martens weren't what he meant, but they were all she had.

He looked at her feet and said, 'I hope they're more comfortable than they look.'

'They'll have to do,' she replied, and he smiled, he didn't really seem that bothered. He wasn't like she expected. And he seemed to be happy with her chatting with him. Though that was a bit weird since he was old enough to be her dad.

She thought they must have looked odd as they walked along, not just because of the age difference. He was taller than her, and walked with the relaxed, loping stride of someone used to roaming the countryside. His clothes were easy-care, unostentatious, though not drab. He was wearing a sea-green jersey top under a grey fleece, the shirt co-ordinating with grey-green socks, visible above his well-worn, laced boots. He had no hat or gloves, but a scarf with a striped weave in blues, greens and greys. When it warmed up, the early morning frost disappearing, he unwound it from his neck and tucked the fringed ends in his pockets. His dark hair carried a soft wave that stopped it flopping in his eyes. She noticed that the back – she saw a lot of his back view – where it came down onto the nape of his neck, was carefully cut.

In contrast to him, she found herself scuttling along to keep up. She couldn't find a steady rhythm. She climbed awkwardly over stiles, stumbled on tree roots. And her outfit felt silly. Her red bouclé top, under a black, quilted satin jacket, didn't quite meet her skinny jeans, and matched neither her bobble hat nor the boots. Her string of large beads, shaped like daisies, swung violently from side to side. She'd not realised that would happen, and it was annoying.

But the walk turned out more interesting than she expected, partly because of Mr Johns going on about stuff. She'd never heard of geocaching, for example, and was fascinated by the contents of the sandwich box when he pulled it out of its hiding place, tucked away between the footpath signpost and the gate. Inside there was an earring, a seaside postcard, a yellow and brown shell he said was from a snail, some buttons, other odds and ends.

'You'll have to explain,' she said.

'There are lots of these caches, all over the place. Biscuit tins, Tupperware boxes. There's a website. You find each one using GPS co-ordinates and you're supposed to leave something, a trinket, something worth nothing much. Some items are travelling across the country.' He picked a small notebook out of the box. 'See, the notebook says that this coin –' he held it up – 'is on its way from a village down south to one in North Yorkshire, where a grand-daughter lives.'

She took it from him and saw it was a farthing. Lizzie had some of them. She had told her the bird on it was a wren.

'Anyone going in the right direction might pocket it then leave it at a different cache further down-track.' A pearl button, a Snoopy brooch. Strangely, at the bottom, under another couple of tattered postcards, there was a new-looking pink mobile phone. Mr Johns thought it must have been left by mistake and said he'd hand it in to the police, returning everything else to the box which he put back in its hidden spot.

The footpath they started on was a muddy track between fields, trees by the fences either side, green buds showing. He talked about the birdsong they could hear. It didn't mean much. She recognised many of the names and had seen a robin sing, and starlings whistle and chatter on the tree by the kitchen window at home, but had never thought of recognising songs. There were so many different types he claimed to hear.

'That loud, musical trill is a wren. Look, there he goes, fast and low down.'

All she saw was a flash of brown. She'd not thought a wren was a real bird.

'Hear that one? A chiff-chaff. Named for its call.'

Past Sawyer's farm, there was a big, old barn, the walls made of corrugated iron painted dusky red. On each side the roof flared out to shelter additional space. It looked elegant. She smiled at herself. Everything around looked so very green and fresh.

He pointed out the hawthorn buds. 'They should be out soon,' he said. 'Next month. May?'

'So that's why it's called May blossom?'

He grinned at her.

They saw a pair of big rabbits racing across an open field in a wide arc. He said they were hares. A green woodpecker, looking like the pterodactyl in her childhood story book. Then, where the field margin merged into a copse, there was a dog that morphed into a muntjac deer.

When he told her what it was, she couldn't stop herself coming out with, 'I've only got your word for that.'

Fortunately, he laughed.

She said, 'We'll be seeing badgers next.'

He smiled patiently at her. 'They're nocturnal. You really don't know what's out there, do you?'

It was true. That's probably what made the walk so interesting, him explaining stuff all the time.

They sat on a bench, and he dug out two apples for them, retrieved the geocache mobile phone and switched it on. It still had enough battery. No password. He found 'home' in its contacts list and called the number. He got an answerphone: 'Mr and Mrs Jenkins are not available to take your call. Please leave a message after the tone.' He ended the call and looked at the 'home' number.

'I should have recognised it if I'd looked: Stuart Jenkins. Who'd have thought?'

'Weird,' said Sharon. 'He's not very good with technology, is he? Doesn't even like emails. A mobile. Pink too. Perhaps it's his wife's. What's her name?'

'Barbara,' Mr Johns replied. 'She used to help with his accountancy business.'

A dull, boring accountant. That figured.

They called in on their way back. It was an old house with a blue front door, an original, black-painted bellpull and a brass door knocker and letter box. Sharon noticed the smears of cleaner round the edges of the brass fittings. Must be a pain to keep them shiny. Mr Jenkins answered the door. He beamed, pushing his specs back in place, when they showed him the phone. It belonged to his daughter, Maggie.

'Where had she secreted it?' he asked. They told him and he laughed, his chins shaking. 'We were that way not so long ago, though I didn't see her with the box. She's like a jackdaw, she conceals glittery things. We bought it for her hoping we'd be able to teach her how to use it, in case she became lost, not that she goes out alone. Suffice it to say, she couldn't operate it. We should have known. I struggled enough myself when they first came out. But always optimistic; has to be that way.'

Sharon was puzzled and it must have shown. 'You haven't met our Maggie? Let me introduce you.' He led them inside and into a broad sitting room with thick carpet and thickly cushioned, stout furniture. Maggie was sitting folding sheets of paper. She had plump arms and bulging ankles, visible below her loose tracksuit bottoms. She might have been anything between forty and sixty. Her face was smooth – no worries to wrinkle it maybe. Maggie looked up and smiled at her father, showing brown peg-shaped teeth in lumpy, pink gums.

Sharon remembered the earlier conversation she'd had with Mr Jenkins. He'd said something about Maggie, and Eileen's daughter Alice. Did he say they were at nursery school together? They must have been the same age, then.

'Did you say she used to play with the little girl who disappeared? Was she also …?' Sharon wished she hadn't started that question. She was always blurting out her thoughts. She could have kicked herself.

'No. Most certainly not.' Mr Jenkins looked flustered. He hesitated, gazing sadly down at his daughter. 'Alice was a charming, bright child.'

# FOUR
## SHARON GETS INVOLVED AFTER THE CRASH

A man appeared at the hatch one morning, in a state. Sharon didn't recognise him – a newcomer to the village, she suspected. A builder's truck loaded with bricks had mounted the pavement outside his house to avoid a parked car and cracked three paving slabs. He had photos on his phone of the damage, which he insisted be taken as evidence. Sharon gave him the council's email address, so he could forward the pictures. Though she'd no idea what she was supposed to do with them. Not that he was the first to complain. There were so many building projects, it was getting to be a daily event, dealing with the moaning. Damage, heavy traffic, dust, noise.

One woman brought in her two young children, insisting, 'Something's got to be done. There'll be an accident, else.'

But what could be done?

She was right, though. Sharon took the call when a woman phoned, just after they opened at eight. 'Is Stuart Jenkins there? There's been a crash. We need his help.'

'I'm sorry? What?'

'Eileen's place. A lorry's taken out her front garden wall.'

'You want Mr Jenkins? Don't you need an ambulance? Or the police?'

'No, sorry. No one's hurt. We might need the police, I suppose. But it's Eileen. She's hysterical. We thought he might know what to do. He's helped her in the past. His wife said he'd gone down to you.'

'Right. Okay. But he's not here yet. I'll tell him as soon as he arrives.'

He was there within minutes. He dumped his briefcase when he heard the news and rushed off.

He returned a couple of hours later, still looking flustered. 'It was just before school. There were children all over the place, lucky none were on that bit of pavement at the time. The brakes failed on a ready-mixed-concrete truck, the drum still rotating, making a dreadful noise, the driver trying to avoid stopping it and having the load set.'

'Oh, dear,' said Janice.

'Yes, indeed. Inevitable, with the racket and the awful mess, Eileen is grievously upset.'

Sharon still didn't understand why they called for him.

'I've not seen her that distressed in years,' he said, seeming upset himself. 'She was wandering about, extracting fragments of broken plants out of the rubble – it looked as if she was trying to stick them back together. Talking to herself. Yes indeed, making no sense at all. Not a bit of sense. Happily, the man who came was very good with her.'

Apparently, Mr Jenkins had a phone number to get emergency psychiatric help for Eileen. Crisis intervention, he called it.

Sharon went to look at the wreckage in her lunch break. The truck was gone by then. It must have needed a massive breakdown vehicle. Barriers had been put up to keep pedestrians off that section of pavement.

Eileen's had taken the brunt of the hit, the rest of the old terrace pretty much unscathed. Her garden was a total mess. It looked like the lorry had come in at an angle. The hawthorn tree on the left had half its branches ripped away, flower petals were scattered like snow over the soil and the road, along with chunks of brick and other wreckage. Her wooden front gate was completely smashed. Some of the seashells lining her front path were broken. A pot of flowers, right up by the front door, was shattered. And a window was cracked. It all looked awful.

A couple of teenagers were taking photos on their phones. 'Looks like a bomb's hit it,' one said.

The girl was right. And it would be a lot of work to make it good again.

Just a few days later, the worst of the rubble was gone, the window re-glazed and the path properly cleared so that it was safe to get to Eileen's front door. Sharon heard that Mr Jenkins had contacted Eileen's insurers and got things moving – Eileen had no family to help out. The plants looked worse, though, all battered and wilted. And she could see that there was still plenty of wreckage left behind. She realised she hadn't seen Eileen in the streets since it happened. Could she not face going out? Was she ill?

Mr Jenkins appeared in the office. 'I'm getting together a working party to help Eileen. Seeking volunteers. It shouldn't be too onerous.'

There was only her, Janice and Geoffrey Johns in the office. No pressure, thought Sharon.

'To do what?' Mr Johns asked.

'First, get the debris out of the garden. The large pieces of detritus are gone, but it's wreaked havoc on the soil, probably needs the worst of it dug out, thrown away and replaced with bags from the garden centre. The dead plants can go on her compost heap.'

So, he knew she had a compost heap.

'Once the wall's been rebuilt, it'll all need replanting. Though she might be well enough by then to do at least some of that herself. We'd surely have to ask her what she'd want.'

Eileen was ill then.

'Okay. But the new soil should probably wait until after the brickwork's done.' Mr Johns seemed to be volunteering. 'When were you thinking for the clear-up?'

'The weekend, if the weather's dry.'

Janice said, 'Not me, then, I'm afraid. My in-laws are visiting.' She pulled a face.

'I could,' Sharon said. 'I could bring my mum, too. She knows about gardens, which is more than I do.'

As she spoke, Sharon suddenly had a picture of Craig. He would have laughed at her. 'Where's the fun in that?' he'd have mocked. But she didn't need to bother any more about what he thought. He was history. She was glad she'd closed her Facebook account and changed her mobile number.

She asked, 'How is Eileen, do you know? I haven't seen her out and about.'

Mr Jenkins looked glum, settled his glasses back up his nose. 'No. She's been quite disturbed, hasn't coped at all well. The doctor had to put her back on medication. Though she seemed a bit more coherent when I saw her yesterday and understood when I talked about people coming to help with the disarray. Pleased. Well, I hope she was. Difficult to tell with her.'

Sharon worried that Eileen might do something, scream at them perhaps, if they invaded. Vivid imagination, me, she thought. Think positive. 'It'd surely help her if it looked less ghastly. Perhaps find some pots, put some temporary, pretty stuff in?'

'Good idea,' said Geoffrey.

'I'll get Lizzie onto that, then.'

They didn't see Eileen at all, on the Saturday. The two men shovelled the most contaminated earth into bags, carried them off in a wheelbarrow. Mr Jenkins had arranged to add them to a skip down the road. Fat old Jenkins was stronger than Sharon would have guessed. But he got all sweaty, great wet patches under his arms. Lizzie was managing to move around okay – the MS sometimes allowed her a good day. But she couldn't easily get down on her knees, and certainly couldn't do any digging. She went off early, with Stuart driving, to buy stuff at the garden centre to go along the front path. A trestle table had appeared from somewhere, a crate and a cushion. She sat filling pots with compost and deciding which plants would go with which. It was down to Sharon to pick out rubble and damaged greenery. There was little that looked worth saving.

The late-spring sunshine was cheerful. The day warmed up enough to take off a layer. Sharon was pleasantly surprised. She'd thought it would be hard, grubby work, and depressing too. But the bright sunlight, the exercise, and the feeling of them doing something useful together lifted her mood. By mid-morning they were all on first-name terms.

'I'd not seen you as a gardener,' Sharon said to Mr Johns, now definitely Geoffrey.

'I've been looking after my mother's patch since my father died. That's years ago. Got to be a habit, I suppose.' He paused, 'What happened to your dad, if you don't mind me asking?'

''S fine. It was a long time ago. I was only little. He was on his motorbike. He was hit by a car. What about yours?' It was only when she'd said it she thought he might think it cheeky, but he wasn't bothered.

'Heart attack. I'll tell you the story, if you're interested. It's quite funny in an awful sort of way.'

Why not? She'd not brought her music because she thought it'd be rude to wear the ear buds. Might as well listen to Geoffrey. She grinned and nodded. 'Go on, then. We've hours of this stuff to do.'

'It was 1992, I was in Oxford, doing my research stint. One afternoon, my mother phoned me. Lucky I happened to be working at home. "I don't know what to do," she said. "Your father's dead. I don't know what to do."' Geoffrey's voice was a high-pitched singsong.

Mean, Sharon thought, mocking her like that.

'In a daze, I drove home to find her hunched in his armchair, in the sitting room. I always hated that room. Dark brown George and Mildred furniture, horrible Toby jugs on the mantlepiece. She was just sitting there, in the cold, her hands white.'

'The poor thing.'

He shivered. 'I found a heater – one of those dreadful single-bar electric things, you might never have seen one. And a blanket. I made her some cocoa.

'She told me she'd been angry with him going on about the birds, looking out of the window through his binoculars, not listening to her. She'd reminded him about the dripping tap, and he'd laughed and said, "But did you tell me when I was paying attention?" It made her cross.' Geoffrey paused.

'Hang on a minute.' Sharon fetched another pair of bin bags and doubled them up. She didn't want the heavy bits she was collecting to tear through. She looked about; there was so much more to do. She caught his eye. 'So then what?'

'Ah. Yes. She told him she was sick of it. He went out into the garden. She didn't look for him till lunchtime. Then she saw him from the kitchen window, sprawled on the path, face down. It must have happened much earlier because when she got to him, he was cold and stiff, and a snail had crawled onto his thumb.'

'Eugh!'

'I was listening to her, thinking I had no idea about what might need to be done. It was ages before I thought to ask where he was.' He gave a hollow laugh. 'She pointed out of the window. Dad was still lying on the garden path. She hadn't called anyone but me.'

'Wow.'

Geoffrey went quiet.

'Was he religious, like your mum?'

'No. But that didn't stop her. Funeral mass and everything.' He grimaced. 'She said things like, "He won't have been in a state of grace, but he wasn't a bad man, so he'll be in purgatory, he won't have gone to hell."'

What was purgatory?

'Dad had deftly ducked and weaved when she talked about God. He didn't argue with her, but he didn't agree either. He would change the subject, without her noticing.'

'So they got on okay?'

'Mmm. S'pose so. I used to wonder how on earth they got together. I've never asked.' His story seemed to be finished.

Sharon was chucking broken shells into her sack.

He said, 'I can't imagine where those came from.'

'All smashed,' Sharon commented.

'There are always scallop shells in the trash at the restaurant,' said Geoffrey. 'I wonder if she'd like some of them?'

What restaurant is that? Sharon wondered.


Later, Geoffrey regaled her with stories about being brought up a Catholic. 'As a lad, she took me to church; I'd been baptised. But, as I grew up, I struggled with it all. Wasn't compatible with science and logic. I "lost my faith", she'd have said.'

'I should count myself lucky I never had any church stuff, you think?'

'Mmm. It was all so illogical. There was a saint's day in the autumn when, if you went to church and said one Our Father, one Hail Mary and one Glory Be, you could transport a soul out of purgatory.'

That word again. Sharon interrupted him to ask, 'What's purgatory?'

'A sort of a staging place between death and heaven.'

'Right.'

'So, the prayers would get a soul into heaven. My mother would take me to church, and we'd pray two or three times, but then we'd leave, she'd do the shopping and we'd go home for dinner. It didn't make sense. If you could achieve something so wonderful with such a simple exercise, why didn't people spend the whole twenty-four hours in and out of church, praying?'

Sharon could see his point.

'You know about wealthy people endowing monasteries? The monks would pray for their benefactors after their death, to move them faster into paradise. I thought, isn't that buying your way into heaven? I was sure that had to be wrong but didn't dare say so.'

Sharon was losing interest. But she was rescued. Lizzie came over and sent her home to fetch a big thermos of tea, make a pile of sandwiches and bring the cake she'd baked. There was a conversation about whether they should knock on the door to offer some to Eileen, but they decided not to. If she were up to company, she'd have already come out to say hello.

By teatime they'd done as much as they could. The garden looked a bit less ravaged and depressing.

At the end of the following week, Eileen appeared at the office. She was carrying a wide pot packed with purple and yellow pansies. She must have walked very carefully with it the half length of the village. Plants from her back garden, perhaps.

She said, 'Three, three,' as she put the pot on the lip of the hatch, then went away.

Sharon and Janice looked at each other.

'Oh dear. What does that mean?' asked Janice. 'She's so strange.'

Sharon got up to have a look. Three? There were four people there on the Saturday. They put in only the one day. Oh well, maybe it's just that Eileen's even madder than usual. Then she noticed, 'Three different pansies – look!' she said, grinning. So not that mad. It was good that Eileen was out and about again.

July, and Sharon had the box of plants her mother had put together and was taking them over to Eileen now the wall was rebuilt. Geoffrey had added a carrier bag of scallop shells to the load. And there she was, standing on Eileen's step with her hands full. The cardboard box was sagging where the damp had worked through, so she had her arms underneath to stop it collapsing, the handles of the plastic carrier bag digging painfully into the crook of her left elbow. Awkward, but she managed to grab the knocker. She waited, hoping the old lady was in.

Lizzie had tried to organise a few people to help restore the ruined garden but had no joy. Geoffrey was busy at his mother's. Stuart's wife was poorly, some problem with her back. Her mum couldn't find anyone else prepared to help. On that earlier Saturday when the four of them worked at Eileen's, several neighbours appeared and made encouraging noises, but they didn't get involved. No one even offered a cup of tea. It was as if people wanted to pretend Eileen wasn't there.

Sharon knocked again. Eventually the door opened a foot or so and she could see Eileen's bright eyes peering at her through the gap. 'Plants,' she said, 'Mum thought you might like…'

Eileen didn't move, was looking suspicious.

Sharon could feel the wet seeping through her rucked-up sleeves; she must be getting all muddy. 'It's Sharon,' she said, 'from the village office. Plants for you.'

Eileen's mouth was working but she still didn't speak.

Sharon shifted her position a little. 'Oh God.' The soggy cardboard was giving way.

'No God,' said Eileen, her forehead creasing in a frown. But she did open the door properly just as Sharon, struggling, had to put everything down. She freed her arm from the plastic bag, rubbed the red grooves it had made in her skin. She righted the plants, hoped they were okay. They didn't look too bad. As she stood up again, wet compost dribbled down one leg.

Eileen looked blankly at the heap deposited at her feet.

Sharon couldn't think what to say. Those small conversations she'd had before had her imagining she could do this. But perhaps, her arriving unannounced like this, it was too much for the poor old thing. She took a step back, looking carefully at the woman's face. Eileen seemed upset. That wasn't what was supposed to happen. Should she just have left everything for her to find?

Eileen leant towards the gift, gazing at it, her arms stretched down. Her fingers fluttered.

Was that a thank you? Or was she being waved away? Sharon managed to say, 'Shall I leave them with you?'

Eileen smiled.

# FIVE
# SHARON TOURS THE VILLAGE WITH GEOFFREY

Geoffrey came in the office after school to talk to Janice about the housing developments. Sharon made them tea, listening in.

She said, in a lull in the conversation, 'I've lived in this village most of my life, so I thought I knew my way around, but I don't know where half these sites are.'

Geoffrey turned to look at her. 'I can't place all of them either, so I was going to have a look, before the next council meeting, make sure I knew what I was talking about. Want to come too?'

She'd enjoyed their last trip out, all those months ago, so she agreed. But on the day, he was in a mood, and she was soon wondering if this was such a good idea.

There were six places on their list. One was on the main street, three were tucked away in corners Sharon didn't know, and two sat outside the current boundary, at either end of the mile of village. They walked first to the site at the eastern end of the village, where building had been progressing for some months. A show home was open, and flags were flying. One hundred houses, what she would call posh. There was some paving already, tarmac, gravel and grassed areas, the edges of the turf strips showing. Some amendments to their planning application had been submitted.

'No trees at all,' Geoffrey pointed out.

Perhaps they'll put them in later, Sharon thought.

They returned via the back streets and passed two small sites with little activity, then on to the one on the main road. She'd noticed this one before. It would have been difficult to miss it: high, steel fencing around a ravaged patch of ground. You could see the footprint of the old house, knocked down weeks ago, the rubble carted off in lorries that blocked the traffic. Today they had diggers grubbing up the stumps of large trees. Sharon thought how she hadn't really noticed they were there until they were ripped out; the whole old, shaded garden had been an invisible fixture.

Geoffrey said, 'They're squeezing six dwellings in here. Now the garden's being cleared you can see that there's more space than you'd have guessed. Even so...'

'Cramped,' she said. 'The paperwork says these'll be five bedrooms, three bathrooms, double garages. They'll be able to read each other's computer screens.'

Geoffrey laughed, but half-heartedly, as if his mind was on other things.

They walked on. At the bus stop a bit further down the road stood a familiar figure, JJ Lock. Lank hair in a loose ponytail, a gangster hat shading his eyes from the cool sun, a long, grey gaberdine coat. They both knew him from the school, where he taught music; Geoffrey must see him all the time. Sharon noticed his laced shoes, made of tan leather, with an intricate pattern cut into it – brogues, she thought they were called, expensive. She wondered how the patterns were made. As they passed, he was absorbed in reading a folded magazine and was smoking a cigarette. Most of the smokers Sharon knew were moving on to vaping. He didn't look up but, even so, Sharon was a bit surprised when Geoffrey didn't speak to him. Perhaps he hadn't noticed him. Mr Lock tossed his stub into the bottom of the hedge, to join other litter. Geoffrey noticed that. She heard his intake of breath. She waited.

He said, once they were out of earshot, 'I did a project on

biodegradation of cigarette ends with year seven. Each child had a plant pot, took it home and brought it back full of soil, or potting compost, or sand, or gravel. Different substrates. We staked out a cigarette butt on top of each one and put them outside, where they could get rained on, and the sun could shine on them, to see how long it took for the butts to disappear.' His tone was angry. He was leaning forwards as he walked, his hands clenched at his sides. 'That was last spring. They're still there. The children will have left school, and nothing will have happened. Cigarette filters are made of a type of acetate that never fully breaks down. Degradation takes decades.'

It wasn't cold, but Sharon was aware of her hunched shoulders, her hands in her pockets. It wouldn't look friendly. She made an effort to be polite. 'I thought the filters were made of paper.'

He replied, 'That's what everyone thinks,' making her feel stupid.

Rude man. But she said, 'That explains why they hang around so long. I had noticed that and wondered why.'

He nodded.

She wasn't sure she should be encouraging him today. He was really grumpy. He usually seemed interested in what she said. He mostly behaved as though he knew he wasn't her biology teacher any more. Though today he must have forgotten. And she wasn't totally comfortable with him as a friend, a man friend. He was so old, and he wasn't married. Maybe the fact that he was single was making her wary, though he'd never made anything like a move on her. Actually, she felt safe with him for some reason. Perhaps because of him being a teacher. She looked sideways at him. I suppose he's quite good-looking for his age, she thought. Dark, wavy hair, a ready smile – normally. His clothes fit neatly on what must be a fairly fit body... No. Don't go there.

Geoffrey interrupted her thoughts, 'Boring, I know, but I can't help noticing litter. I think most people haven't a clue about biodegradation. Do they think crisp packets rot down over a week or two? I know, I know. *What else am I supposed to do with it? I can't see a bin... It's harmless, it's just a crisp packet... Everybody else does* it... If they don't make them biodegradable that's not my fault. That last one makes me laugh. I can see damp crisps being popular.'

Wasn't there a pack that was waterproof and biodegradable? He continued, 'And since we're talking about crisps...'

Well, you are, Sharon thought.

'I can bore for England on that subject. Food of the devil... People on benefit buy crisps! The most expensive way to eat potatoes. So delicious with their impregnated fat, they're irresistible. Significant contribution to the obesity crisis. Huh!'

She'd better hide her lunchtime crisps, made a mental note to take the packet home from the office to bin it. She laughed at him anyway. 'I see what you mean about boring for England.' Would he take the hint?

As they continued down the main road Sharon looked at what used to be front gardens, many now paved, tarmacked or covered in gravel. Some late summer flowers were in bloom in the few that were planted; she didn't know what most of them were. Those blue flowers might be Michaelmas daisies, they had some at home. Geoffrey was due to give his report on front gardens soon. She decided not to ask him, today, where he'd got with it.

Geoffrey said, 'Changing the subject slightly, had you noticed that Eileen counts litter? People think she's just mad and says random rubbish, excuse the pun, but she doesn't, she talks about what she sees on the ground. And she handed me this outside the library the other day. I imagine she found it – she didn't say anything, she rarely speaks to me.' He pulled from his pocket a small, shiny, white-metal cylinder, like a cartridge for a fizzy-drinks dispenser, with no label. 'I don't know what it is.'

'Nitrous oxide,' she said with an inward shudder. Craig, rearing his ugly head again.

'Right.' He raised an eyebrow at her but didn't ask how she knew, just dropped it in a bin.

At the western end of the village, past the last houses, there were two fields on the left, sloping gently down to a stream.

Sharon said, 'This is the plot for the three hundred not-particularly-affordable homes – plus another hundred and fifty later, if you believe the rumours. Where the developer leafleted people who lived nearby, asking for their comments?'

He nodded. 'They bought the fields years ago and the farmer's continued to work them, so no one noticed. They've been waiting for the right time. In the past, no one would have thought of an estate here; the bottom section's on the flood plain.'

'You think of it as farmland, and suddenly it isn't any more.' Sharon had seen this view so many times and was now looking at it differently.

'"They've paved paradise, put up a parking lot",' he said ill-temperedly.

She stopped and stared at him.

'Sorry. Before your time? "Big Yellow Taxi", the Joni Mitchell song. Written long before it was obvious what was happening. Clever woman.'

Sharon scuffed her feet in the gravel. She didn't know the song.

'And clever idea, the leaflet, quite nicely done. They asked for opinions, and suggestions about what might be included. Trees, perhaps, I thought, a park. Not that I live near enough to have been asked. Meant they could use any good stuff as evidence of local support for the planning application, have proof that they're "collaborating with the community". I don't know what else they got, but I don't imagine they were happy with the traffic survey some locals did. It showed the junction at the top is grid-locked already at peak times, and this estate could only make it worse.' He was kicking a stone along the verge.

'I think the planning application comes up next month,' Sharon replied.

They walked on down and turned left into a single-track road that passed through trees and then climbed into open countryside. In the tree-shaded section, it was impossible to ignore the rubbish on the verge. Bottles, cans, plastic cartons. Half-buried in the earth, broken and dirty where they'd been driven over. There was builders' waste too. A smashed toilet, part-used sheets of plaster-board, sacks with left-over cement and gravel, old electric fittings... Even more revolting, she noticed condoms draped over the field gate. Outdoor sex, or in cars? Why would anyone hang them up like that? She imagined some gross lads' competition.

Geoffrey said gloomily, 'There are bluebells here in May. Difficult to believe, isn't it? I think they make it look worse, the flowers innocently appearing through the mess. Oh, and here's a favourite.' He pointed to a small, knotted black plastic bag, hung on a twig by its tie-handles. 'It's ugly and offensive. And the poo can't easily decompose, because it's in the plastic. It would be better if they just shifted their dog turds away from where people walk and left them exposed.' He was banging his closed fist against the gate post.

Sharon winced at the word 'turd'.

'A friend who has a dog said it might be left like that for the dog-walker to collect on the way home, so they don't have to carry it the whole time. If that's the case, how come they forget so often? How can they fail to see it, staring them in the face? Maybe they resent being told to pick it up, they're making a protest.'

'Hmm,' said Sharon. More ranting about litter. The man's obsessed.

'On the subject of poo, while I was outside the school, waiting for someone, I heard a man talking to another parent. His children have pets: a dog and a cat and now a corn snake. Did you know they feed pet snakes on mouse carcasses, sold frozen? And they've sanitised the names: pinkies for new-born mice, fluffies if they're older and bigger?'

'Yeuch,' said Sharon, wondering where this gruesome tale was going.

'Anyway, three kinds of animal in their home, smearing their grubby bottoms around, with bugs like toxoplasma, but this man was telling how he'd had the house-martin nests knocked out from under the eaves, because of the mess the droppings make.'

Sharon thought, toxo what?

Geoffrey continued, '"Because of the children", the man said. But that's outside the house! How is it a real risk? I wanted to shake him. He won't have thought that there are only a finite number of sites for house-martins to nest, that he's personally responsible for depressing the numbers of birds, as if there isn't enough already doing that. I despair.'

On the way back, Sharon spotted a kestrel hunting along the verge. She pointed it out to Geoffrey. It hovered, its head held still while its wings and flared tail worked the gusts. It dived, hovered lower for a while, then glid off to patrol further along.

He said, warmth in his voice, 'I never tire of watching them, so skilled, precise. Beautiful.'

Sharon looked sideways at him, plucked up courage. 'That's the first nice thing you've said.'

There was a silence, then, 'I am so sorry. You're absolutely right. I'm still fuming from yesterday, and I've been taking it out on you. Unforgiveable. My mother, as usual. And I should have learnt by now.'

'Religion again?' she asked, remembering him talking before about their differences on the subject.

'Partly. I should be laughing really, it was absurd.' He paused, then decided to continue. 'She tried to set me up with a woman from the church.' He looked up at the sky, squinting.

Sharon had to laugh.

'I should have known. She phoned about another stupid problem with the house, like she does all the time, but she was quite specific about when I was to come. I should have spotted it. And the poor girl looked so keen. It was excruciating. I've been steaming ever since. And I've been taking it out on you. I am so sorry. Please accept my apologies.' He looked genuinely sorry.

She couldn't help herself, she laughed even more. Then pulled herself together and said, ''S fine. I can just imagine your face...'

He seemed to cheer up after that, and she felt better too. She wondered, though, if she fully understood what he'd said. Okay, he wasn't religious, but was there more to it than that?

They stopped and looked back as they reached the houses. Viewed down-slope into the low sun, the green of the nearest field caught the light and turned silver.

'Wow. Look at that!' Sharon exclaimed.

Coated with spider silk from myriads of tiny spiderlings, Geoffrey explained. 'Beautiful, isn't it?'

Sharon had to agree. Shimmering, as if it was all covered in a metallic gauze. Fairy-tale. Magical.

Geoffrey said ruefully, 'Once the development's underway, all those tiny creatures will be displaced. And we're doing it everywhere. To every species. We're over-running all our co-habitants on this planet.'

That brought her back down to earth. She'd run out of pacifying replies. She knew there were extinctions all the time, it was part of natural selection, wasn't it? But were people really taking over and wiping out other species? He seemed to think it had gone way beyond natural. She hoped he was wrong.

## SIX
## SHARON GETS TO KNOW MAGGIE

Sharon was almost at the office when she saw Stuart Jenkins. The Toad, she now privately called him. He was with Maggie, coming from the opposite direction. He seemed to be muttering impatiently at his daughter, who was leaning into him. Sharon watched them veer towards the kerb and back again. Did he shove her then? Can't have done, she must have stumbled. Maggie had a lopsided walk, slightly twisted to the right, her toes turned in. Must make it easy for her to trip. In floppy, warm, comfortable clothes, a few streaks of grey in her untidy hair. As they approached Stuart looked up and beamed, nice as pie, as always.

'Sharon! How are you? How's the work going? I'm hearing good things about your tremendous achievements, yes indeed.'

''S fine.' He could be a bit over the top.

'I'm bringing Maggie to the office while I visit the dentist. Janice has given her approval. It wouldn't normally be necessary, she'd be at the day centre, but it's shut while they're having new flooring put down in the entrance hall. And Barbara isn't well, her back's playing up badly.'

'Right,' said Sharon.

Maggie was taking no notice of this conversation, wobbling

slightly as she waited, looking away from them, her free hand waving vaguely.

'Your mother keeping well?' Stuart enquired.

'Not too bad, thank you.' Not that it's any of your business.

They turned down the path to the council office.

I never want to talk to him about personal stuff, Sharon mused. Why is that? He's just trying to be helpful. Everyone says how helpful he is. It must be just me. Though there's something about him. Tries too hard? Compensating for being a hideous lardball? Sharon! Stop that. She knew she had a thing against fat people, and she also tended to say too readily what she thought. She was trying to do better since Geoffrey'd had words with her. She cringed, remembering it.

They'd been in the office, and she'd asked him, 'Did you see The Budgerigar yesterday, twittering over the report on the play area?'

There was no reply.

He didn't seem to have heard. 'Did you see—?'

He interrupted her. 'I imagine you mean our esteemed chairman, Mrs Hilary?' His tone was flat.

'Er, yes. Don't you think she's a bit like—?'

'Well, maybe,' his tone a little softer, 'but you should be more careful what you say in the office. I heard you refer to Mrs Rubbidge the other day. That's Eileen, isn't it?'

Sharon felt the blush rise up her neck and onto her face. He was right. And I'd hate him to find out what I call him. In fact, I must stop even thinking about him as The Conker. At school was one thing. Now he's a colleague. I should be more respectful. Though I know I'll find it difficult. I've always given people nicknames.

She was brought back to the present by her usual struggle with the awkward door. Though she didn't let Stuart help. 'I can manage,' she insisted cheerfully.

. . .

39

The parish council office was a big, square room with large windows on two adjacent walls. Desks, computers, one for the parish councillors to use when they came in. Sharon's spot was by the main door and the hatch where people came to ask questions or make bookings or complain about something. Council meetings were held at a long table. There were a few splashes of colour: a copper begonia on Janice's windowsill, a collection of mugs and a red electric kettle on top of one filing cabinet, next to the small sink. Sharon had plastic pots for pens and paper clips in that acid shade of light green that was almost fluorescent.

Janice was already at work, and smiled as they came in.

Stuart said, 'I think she'll be no trouble. I've brought a picture book and her beaker. I don't expect to be long. Not long.' He took off Maggie's coat and settled her in a chair with arms, at the meetings table, with her things to hand, and he left.

Sharon had only seen her close up the once before. She kept an eye on her. Lizzie was getting more disabled, so she was curious about what Maggie could and couldn't do. What was it like living with someone who needed so much help? Sharon spotted the edge of a pair of incontinence pants peeking out above the elastic waistband of Maggie's soft trousers. She sat with one leg stuck out to the side and Sharon could see the worn angle on the sole of her furry boot, remembered her awkward gait. The boots had Velcro fastenings. She looked like a giant baby.

She asked Janice, 'Did Stuart say if she drinks tea?'

A shrug.

She hesitated, wondering how she should talk to Maggie. She couldn't make tea for Janice and herself and just ignore her.

She walked across. 'Hello,' she said.

There was only a little tilt to the head to say that Maggie heard her.

Sharon perched on the next seat, so she wasn't towering over her. She could smell baby powder. 'I'm making tea. D'you want some?'

She found Maggie's bright, brown eyes were fixed on her and a slow smile emerged.

'I'll take that as a "yes",' Sharon told her. 'May I take your beaker?'

Janice looked up. 'She didn't say anything did she? I thought she couldn't speak.'

'No, but she looked. That's good enough for me.' Sharon was pleased with herself.

She was thinking hard now. Perhaps not give her the drink until it's cooler. She noticed Stuart had left a towel in the bag on the floor. Maybe tuck it under her chin? That seemed familiar: Maggie beamed, her strange, brown teeth appearing, all crooked. Her tongue seemed almost too big for her mouth. Maggie took the plastic beaker carefully. Her fingertips were pink, the skin ragged. She had small nails that looked bitten, half-buried in the flesh. She grunted as she slurped. She sounded happy.

When she took the mugs to the sink to wash up, Sharon squatted by Maggie to take hers too. There was only a small dribble to mop up. Maggie was staring vacantly, one handle of the drinker hung on a thumb.

'Shall I take that for you?'

Sharon got the smile again.

Maggie reached for her big book but couldn't quite grab it where she'd shoved it away across the table. She looked up and waved a random shape. Sharon slid the book towards her and was rewarded by a squeak. Wordless Maggie could actually communicate quite a bit. Sharon returned to her desk.

As she got on with her work, she could see what Maggie was doing. Her expression solemn, she carefully turned the tattered pages of the book. There were a lot of pictures. Maggie liked the flowery ones, stopped and gently touched the images, making the small, happy, grunting sound.

Stuart was soon back, looking as if he was in pain, one side of his face swollen.

'Thank you so much, ladies!' His tone was artificially jolly. To Maggie, 'Up you get.'

But she struggled.

He turned to the women. 'Can you give me some assistance? The arms on this chair are too high for her to push down.'

They heaved her up. What a weight she was, thought Sharon. Maggie's sleeve rucked up, showing her dimpled elbow. Took after Stuart, didn't she. The talcum powder scent again. Big coat, mittens and a scarf took a while.

She and Janice watched the pair depart, Maggie with that half-turned gait, twisted a little away from Stuart's supporting arm. It must make her back ache, thought Sharon.

'You did well there,' Janice said as they settled back at their desks. 'I'd not have guessed she'd understand so much. Well done.'

Sharon blushed with pride.

# SEVEN
# EILEEN RECOVERS FROM THE CRASH

She stands in her habitual place by the window overlooking her back garden, talking to herself. The carpet is worn thin here, from all the times she's stood on this same spot. Months now, since the lorry came in the garden... Every day, the memory of the terrible noise when it hit the wall, and the screeching rumble that continued for hours afterwards.

Someone still comes, every once in a while, to check on her. Encourage her to eat and drink regularly. She eats a proper meal, most days. She thinks she does. To begin with she couldn't eat at all, apart from custard creams.

Tea tastes like tea again.

She's not having to take the tablets now.

She's thinking. I know it's not Ian, the man who comes. Ian moved away years ago. I don't know this one's name, though he's told me, I'm sure. But he's alright. Doesn't say much. Doesn't expect me to say anything. Though I did speak to him last time. About the roaring noise in my head whenever I remembered what had happened. I'm glad I asked. Helped, what he said. He must have been the man who came that day. Must have been here.

In her mind's eye she can see him looking sideways at her.

'There *was* a dreadful noise,' he said. 'From the concrete mixer going round and round. All the stones in the mix, hitting the blades. I don't think the sound comes from your head,' he said. 'It's part of the memory.'

Outside is misty. A cobweb across the bottom of the window is beaded with tiny water droplets. She can see the hips on the nearby rosebush, making dull red smudges in the poor light, on spindly, bare branches. She doesn't mind these grey autumn days. Fog is comfortable. She's never confident with strangers, is easier when there's no one in sight.

The roaring sound is part of the memory, it's not coming from madness.

When the sun was out yesterday, she made herself go out the front and pick up more broken bits from the earth.

Ian-not-Ian had said, it smashed into your life. Into your private, quiet life. It's bound to take time to recover.

I'm doing really well.

Other people invaded too. 'Stuart, though I'm used to him,' she says out loud. And the girl from the council office. Sharon. I think her name's Sharon. Kind. So confident. I wasn't, at that age. Never have been. She listens. Yes, she seems kind.

Eileen thinks about when she first went to work, how hard it was, even though it was long before she was ill. She always felt nervous, with the loud men in the office, the gaudy women. They were mean. Didn't know to do differently with a mouse. Are things better nowadays? That girl, Sharon, seems so confident.

A small, sharp sound from outside. Eileen tips her head. Another one and then a crack. A thrush, invisible in the gloom, has broken into a snail on the paving slab it favours. She smiles.

# EIGHT
# GEOFFREY TALKS ABOUT THE PAST

JJ was waiting for Geoffrey outside school one afternoon, 'Hi, Gee, my pompous friend.' He punched him gently in the arm.

'What you after?' Geoffrey parried, smiling. They knew each other well, had been at school and in a band together. Though, these days, JJ didn't talk to him that often. Geoffrey had almost forgotten how – assertive, direct, confrontational, what was the word? – he could be. Always gentle and encouraging with the kids, though.

'Fancy a drink later?'

That was a surprise. 'Okay.'

In the pub, JJ took a while to get to the point. 'I was chatting with my dad.'

'Oh yes?'

'That warm day a bit back, I went out with him for a walk, and we sat in the park, talking. Nice it was. Pigeons pecking. Warm wind through that line of poplars that runs down the edge. Squirrels. Dog-walkers.'

Did JJ have something particular to say but was finding it difficult to get started?

JJ coughed. 'You know I gave up on a career making music because of the pressure, the endless fighting for your corner you had to do? Never knowing where the next penny would come from. To be honest it had got to the point where I thought I wasn't good enough. But the other week I was Googling and found some stuff from a music rag, years back, that really set me thinking. This journalist was writing about promising bands that never made it and mentioned ours, Lakenheath. He said my songs were good, but "the whiff of paedophilia", from my dad's history, had maybe made it difficult for me to find work. Blocked any chance I might have had.'

'What?'

'I knew he was investigated, all those years ago, when mad Eileen's little girl went missing. That was when he left his group. But I never knew the details. I asked him outright whether that was what the writer might have meant.'

'He talked about it?'

'Yeah. He did. He said that must have been what the man was referring to, there wasn't anything else. That was a relief. But he told me things I'd not heard before. What happened to him when Alice disappeared. Said he was gutted if it had blighted my chances.'

Geoffrey sat back to listen.

JJ launched into the tale. 'He was interviewed at home by a police officer. Pretty much any man in the village who could walk unaided was interviewed, he said. The copper asked where he was that Saturday. He'd just got back from Scotland on the Friday, after a gruelling tour, and he was wrecked. In bed all that Saturday, he said. Alone. Asleep. Totally out of it.

'My mum, Justine, had told him the girl went missing sometime in the afternoon. Eileen had gone to the shop, leaving her playing in the garden. Justine had taken me to the park and then on to a friend's, we weren't back until the early evening.

'When he was being asked the questions, Mum was sat by the window. Sniffing, looking icy, he said. Angry with him.' JJ paused.

'Took a while for him to tell the next part, the crucial part.' He fell silent.

'I'll get us another beer, shall I?' Geoffrey took their glasses to the bar. What's coming next? he wondered.

JJ soon collected himself. 'You know how tiny my mother is? Weighs nothing, always did.'

Geoffrey nodded.

'It's one of the things that attracted Steve to her. When they were young, he used to pick her up. He's got big mits, could have his hands almost meet round her waist. She'd wrap her legs round him.' He hesitated. 'No matter how old you get it's never easy to think of your parents having sex, is it?'

Geoffrey pushed away an off-putting image of his own mother.

'Anyway, Mum knew that Steve's tour had ended nearly a week before he got home. She thought he'd taken off with a groupie. Before I was born, she travelled with him, she knew what tours were like. Actually, he'd gone to see another band, but he was pissed off by her suspicion, worn out. So he was cruel – his word.'

Geoffrey turned so he could see JJ's face.

'He didn't even try to reassure her. He said, "There was this lovely blond, waist so small I could put my hands round it, thumbs and fingers touching front and back. And supple; used to be a gymnast." Said he was thinking of Olga Korbut.'

Geoffrey raised his eyebrows.

'No, I didn't know who that was either. "The Sparrow from Minsk", 1972 Olympics, apparently. Well before our time.

'Justine was still slim, but he knew she hated that her waist, after carrying me, hadn't got back to how it was. She said later she thought the bendy girl was all fantasy. But she was exhausted. Caring for me on her own most of the time. Broken sleep. The tedious, mindless trivia of it all.' He paused.

Geoffrey waited, tense.

'She must've been very tired. Not thought what she was

47

saying. With the police constable sitting there, out of the blue she announced that "he liked waif-like females."

'And that's what started it. The policeman looked at Justine, must have been wondering why she'd said that, what she might mean. He wrote something down. Steve couldn't look at her, worried this could cause trouble.'

'I can see that might sound suspicious.' Geoffrey looked at the glass, forgotten in his hand, and took a swallow.

'Then it got worse. Picked up by the media. Steve told me, on that last tour in Scotland, how he'd lost his temper and punched a reporter who'd been bad-mouthing his latest song. That bloke, no idea how he got the story, led a merciless crusade against Steve. Justine's words became, "He likes little girls".' JJ took his mobile out. He found the articles with just a few thumb flicks, must have pulled them up very recently. He showed Geoffrey.

**Pop star Lock shock revelation.**

**Steve Lock accused of paedophilia.**

Wife points the finger at Steve the singer.

'They say there's no such thing as bad publicity, but child molestation… He was thrown out of the group, their manager trying to limit the commercial damage.

'They'd been successful. He thought there'd be no problem, financially. At least for a while. But there was suddenly no money. "A fucking mountain of debt" he said. He still thinks he was stitched up. Dubious contracts and the like. I saw some of that. Between the debtors and the police there was no let-up for months.

'A few people in the village put the boot in too. Stuart Jenkins was his usual "helpful" self. Told the police he thought he'd seen Dad talking to Alice the week before. Fortunately, Dad could prove he was still up north then. He was crushed by it all, the suspicion, the injustice. There was nothing he could do. But there was no actual evidence against him. The fuzz gave up eventually.'

They watched a red setter wrap its lead round the shapely legs of a woman at the bar. She sat on a stool and threaded it back out, as if she'd done it many times before.

'He told me I kept him grounded. Toddling and crowing. Learning to use the toilet, finding new words, discovering how to sing.' JJ smiled at Gee. 'Seems I took an interest in muck for a while. He'd find me with a worm wriggling in my teeth, mud smeared across my grinning face. Then it was biting. Didn't know I did that.'

'I ate coal. Got filthy,' Geoffrey remembered.

JJ grinned. 'Apparently I bit the cat, and Justine, and then the girl next door. Dad bit me back and I stopped.' He hesitated, thinking. 'But that kept him going, looking after me. Gave him a sense that he could be useful. Kept him sane. Ish.'

'Ish?'

'Mmm. Him and Mum scarcely spoke for ages. She found a vacancy in a poncy gift shop in town, selling scented candles, crystals and stuff, using her maiden name. She was the breadwinner. Meanwhile he took me to nursery school. Though he daren't linger around other children. Avoided talking to parents. They'd be cold with him, anyway.'

'I can imagine.'

'He learned to cook.'

There was a silence.

'I don't remember any of this. He thought I might. Was pleased I didn't. Said "We tried not to let you see." They got talking again eventually. No one else to talk to, he said. And Justine was horrified when she realised what she'd started. He told her he should never have taunted her. They eventually got to like each other again. Though he said he was a miserable sod to live with for quite a while.'

'Must have been depressing, after the stardom,' Geoffrey said.

'Yeah. Proper depressing. With a capital D.'

Gee looked at him.

'He was on antidepressants for a while. Went to the doctor's 'cos of something else. In-growing toenail, I think he said. The bloke spotted the black dog, suggested pills. Course, he didn't want them. But the man guessed he'd used in the past. Pointed out it was the same sort of thing, only might actually do him good. He couldn't argue with that, and it did the trick.

'He said I seemed to know. Only a toddler, but I sensed... something. He told me, one time, it was raining, he was carrying me, tears mixing with the wet on his face. My little finger wiping the wet away, my little face all worried looking.'

'Could make a song,' Geoffrey said. It would be good to lighten the mood.

JJ ignored that. "Course, he couldn't find work like he'd had. No more limelight. The first job was in a record shop. He did know something about pop music, after all. But he said he couldn't sell vinyl forever.'

'Ended up in the prison service, didn't he?'

Seemed that happened almost by chance.

During his long speech, JJ had slipped progressively down in his chair. He sat up abruptly. 'So, having given up on making music, I went for teacher training, as you know. I stopped writing and singing my own stuff altogether. Because I thought my songs must be rubbish. Now I'm wondering if I might give it another go. Wondered if you'd join me.'

That made Geoffrey sit up too. 'Can I think about that?' He smiled. 'You could be a mean bastard, you know.'

JJ beamed, said, 'And you're a tedious twat,' and went to get another round in.

They talked about their band days as they continued to drink.

The cycle ride home for Geoffrey was definitely illegal. He was relieved when he made it back.

# NINE
# SHARON LISTENS WHILE GEOFFREY BANGS ON

The next time they walked together, Sharon and Geoffrey headed south. The trail was an old drovers' road, he told her. He talked non-stop. And not just about the wildlife. He told her about the modern windmills, dominating the distant view. How the roots of the blades are big enough for a man to stand in, how they climb up into them for maintenance. One man died up there, tangled in the turbine machinery. Others had fallen. Blades had broken off in high winds, the fragments flung for a mile. There'd been fires, the fire brigade unable to put them out, their equipment too short to reach.

'There are thousands of bird strikes. One got in the news a while back, a rare migrant – lots of people came to see it. There were photos on the net. Then a video of it being killed, hit by a turbine blade.' He gave a wry chuckle. 'I guess they got to be certain of its identity, anyway.' He paused. 'Windfarms don't ever generate enough electricity to compensate for the resources used in their construction.'

Isn't it too soon to know that? Sharon wondered. Though she didn't feel bold enough to say it.

Many of the fields they passed were empty, but that didn't stop him talking about farm crop management. 'Fiendishly controlled,' he said. 'Growing potatoes for crisps is a good example. They need a uniform, smallish size – think the diameter of a crisp – so they do test digs, water them to get the exact right size when they're lifted.'

'Pringles are all the exact same size,' Sharon said.

He turned and gave her a withering look. 'Stamped out from potato mush mixed with flour and fat.'

Well, that's me told, she thought.

He pointed out there were no weeds in the beginnings of winter-planted rape and wheat in the fields they passed. She didn't recognise the crops. She hadn't looked that closely before at grass, either, but he was right, even that was unnaturally uniform. He talked about sterile fields. 'Swamped with herbicides, no weeds, so no succession of nectar sources for insects or seeds for birds.'

Listening to Geoffrey drone on, one of her mother's favourite books, *The Hitchhiker's Guide to the Galaxy*, came to mind. Marvin, the depressive android. Moaning all the time.

'We haven't any organic farms around the village,' he said, 'so it's simple here. Every field, including the grass, is pretty much sterile. If you looked at the area on Google Earth, and painted all those fields grey, and half the gardens too, you'd see how little really green space there is. And we're in a rural area. People have no idea. They hear about Wildlife Trusts trying to develop green corridors, but they don't realise that those little strips are the only places wild things can live.'

Sharon made an effort to smile. He knows he rants, she thought.

And he did. 'Sorry. Sermonising again,' and he grinned apologetically. He was quiet after that. Seemed preoccupied.

Later that week, Geoffrey came in the office to work for a while at the hot desk. He was moody again. He kept muttering. Sharon tried to ignore him, she had work to do, they were busy in the run-up to Christmas. He got up to gaze out of the window then turned towards her with, 'Did you know I was in a band with JJ?'

What? she thought, half-closing her eyes. But maybe that's where JJ always calling him Gee came from.

'Lakenheath, we called it. Christopher Moore was in it too, though you probably don't know him. We got together at school, used to practise in a barn.'

Sharon grunted.

'I played guitar, but mostly made a racket on drums.'

'Really?' She wasn't looking to be distracted.

'We were sixteen, when we started; 1986. The miners' strike quashed the previous year, Margaret Thatcher prime minister, shops closed on Sundays. That was the year Ronald Reagan bombed Libya using planes that took off from UK airfields, F111s out of RAF Lakenheath – hence the name. No internet then, so we didn't know there was a silver band with the same name, set up decades earlier.'

'Sorry, noise, have to make photocopies.' Sharon looked at him as the machine grumbled. He'd moved to the long table, was leafing through the village newsletter, but didn't seem to be reading it. Bothered by something. Did he have no one to talk to? Like me, she thought. She didn't chat much herself these days. Schoolfriends away to another life at uni. And she hardly saw the ones still around, now she rarely stopped out late partying. She didn't like to disturb her mother's sleep.

It was five o'clock, almost, so she gave up on her work, made them mugs of tea, and settled across from him. 'Tell me about this band, then. You know you want to.'

He looked at her. 'Right. Well. I guess you'll know some music from the eighties... 1981, the charts topped by The Specials' "Ghost town". JJ liked that moody, rather eerie effect. "Money for Nothing", Dire Straits, 1985. Had the line "Bangin on the bongos like a chimpanzee" – he would taunt me with it. He liked lyrics that said something...' He trailed off.

Sharon tried to imagine what life was like then. Her dad must have been around the same age as Geoffrey. She wasn't even born then. Shops closed on Sundays? Were there computers? Or mobiles? 'I'm going to give up and ask. What's brought this on? Nostalgia. What's this about?'

He focused on her, put his mug down, his mouth in a twisted smile. 'Here's the thing,' he said. 'JJ's asked if I want to start playing with him again. I said I'd need to think about it, my guitar might need re-stringing, I haven't played in ages. So I'm thinking about it.'

Ah, so that's it. She smiled to herself. 'Sounds like fun. Why wouldn't you?'

'That's the thing. It wasn't always fun. He could be a hard man. Called me Pee-Pee when he didn't call me Gee. Pompous Prat.' He grimaced.

She grinned, pompous prat, yeah, she could see that. Though she couldn't imagine the teenage version of him. 'So you weren't exactly Mr Sunshine either, then?'

'No, I suppose not. Actually, I don't know if JJ's approached Chris too – should've asked. And it might be good to get back to making music.' He mimed an energetic drum sequence.

It was getting dark as they locked up and left, the streetlights wrapped in misty halos, the air chilly. Sharon wound her scarf an extra turn around her neck, buried her nose in it. As they walked together in silence, Geoffrey pushing his bike, she watched a black and white cat stalk a large leaf, shoved along erratically by the soft breeze. She asked, 'What've you got to lose?'

He looked at her, his forehead wrinkled. 'Maybe. Yes. You're right. I should give it a go. It won't be how it was.'

# PART TWO

# TEN
# EILEEN IS AT JUNIOR SCHOOL
## 1949

She's waiting in the cold, dark corridor outside the headmistress's office. Looking down, her shoes are grubby, the toes scuffed. Rubbing the top of one shoe against the other sagging sock doesn't make it any better. She fiddles with the repair her mother made where her gymslip got torn. A strand of hair falls across her eyes. It feels crinkly and lank – it's nearly a week since the last hair wash. She pushes it behind her ear. She wants to go to the toilet. But she knows she can't do that now.

It wasn't her fault, it was Fred tipped the ink onto her book, but she couldn't say that. She couldn't say anything, which made Miss Hartrup really cross.

The door opens suddenly. The headmistress is towering over her. 'I said for you to come in.'

'Sorry, Miss Scott.' Eileen follows her. She sits where Miss Scott tells her, on the chair in front of the desk. Her legs dangle because the chair is too high. Miss Scott sits back down and is writing, and Eileen can see the straight line of her parting. Her hair, on each side, is pulled back tight towards her bun. Wouldn't that hurt? I mustn't be caught staring, Eileen thinks, and she looks away. Through the window overlooking the playground there are sparrows fighting over a broken biscuit. She tries not to fidget.

She jumps when Miss Scott speaks.

'Miss Hartrup tells me you've ruined your writing book. Covered it in ink. What were you thinking?'

Eileen stares at her lap, twisting the skirt fabric in her fingers.

'Even if it was an accident, you're a very careless girl. What have you to say for yourself?'

There is nothing she can say. Her eyes are blurring with tears and slime is dribbling from her nose. She sucks it off her top lip into her mouth. She hears a gasp, and she looks up and sees the headmistress's face screwed up in disgust.

'Have you no handkerchief?'

Eileen shakes her head. A sob bursts out.

Miss Scott gets up, picks up a ruler and walks round the desk. She takes hold of Eileen's collar and pulls her off the chair onto her feet, then she whacks her calves, three times each side. The stinging pain is so bad she can't see and her knees go to jelly. A hot stream of pee runs down her left leg into her shoe. Through her tears, she glimpses the yellow stain on her sock. She falls over when Miss Scott lets go of her, then clumsily gets to her feet, twisting to see the red marks on the backs of her legs.

She is sent back to class where she sits, stiff, at her desk, and the pee makes her feel sore. She is certain that others can tell she's wet herself. She can smell it. She wipes her face on her sleeve, smearing snot.

Miss Hartrup sees. 'Eileen, that's disgusting.' She points to the corner at the front of the class. 'Go and stand facing the wall.'

Eileen stumbles between the desks, head down. Once there, she crosses her feet to hide the yellow sock and tries to tell herself the class isn't staring at her. But she hears the whisper.

'Look, Eileen's skirt's all wet, she's weed her pants!'

Tittering.

A burning blush climbs to the top of her head.

They were never nice to her. Now, they say she stinks. They sing.

*'Roses are red,*

*Violets are blue.
You look like a monkey
And smell like one too.'*

She tries to ignore them.

Once a week, she has a tepid bath. Mummy says just a few inches of water is all they can afford. She scrubs herself. In between baths she rubs and rubs with her face cloth. They're still mean.

After Easter, Mummy gives her a broken chocolate egg from the shop. It tastes wonderful. The Easter holiday is soon over.

Warmer days come. There are gold daffodils along the edge of the school drive. Bumble bees are busy. Everyone plays outside in the break. But no one will ask Eileen to join in a game. Not after what happened.

'Joy, you're it.'

'Can't catch me.'

A mob of girls rushes by and Eileen has to step aside to avoid being barged. She's always clumsy when she tries to skip, and she can't catch. But they don't even let her play hopscotch or jacks any more. She walks slowly around the edge of the playground, scuffing her feet, trying to look as if she doesn't care. She leans against the wall, chewing the split ends of her hair though Mummy has told her not to. She watches as children come and go, avoiding her. She must be a horrible person, she thinks.

But she can't be all bad because she has a secret friend.

# ELEVEN
## EILEEN HAS A FRIEND CALLED MARY

It started a few weeks earlier. Easter Saturday, she is wandering in the warm sunshine, and there's a dog by the brook, snuffling among the reeds. His lead is trailing behind him. She recognises him. Black, with a red collar, a terrier called Sammy. She's seen him with Mary from the class above. Mary lives at the end of the road. She has a thick, dark, glossy plait. It's beautiful.

'Sammy,' Eileen calls. 'Nice Sammy, good dog.'

He takes no notice as she creeps towards him to catch hold of the lead. She doesn't tug. He's rootling through the weeds. She winds the loop of the lead around her hand and squats down to watch him, wishing he was hers. Suddenly Mary arrives, all puffed out, sweaty and dirty.

'Have you got him?' she cries. 'Oh, hurrah! Don't let go. Naughty Sammy, bad dog.' She smacks him on the nose.

'He's not bad!' Eileen says. 'He's nice. I think he's pretty.' She doesn't want to hand over the lead, but she does.

Mary makes a face. 'He's been bad today though. He pulled me over. I think he saw a rabbit. He went straight under a bush and out the other side. I couldn't hold him. I had to let go, and then I fell in the bush. Look at me!' She gazes down at her scraped shoes and her grubby frock with bits of leaf and twig clinging to it. 'I'm going to be in so much trouble.' Then she looks at Eileen and says, 'It would have been worse if I'd come home without Sammy, though. I'm so glad you found him.' She smiles cheerfully at the dog. She seems to have forgotten how cross she was. Then Sammy gets bored with the grass and turns to bounce between them, panting and licking their hands and making happy noises. His tail is wagging furiously. It's lovely.

'He likes you,' Mary says and she's grinning.

'We don't have a dog. I've always wanted one.'

'You can play with him, if you like. We could play with him together.'

Eileen looks at Mary. Can she mean it?

'I couldn't be your friend at school,' Mary says seriously.

Eileen nods, understanding.

'But we could walk Sammy. No one at school would have to know.'

Eileen nods again.

'Would you come home with me now? Mummy might not be so angry if you came too, to help explain.'


Her mother doesn't seem very cross at all. She laughs, squatting to pick the bits from Mary's clothes. 'I'm sorry, pigeon,' she says. 'I thought you were big enough he couldn't pull you over now. Obviously, I was wrong. You'll have to grow a bit more before you can take him on your own again.'

'Nooo!' cries Mary. 'Eileen can come with me!'

Mrs Murgatroyd looks down at Eileen. She bites her lip and holds her breath because Mary's mother will see she's dirty. But there's a gleam of hope when she smiles and asks, 'Would you like that?'

Eileen nods.

'Well, we'd better make sure he can't run off again.' She takes the dog's lead and threads a yard of washing line through the hand loop, knotting it in place. She fashions handles at the ends of

61

the line, gives one to each girl and they go into the garden to try it out.

Eileen has never done anything like this before. It's marvellous. And afterwards Mrs Murgatroyd makes them buttered toast and sprinkles it with something delicious.

Her mouth full, Eileen mumbles, 'It's lovely. Thank you.'

'Cinnamon and brown sugar,' she says. 'Haven't you had it before? Mary's favourite,' and she smiles.

Most weekends now, Mary and Eileen walk Sammy along the lanes that lead away from the village, so they aren't seen by other children. Mary talks constantly, and Eileen gradually feels more confident. Mary doesn't know much about insects and flowers and things. When Eileen tells her about them, Mary listens to her! Eileen loves that.

It's so wonderful to be with Mary, she doesn't want to spoil it. So she doesn't say anything about what's wrong at home. Actually, she doesn't know what's wrong, so it would be difficult to tell Mary anyway. But she knows something's not right.

Maybe Mummy is ill, she'd thought at first. Mummy always looks sad and her face keeps going blotchy. Or perhaps it's Daddy who's sick.

Before, when Daddy was away 'in Signals', with just Mummy there, it was nice. But he came back, wasn't in the army any more and was around the house for a while because he didn't have a job. He would play with her, but then he didn't want to. He seemed cross with her and she didn't know what she'd done wrong. Then he was driving a lorry, delivering boxes of biscuits, and things were better again. One time he took her for a ride in the cab. It was so high up he had to lift her in. All the noise from the engine was really loud. She'd never even been in a car. It was a bit scary, but exciting... wonderful.

Then he got cross again.

Now he goes to work and when he comes home to eat his dinner he doesn't talk to her, or Mummy. He goes out again most evenings until after Eileen's gone to bed. But sometimes, on the way to the toilet, she sees him on the landing and he looks flushed and smells funny. So perhaps it is him that's ill. That wouldn't be as bad as Mummy being poorly.

At night she hears him shouting. 'I'm sick of it, Ena. You're like a tame rabbit. Timid, pathetic, nibbling at life. All you talk about is trivia. What Mrs Jessop said, how one of the tomatoes you bought was rotten, whether it's going to rain! I'm sick of it!'

She can't hear Mummy's reply, just the sound of her voice, upset.

'What did you do when I was away? Nothing, that's what. There's a world out there! There's more to life than recipes in *Woman's Own* for that disgusting fish, what do they call it? Snoek! Foul muck. Don't you try and feed me that again!'

School ends, and July finishes with long, sunny days exploring, talking. Eileen and Mary make daisy chains to loop round Sammy's neck. Mary has a ball for him to chase. It's so hot, they spend the afternoons lazing in the grass under the huge conker tree behind the pub. They take turns reading *Alice in Wonderland* to each other, or pore over Mary's weekly story paper. *Girls' Crystal* has tales about Cliff House School which sounds like a jolly nice place.

Mary tells Eileen about the cliffs at Broadstairs, where she went with her parents last summer. Some of the beach was still out of bounds because of buried mines.

Eileen says, 'I've never been to the seaside.'

Mary says, 'The sea's very big. The water's salty and comes in waves, making a shushing sound on the sand. Sometimes there's lots of sand, sometimes the water comes up the beach and covers it.'

'Why does it do that?'

'Don't know. It's called "the tide". But when it goes away it leaves little pools with weed and crabs and fishes and things. You can catch them.'

Eileen can't imagine a crab. 'You're so lucky,' she says sadly.

Mary puts a blue flower behind Eileen's ear. 'Now you're lucky too.' She giggles at her.

One hot day, they're walking Sammy in the back field. There are grasshoppers to catch, gorse pods to pop. Eileen squeals and calls to Mary, pointing to where a plume of dust is caught up in a little whirlwind, with bits of grass and dry leaves. But Mary doesn't really look. She hasn't said much all day. She seems unhappy.

'Are you poorly?' Eileen asks.

'No, no not really. But I have to tell you something. Mummy said to tell you. My daddy's got a new job at a place called Shawell. I don't know where that is, but it's a long way away. We have to move. I'll have a new school.'

Eileen stares at her. This mustn't be true. 'Are you taking Sammy?' she asks.

'Yes. We have to.'

'Will you be here for my birthday?'

Mary shakes her head.

Two weeks later she's gone.

'Mummy, Mary's gone away.'

Her mother's busy with the washing, 'What's that, Eileen? They on holiday?'

Eileen stares blankly out of the foggy windows. She can't tell her it's much worse than that.

# TWELVE
## EILEEN'S PARENTS ARGUE

Eileen can't stop herself picking at the flesh by her thumb nail, making it bleed. No need to wash when she's not at school. Some days she forgets to comb her hair. Her mother impatiently reminds her, flicking the back of her hand against the side of Eileen's head.

The fifteenth of August is Eileen's ninth birthday. Her mother gives her the sky-blue jumper she's just finished knitting, as Eileen knew she would. It's too hot to wear it.

But there's another present, which Daddy hands her. 'Here, poppet. I thought you might like this.' He hasn't called her poppet in ages. And he's smiling. Most days he's been scowling at her, telling her off. She peels the wrapping paper carefully away. A book. *The Gypsy Princess*, with pictures of a pretty, barefoot girl with a fairy dress and an embroidered waistcoat, beads plaited into her hair. It's beautiful.

'Thank you, Daddy,' she says.

There's a cake, too, with pale green icing and glacé cherries on the top. Nine candles, eighteen cherries.

'The piping's a bit of a mess,' Mummy says. 'Should taste alright, though.' They sing to her and she blows the candles out and wishes Mary was here.

Soon, the summer holidays are nearly over. Eileen drifts down the lanes where she has been with Mary.

Daddy's job has changed again, and sometimes he's out all night and sleeps in the day. Mummy tells Eileen that he's working 'shifts'. Is that the word for being home at different times, or is that the job? She hears him muttering about the work, and the bosses. She tries to be quiet so's not to disturb him when he's sleeping in the day. Mummy is constantly telling her to hush.

The book is lovely. The girl's name is Ethelinda. In the story, her father is put in prison while her mother is away working as a trapeze artist in a travelling circus. Ethelinda does her best to look after herself and care for their horse and their three dogs. When anyone comes by, she hides in a blanket box under her bed in the caravan. Eileen likes how the gypsy girl talks to her animals, and she copies her.

'Now I know you're young and have a lot to learn but, Spotty-Bear, you must be good. Don't whine and give me away.'

Mummy is busy shelling peas. 'Who's that you're talking to?'

'Spotty-Bear. He's the youngest dog.' Eileen points at the book.

Mummy raises an eyebrow but doesn't say anything. The puppy never gives Eileen away when she tucks herself in the airing cupboard to escape Daddy's bad temper.

One night, in bed, Eileen hears him talking loudly on the landing. 'It's the same thing, over and over. Dull, boring, repetitive, pointless. At least in the war I had something that was interesting. Could use a bit of initiative. Now… And Mr Burnham tells me I should be grateful to have a job at all. That little weasel. Spent his war profiteering is how I see it.'

'But he was a real help when you were away,' Eileen hears her mother say. 'Brought us food, a rabbit one time. And a rag doll for Eileen. I think it's 'cos of that, him being friendly to the family, that got you the job.'

There's a long silence. Then Daddy shouting. 'You harlot! You went with him! When my back was turned!' His words are spluttered out. He sounds furious.

What's a harlot, thinks Eileen, feeling very frightened. She doesn't catch her mother's soft reply, but she hears a thud followed by sobbing. Then another thud. And silence.

Eileen lies awake. She's so scared she can't even move. In the morning Daddy goes off to work as usual. Mummy behaves as if nothing has happened. Eileen doesn't understand. She doesn't think it was a dream.

The next night she wakes to hear a kind of thrashing sound, coming from her parents' bedroom. Then a noise a bit like an animal grunting. She can't sleep, again. But next morning they are having breakfast and smiling at each other. They almost look shy. Her father nips out into the garden and returns with a few fat blackberries, and pops one in Mummy's mouth. Eileen looks away. Then he ruffles Eileen's hair so that the bow comes undone. He goes off whistling.

But that's the last cheerful breakfast. Two days later her mother has a gash across her eyebrow and a black eye. Another week and she has a cut lip and a line of bruises on her upper arm.

Eileen arrives home a bit late, to find her father standing at the open front door. He scowls at her. 'Is it too much to ask that you come home on time? What've you been doing? Messing about, I suppose, playing, while I've had to wait for my tea.'

Eileen quakes with fright. Is he going to hit her?

Her mother steps between them and looks up at him apologetically, saying, 'It's only been a few minutes. And the meal's ready. It's not as if you have to be anywhere.' She smiles up at him, but Eileen can see Mummy's hand behind her back, gripped tight on her pinny ties.

He glares at her. 'That's what you think, is it, Ena?'

Daddy is so angry, and Eileen knows she's somehow to blame. As she eats her tea, the sound of her cutlery scraping the plate is deafening. He sends her to bed. She lies there, waiting for their raised voices, but not this time. The quiet is somehow worse. She falls asleep and dreams of a howling dog in a cage, looking like Sam, but not him.

The next morning, a Saturday, she wakes to find it's late. Mummy hasn't called her. She's sitting at the kitchen table, a wet handkerchief clutched in her hands, her face puffy and pink around the eyes.

She says, 'Your father's gone.'

Has he died? Eileen feels numb and sick with guilt. It must be because she was bad. I don't understand how, she thinks, but it's my fault. Her stomach hurts.

But later she hears Freda, next door, talking to the milkman.

'He's gone off. The Lord knows if he'll be back or not. At least I won't have to listen to them rowing. But I'd watch out, if I were you. I don't know how she'll pay the bills.'

So Daddy hasn't died.

Mummy doesn't talk about where or why he's gone. She doesn't say much at all. Home is a cold place, not just because it's autumn. It's almost nice to go to school.

The next Saturday when Eileen gets up, the kitchen is very chilly. The Aga has gone out. She goes to fill the coal scuttle to find the bunker is empty. When she comes back into the kitchen, her mother gives her a hard look.

'There isn't any. You'll just have to put up with it. Your father left us no money.'

Eileen hasn't eaten cold baked beans before. And she never liked Spam, even when it was fried. Freda brings them half a loaf of bread, some sprouting onions and some other bits of food in a basket. When she's gone, her mother says, 'Taken pity on us. I should be grateful. Though I don't suppose she'd have done that if bread was still rationed.'

Three days running, tea is onions stewed on the top of the paraffin heater in a lumpy brown liquid made with a packet from the back of the cupboard. Eileen is hungry, so she gets it down. Anyway, she's used to dull meals, with everything made from powder: mashed potato, tomato soup, those horrible scrambled eggs. Her mother said it would get better once peace was declared, but it hasn't.

. . .

'I need a job,' Mummy says, talking to herself. 'I must find a job.' She's got the local paper open on the table. Eileen finds pencil circles round advertisements. She reads them carefully. *Cleaner wanted 6–9 and 5–8.* Did that mean Mummy wasn't going to be there at home? When Eileen was little, her mother had a job in the biscuit factory. She made special biscuits, she said, for the soldiers. Iron rations. You couldn't bite into them, they were so hard. And Eileen had to be at the neighbours', with other children. She would be waiting, all the time, for Mummy to come back. Is that going to happen again? She reads: *Vacancy for home help.* What's a home help? *Receptionist/telephonist, typing skills preferred.* She didn't know her mother could type.

Mummy gets a job in the village Co-op. She works long hours, from early in the morning, but it's not too bad because Eileen can be with her some of the time. Porridge for breakfast at six, leave the house just before seven. She helps her mother stack shelves and then when the shop opens at eight her mother sends her off to school. She doesn't want to arrive far too early, so she soon settles into walking the short distance very slowly, playing a game with herself of two steps forwards and one back. She sings, 'One, and two, and back,' as she skips. She likes counting.

After school, she goes back to the shop and sits under the counter, trying not to get in the way of her mother's feet. Mummy finds drawing pins so Eileen can tack pictures she likes onto the wooden sides of her cosy cave. A robin, a puppy that reminds her of Spotty-Bear, a waterfall with a rainbow in the spray. Mummy gives her a photo from the paper of the Leicester football squad that nearly wins the FA Cup Final. Eileen doesn't keep that one for long. After closing time, she helps as her mother tidies and cleans, and she learns to count the takings.

'You're better than me at totting up the money,' Mummy says. 'What would I do without you?'

Eileen is proud of herself.

But when the other children notice her skipping steps and the counting, Eileen realises too late how it looks.

'Spastic. Mental.'

More singsong jeering.

'Your dad's done a runner! He's done a bunk!'

And it's my fault, Eileen thinks.

The children get bored sometimes. It's better when they ignore her.

In those early days, Eileen and her mother don't talk much.

Eileen sees her mother working hard at the shop. She has just Thursday afternoon off, and Sunday. 'On my feet all day,' she says, sitting by the Aga of an evening, soaking them in a bowl of warm water. But she never stays still for long. Cooking, laundry, keeping the house clean. Sunday is now washing day, and as well as that, all the hot water is used to clean the house, top to bottom. Mummy works constantly. 'No time for anything else,' she says. Eileen tries not to be a nuisance, not to make extra work, but it happens anyway.

'What happened to this blouse?' Mummy asks. There are holes where three buttons down the front have been ripped out.

'I fell off the swing.' Eileen holds her breath. Three girls at school had grabbed her. They pushed and shoved until she tripped over. She thought the biggest was going to kick her, but she didn't.

Luckily, Mummy is busy and doesn't ask any more questions. The rest of the evening she's darning a pair of socks then turning the worn-down sheets sides to middle.

'Make do and mend,' she says, sighing. She repairs Eileen's school uniform over and over.

'I've no money to spare for school trips,' Mummy says when Eileen asks.

Clothes come from the jumble sale. 'It's come to something that I have to go to the *church* for clothes.' Mummy looks cross and sad at the same time.

Sometimes gifts arrive, hand-me-downs for Eileen from villagers with older children. Mummy smiles but Eileen knows she's not happy having to take them. They eat well, though. The meals can be strange, often made from the vegetables that Mummy says are too sad for the shop to sell, and the badly dented tinned goods that nobody wants to buy. There are no cakes or sweets for them even when sugar comes off ration, and hardly any fruit, except when the apples ripen on the tree in the garden. Eileen has her milk at school and that bottle of delicious sugary orange juice that's sweeter than anything they ever have at home.

The winter after Daddy leaves is very cold. She finds more books to read, from jumble sales and the library. She curls up with them in the cubbyhole by the Aga. She reads *Swallows and Amazons*, *Oliver Twist* and *The Lion, the Witch and the Wardrobe*. Engrossed in the stories, seeing those other worlds, Eileen is happy.

Then, at last, spring comes. Mummy's mostly more cheerful. But she says things like, 'You can't trust people,' and, 'Don't speak to strangers. Keep yourself to yourself, we don't want more trouble.'

## THIRTEEN
## EILEEN IS LIVING WITH JUST MUMMY

The row of houses where they live is in one of the small streets near the church. They are built of red brick, and '1887' shows high on the front wall. Under the edge of the slate roof, each house has a line of bricks with their corners sticking out at an angle. Underneath them is another line, this time of patterned tiles. The tiles are white and blue, and even though they are so high up that Eileen can't make out their details, this band of colour looks pretty. The house belonged to Mummy's father. Eileen doesn't remember him. It sits at the sunny end of the terrace, with a bit of extra garden at the side.

She likes it when she's helping Mummy in the garden. It doesn't feel like a chore. Not like the housework. Dusting, always dusting. Scrubbing, mopping, and it all just gets grubby again.

One day when they are changing the sheets, Mummy says, 'Your body will soon change. You'll go from a girl to a woman. You're already beginning with little breasts. We might get you a bra soon.'

Eileen feels her cheeks go hot. She wants to disappear back into her book.

'You'll bleed, down below, every month. You'll need to wear

pads to absorb the blood and keep clean. I've a belt for you in the bathroom cupboard, and there are pads. You mustn't let others know; it's not nice.'
    She's heard of this at school.
    'I've got my period,' a girl will say. 'I'm not doing PE.'
    She doesn't want to think about it.

She's eleven and just starting at grammar school when it happens to her. The brown goo isn't like any kind of blood that she's seen before and it makes her feel dirty. She's growing some hairs down there too, and she hates the way they stick to the pad and pull, hurting her as she walks. She'd hoped the new school would be easier, but the smell from her pad brings back memories of all the taunting. She can't bear the smell.
    Some of the other girls at school talk about using tampons They say they're not as horrible as the pads.
    'They're for married women,' Mummy says. 'They have to go inside you, and you shouldn't do that at your age.'
    How can they go inside? But Mummy is busy polishing, and Eileen doesn't like to ask.


It's the morning of June 2nd, 1953, and Eileen has been looking forward to this day for weeks. She and Mummy are getting on the train up to town. The station, down the road from the village centre, is crowded and noisy, but the racket of the train arriving swamps all the other sounds. Hissing and grinding, it stops. No one gets off. They follow a line of other people through an open carriage door and make their way down the narrow corridor until they see two seats free in one of the compartments. They're lucky they aren't the last getting on; there aren't enough seats for everyone. Neither of them is by the window, and Eileen can't see much past the other passengers. As the train chugs out of the village she can tell they're in the cutting, then the light brightens and she catches glimpses of fields. A pigeon flies alongside the carriage for a while. Then she sees the upper parts of houses and larger buildings. All too soon the rattling slows. And in no time they're in the middle of the city, getting off into the huge, lofty space of the station. Mummy complains about arriving all smutty from the smoke, but Eileen doesn't care.

A few streets away, they join a small crowd collected on the pavement outside a shop selling electrical goods, to watch the coronation of the new queen, Elizabeth II. The window is packed with televisions and the one in the middle is switched on.

'There's usually all sorts of gadgets on show,' her mother tells Eileen. 'Different electrical things. Wireless sets, lamps, heaters. There's a new machine for making toast, can you believe? And an electric mixer for cakes. Look through the door. That big thing like a cupboard is called a refrigerator. It's to keep food cool. I can't see one today, but they have machines that wash clothes too.'

Eileen can't imagine what that would look like.

'Now, keep with me. I've sharpened my elbows specially,' Mummy tells her.

Eileen knows she is small for a twelve-year-old, and she easily tucks herself in front of her mother. The television screen isn't very big and, even from the front of the assembled group, the sound's difficult to hear, though the shopkeeper has the door wide open. The shop's supposed to be shut, the day's a public holiday, but he's there and he keeps popping out and saying things like, 'You could be watching this in the comfort of your own home. Easy payments.'

Her mother mutters, 'If he's letting us watch, why doesn't he shut up? Far too expensive for the likes of us. And I'm not buying on the never-never.'

The fathers of several girls from Eileen's class have invested in a 'box' especially for the day.

Eileen had overheard Angela say, 'My dad's got us one of those Ambassador ones, with the wood veneer cabinet. Really expensive but worth the money, he said.' Angela had laughed. 'For the better class of person, he said.'

Eileen told Mummy this, and she said, 'That'll be her mum

talking. Pretentious, she is. They don't belong to the "better class of people" any more than we do. They'll have had to buy it on HP.' She explained about hire purchase.

'Miss Turnham at school said it was all rubbish on the telly anyway. A waste of time.'

Her mother had laughed. 'People said that about the wireless, when it was new.'

They often listen to the BBC Light Programme together. That morning, *Family Favourites* had records chosen by members of the crowd along the Coronation Route. And when they eat their evening meal there will be a special *Coronation Hit Parade* instead of *The Archers*.

The solemn, deep voices. The massive abbey, crammed with important people. A throne, an actual crown. Strangely dressed men, some in frocks and jewels and great, decorated hats.

'Those are religious garments,' Eileen's mother tells her.

The women around her exclaim at Elizabeth's shiny dress, her jewellery, the long train, her make-up. On the little screen, the dress looks white, like a wedding dress. Eileen wishes she could see the pale colours of the silk embroidery. She's read there are roses in pale pink, very pale green for the Welsh leeks and the Irish shamrocks, mauve for the Scottish thistle. The thistle even has amethysts sewn into it, like the tiny one in Mummy's engagement ring.

One of the men boasts he can identify all the medals Prince Philip is wearing.

There do seem to be a lot of them.

He says, 'After today, it'll be her wearing the trousers,' and there's a wave of tittering.

Eileen remembers, in Mary's *Girls' Crystal*, the girls wearing jodhpurs for horse riding. What's so funny about that?

Her mother whispers, 'When they married, she promised to obey him. But, now she's the queen...?'

It's like watching a film. Eileen half expects an usherette to appear, with a tray of ice creams. The year before, Mummy took her to see *Singin' in the Rain* as a birthday treat, and they had ice cream then. It was one of the best things she had ever tasted. And the film was in colour.

The new queen looks so young and pretty, so unlike all the other people in the abbey. She is handed a Bible.

A man says, 'We present you with this Book, the most valuable thing that this world affords. Here is Wisdom; This is the Royal Law; These are the lively Oracles of God.'

Her mother chuckles. 'Look, she's just given it to that chap behind her, as if it's of no consequence. Good for her.' But then she draws Eileen away. 'Pompous lot, those royals. I can't hear properly either.' She whispers, 'The man behind me keeps shoving me. I've had enough of the smell of his sweat.'

The last thing Eileen hears is the commentator saying, 'Now wearing the imperial state crown and holding the sceptre with the cross and the orb…', as the queen, weighed down, walks down the aisle.

When they get home Eileen finds a two-pound bag of sugar and tries walking up and down their hallway, balancing it on her head with one hand. Her mother laughs.

'And the crown was much heavier than this!' Eileen says.

Another sheet-changing day, her mother says, 'What do they teach you about babies and such at school?'

'Not much,' says Eileen. She's already squirming. She'd recently heard a joke about a penis. It was something to do with making babies. A boy once showed her his willy in the churchyard. He was proud of how he could aim his stream of wee. He said that was one of the reasons boys were better than girls. But the joke wasn't about that. There is something about willies she's missing. She tries to change the subject. 'I saw Misty's kittens being born.'

Mummy isn't put off. But she doesn't want to speak about babies so much as 'lust'.

'Men think about what they might do with women, sex, all the time; they can't help it. It's such a powerful urge for them that it takes very little for a man to lose control. If you provoke him, he can quickly become incapable of restraining himself. You must be very careful.'

Eileen is concentrating on the pillowcase she is putting on. What is she supposed to say?

'When you hear people say, "She had it coming to her", that's what they mean. Flirting, dressing provocatively, sitting on a boy's lap, they're all dangerous. It's not their fault. You have to take responsibility, be modest.'

Modest means not boasting. Eileen never boasts. How could she? Though she knows Mummy doesn't mean that kind of modesty. She thinks of Debra, two years ahead of her, thrusting out her chest at the boy who delivers their newspaper, the top of her blouse gaping open to show the deep cleft between her breasts. Does that mean Debra has it coming to her?

'If you have to sit on a lap, say in a car, sit on a newspaper or a folded coat. If you're not careful, you could become pregnant.'

Eileen has never been in a car, and she can't imagine how she might come to be sitting on a boy's lap.

She is riveted. A man might easily go berserk. And it would be her fault.


At the small grammar school, Eileen knows a few girls, from before. There's Angela, who'd boasted about the television set her father had bought. She and a couple of others are often chatting together in the playground. Eileen hovers nearby.

'Mummy showed me how to make ice cream from condensed milk,' Angela is saying one day. 'Our Frigidaire,' and she pauses to toss her hair and smile round at her friends, 'has a metal tray to make ice cubes. It goes in the freezer compartment. You can take out the part that divides it up for cubes and make ice cream. Or sorbet.'

Eileen says, 'What is that? Sorb...' Then she sees the look on Muriel's face.

'Sore bay!' says Angela.

'Your mum not make that, then?' says Muriel, tittering.

Eileen moves away, biting her lip. At least the sing-song taunting has stopped.

The teacher speaks to Eileen's mother. 'She said...' Her mother is putting on her BBC voice. '"Eileen is frustrating to teach. I don't think she's stupid, but she says silly things. And if she gets a good mark for a piece of homework, you can be sure she'll get a bad one next time. It's as if she wants us to think she's a dullard." She asked me to try talking to you.'

'I don't know what she means. I just get tongue-tied when I'm asked in class. And I do the homework properly.'

But she forgets to be careful sometimes.

In English class, they are reading Jane Austen's *Pride and Prejudice*. One homework question is from a past O level paper: 'How do money and social position affect Mr Collins?' Eileen finds herself wholly absorbed in the exercise, which, unexpectedly, has her thinking of her mother.

She writes: 'Mr Collins has no income or status without the benevolence of Lady Katherine de Burgh. His behaviour reflects this: he is cringing, horribly uncritical of her, pretending to be humble. He behaves, in relation to her, without integrity.' It's satisfying to find a place for this new word she's found, *integrity*.

She expands on the theme, giving examples and quoting from the novel. She's thinking of her mother's dislike of charity. Mummy can seem ungrateful, even angry, but Eileen recognises that as preferable to *servility*. That's another new word she likes. She receives a good mark for her essay. Then she's asked to read it aloud in class. She stands, horrified, looking down at her page.

She improvises. 'Mr Collins needs money, so he accepts it from Lady de Burgh. He has to do as she tells him. He is dependent on her...'

Miss Brandon stares at her.

She knows I'm not reading it properly, Eileen thinks, but Miss Brandon doesn't interrupt, or protest afterwards. She just sighs disappointedly and says, 'Thank you, Eileen. You may sit down.'

Her mother cuts Eileen's hair. In a straight line at the level of her ear lobes. At least, it's straight when it's wet, but then it curls itself into a bush as it dries. She has a side parting, and the bulk of her hair is scooped to the left with a large clip. The hair framing her face is particularly frizzy and uncooperative. She hates it. Looking at herself in the mirror, she tugs at the crinkly ends. She wets them and stretches them out, but they spring back. She soaps them and sticks them down.

Her mother laughs. 'What have you done to your hair?'

Eileen feels foolish and rubs the stiff strands away.

'It's nice hair,' Mummy says. 'Lively.' She gets on with the washing up.

Eileen's not convinced.

'D'you want to try a fringe? I could do that, if you like. Though those curly bits at the front might not behave.'

Eileen shakes her head glumly. 'I think I'll let it grow.'

'Alright, if that's what you want.'

Her hair grows out into a great mass, like straw-coloured wire wool. She hates it even more. One day, she plucks up the courage to ask at school. There are three girls in her year who weren't at her junior school and aren't so mean to her. Catherine, Ruth and Christine were friends before they arrived, and tend to keep each other's company. And she so admires their hair: glossy waves and smooth curls that bounce with each shake of the head.

She sees them coming down the corridor. Christine is singing 'You Belong to Me', twirling around and waving her arms in the air.

Eileen stops to watch.

Catherine sees her and pauses, saying, 'Jo Stafford, you know.

Beautiful voice.' She turns to Christine and adds, 'Desist! Please! You're making me dizzy. And murdering the song!' and all three collapse with laughter.

Ruth says, to no one in particular, 'She's married again, Paul Weston, the leader of her backing orchestra. There was a picture in *Woman*. She looked wonderful.'

Eileen swallows. She stammers out, 'H-how d'you get your hair so smooth and w-wavy?'

'Use rollers,' Ruth says. She smiles in quite a friendly way. 'I use spongey ones so they don't hurt too much to sleep in. But I can't get it as nice as hers. I wish I could.'

'But your hair is beautiful,' Eileen whispers. They've gone by then.


She makes some rollers with sponge from Mummy's sewing cupboard, fixed in place with Kirby grips. But next morning when she takes the fixings out, her hair explodes into a great, stiff halo. She stands at the bathroom mirror. Nothing will smooth it down, it just wants to stick out. She takes up the nail scissors and snips a bit off. A hole appears. She cuts some more, to try and even it up. Clumps of cut hair accumulate in the sink, in the bath, on the floor. It clings to her fingers. It doesn't flush down the toilet. It looks disgusting, like her pubic hair. It's revolting. Tugging at the mess makes her scalp ache. When she stops, an unfamiliar face is staring back at her. Boyish. Ragged. Urchin-like. Just as well Mummy's at work, but what will she say when she comes home? What will they say at school? Oh, what will they say at school?

Eileen has never dared truant before. But today she can't face the mockery. One of Mummy's headscarves round her head, her coat tied tight, the collar turned up, she marches for miles. Her pocket handkerchief is sodden. She eventually stops at the top of a hill. At her back, poplars creak and rustle in the wind. The fields stretch out below her, criss-crossed by hedges. Rooks soar above a copse. She can see a big green barn with its flared roof sweeping down to cover shelters on either side. There's the old windmill in the distance, the sewage works, traffic on the trunk road. She removes the headscarf, shakes it out. Tufts of cut hair break loose and fly away on the breeze as she pushes her fingers through the short clumps.

'Mummy will have to help me,' she says, hearing the catch in her voice. 'She'll just have to help.'

Mummy's key in the lock. Eileen is sitting stiffly on a kitchen chair.

'Hello!' her mother says as she shuts the front door and comes into the kitchen, taking tinned food out of her bag, 'I've had such a day. Trapped my finger in that counter flap again. It's all purple. And Mrs Johnstone's horrid sausage dog messed on the floor for the umpteenth time. I wanted to tell her to clear it up herself but The Righteous must have read my mind, he gave me such a look, I thought… Oh my word, you look like you've been through a combine harvester.'

Eileen is trying not to cry.

Astonishingly, Mummy sets down her bags, bends down beside her and circles her with her big, strong arms. 'Oh dear me,' she says. 'What a mess. We'll have to do some repairs here. Poor you. Don't cry.'

She mops Eileen's wet face and dribbling nose.

Mummy rocks her gently. 'It'll be alright. Don't fret so.'

With the good scissors and a great deal of muttering, laughing and groaning, Eileen's head is tidied enough for her to go to school the next day.

Janice calls out on seeing her, 'Oh, look at big George!' George is the name of her ragamuffin younger brother.

Ruth asks, 'I thought you were going to put it in rollers?'

'I changed my mind, decided to have it short.'

And that was that. What a relief.

• • •

81

'I don't want to wear the twinset. Or that necklace. The pearls look awful, you can see the shiny paint peeling off. I'll wear my skirt and the brown jumper.'

'You've worn them for ages now. They're getting grubby, they need a wash.'

'They'll be alright one more day. And maybe I'll find something this afternoon.'

It's Saturday, and they're setting off together to a jumble sale.

As they reach the church hall, Mummy stops Eileen to say, 'If you're going to be so fussy about what you wear, you'll have to choose it yourself. You can have five shillings. Off you go.'

The hall is gloomy despite the yellow lights. It's already busy with women after a bargain. Eileen takes a deep breath and sets off for the table loaded with women's clothes. She knows she'll have to dodge the elbows and keep hold of anything good she finds, or it'll be snatched away. Freda, from next door, and another woman Eileen knows slightly, Jean something, are on duty there. She's determined not to be put off by the smell of mothballs, and she starts to rummage among the fabrics to pull out what's underneath. The clothes feel slightly greasy. She finds a navy fisherman's sweater, with a hole in one elbow, small enough to darn. She fingers it. How much might it cost?

Jean says, 'That's good, oiled wool. Would go with...' She digs into the heap, looking Eileen up and down as she does so. She pulls out a pleated skirt in a muted tartan of brown, forest green and shades of blue. Coming round to hold it up against Eileen, she says encouragingly, 'It's about the right size.'

Eileen looks nervously at the purse she's clutching.

'How much have you got, Eileen?'

'Five shillings.'

'Well, you could buy a lot for that.'

Eileen hears Freda sniff, but Jean seems not to notice.

A pair of brown leather gloves, scarcely worn. Grey leather shoes with a little heel and a tiny bow at the front. So pretty – though she can't imagine when she might wear them, and she puts them back. Navy stockings in their original packet. Jean brings out a sheepskin-lined coat from somewhere.

Freda looks alarmed. 'I thought you were keeping that for Margaret?'

Jean brushes her hand aside, saying, 'No, it's too small for her, now I look at it.' She turns back to Eileen. 'There's a rip in the back of the lining, but it could be mended. And you can't see it when it's on anyway. Here.' She holds it up for Eileen to try on.

It's lovely and warm.

Jean tots it all up: four shillings and nine pence ha'penny.

Freda sniffs again, looking the other way.

Actually, buying on her own is better. Mummy always seems uneasy if anyone's kind.

Eileen shows Mummy what she's bought and proudly returns the tuppence ha'penny change.

'Freda sold you all this?' her mother asks, looking across the hall. 'Ah, no. Jean Jones.'

Eileen nods happily.

Her mother's beaming. 'We were at school together. Nice woman. Well done. But we'd better hop it now. Before they change their minds.'


Eileen finds herself fretful and angry. Her mother is irritating, nagging.

'Can you fetch me a clean towel? And then peel the potatoes? I want to get the dinner on before we do the bathroom.'

She finds the towel and hands it over in silence, her head down.

'Did you empty the upstairs bins? We need to get the dustbin out the front.'

Silence.

'Eileen?'

'I'll do it!'

She sees her mother's face. What is the matter with me? she thinks. That time of the month, 'hormones' is what she's heard

83

Ruth say, but that doesn't mean Mummy isn't annoying. Treating her like a child. Why does she always want to fill every day with dull chores? Eileen's itching to get back to *Northanger Abbey*.

'I've decided' – Eileen surprises them both – 'I'm too old to call you "Mummy". I'm going to call you by your name.' It feels so naughty, she can't bring herself to actually say 'Ena'. She turns her back on her mother, so she doesn't have to look at her, and waits. There's a hush. She hears her mother sigh.

'Alright. If you must.'

It feels strange, calling her Ena. But feels grown-up, good, too.

'What'll we have for tea, Ena?'

'Ena, you should read *Pride and Prejudice*. I'd thought it was all so serious, but actually, bits of it are funny. See here, right at the beginning: "It is a truth universally acknowledged, that a single man in possession of a good fortune, must be in want of a wife."'

Ena chuckles. She seems to adapt more quickly than Eileen does. Even so, it's a long time before Eileen tries it in public. Not confident enough for that


Eileen's school takes only girls. She realises, as she reaches her mid-teens, that most of them end up in the same kind of life. There's a lady doctor in the next village, but Eileen has no idea how that could have happened. The brightest pupils might go on to teacher training college. But most of the teenagers are preparing for secretarial work until they marry and become respectable housewives and mothers. In the year above her, there was a girl who became pregnant. She left school, defiant. Everyone was shocked. Eileen sees her months later. She looks shabby, pushing a pram out of a dismal prefab on the council estate.

Alongside schoolwork, Eileen has some time to herself. Folded into odd corners, she loses herself in tales of adventure, hardship and stormy relationships. Charles Dickens, Wilkie Collins, Thomas Hardy, Jane Austen, found on the musty book tables at the jumble sales, or in the library. '*You must allow me to tell you how ardently I admire and love you*,' she reads. There's no tedium; no humdrum, boring bits in the stories; they take her to worlds not remotely like hers. When it comes to Eileen choosing school subjects there's little discussion. She likes English. She doesn't argue about doing domestic science – not that there is much more there for her to learn – and typing, rather than serious subjects or real science. Only three in her year do sciences, and they're really clever. She becomes a good, plain cook and a competent typist, knows about Henry VIII and the rivers of East Anglia. The small amount of animal biology Eileen learns doesn't seem to connect with what Ena has told her about sex.

Eileen has an inkling of her own ignorance but can only infrequently overhear the kind of knowledgeable conversations that might help. She rarely asks questions. She leaves school at fifteen with five O-levels, a reasonable typing speed and the suspicion that there is a great deal she doesn't know.

# FOURTEEN
## EILEEN WORKS AT LIBERTY SHOES
### 1956

Everyone knows the story of the Liberty factory on Eastern Boulevard. How two of the company directors travelled to New York after the Great War, in search of ideas on how to develop *Lennards Boots and Shoes*. The business burgeoned and the firm had a new building constructed. Four floors of reinforced concrete with huge windows facing the river and Walnut Street, it was topped with a replica Statue of Liberty. The company name was changed to Liberty Shoes Ltd, and advertisements featured a modern message: *walk with liberty*. However, when Eileen leaves school and takes her first job there, she finds her work is much less splendid than the factory façade.

Slightly built, Eileen is five foot two inches tall by then. She wears her hair short – she's given up trying for the smooth shapes that are fashionable. She experimented with wearing make-up and didn't like it. It looks too garish and attracts attention, which she hates. Sometimes she uses a little powder from a compact, and pale lipstick, and she has a clear nail varnish for special occasions like going to the cinema with Ena. She doesn't wear it to work, it would only get chipped.

At Liberty's she always avoids the clanking lift with its crowded-together occupants. She enters by the side door, takes the cold concrete stairs that are lit by bright, flickering fluorescent lights. There's a fire extinguisher at each level, beside a chipped red bucket of sand coated with cigarette butts and sweet wrappers. She notices it every day and hates it. On the first floor, if the door is open, she may get a glimpse of one of the barn-like areas where boots and shoes are made. The smell of leather and men's sweat wafts, with the racket, into the stairwell. On the second floor, her floor, the corridor walls are gloss-painted cream, all scraped and gouged by the post trolleys that are constantly trundled up and down.

She takes the door on the left into a noisy, open office, which is always full of cigarette smoke, always too hot or too cold. The metal windows rattle when it's windy. Condensation trickles down and pools on the sills, collecting dirt and dead insects. From this, the rear of the building, the view outside is dreary. Brick walls, decorated with pigeon droppings, weeds in gutters. Though the buddleia growing out of a nearby chimney is pretty when it flowers. And there's a regular pair of collared doves, daintier than the ordinary pigeons. When she sees one of them, she knows to watch for the other, they're almost always together. She privately calls them Paul and Joanne, after Paul Newman and Joanne Woodward, stars of *The Long Hot Summer*. Though she can't tell which bird is which.

Eileen doesn't have her own desk, she uses one of the typewriters on a long table against the wall under more glaring fluorescent lights. Her official job is typist, but she does whatever needs doing. Most of the staff ignore her. It's not that different from school, really. They talk over her head about their busy social lives, drinks in the pub after work, trips to the cinema, plans for package holidays in sunny places abroad. She doesn't want to go to the pub with them, but all the same...

When there's a special event like a birthday, or someone is leaving, there might be a token effort. 'We're going over to the Marquis, Friday, say goodbye to Jane. You could come if you wanted. Might go on a bit late for you, though...' She doesn't even need to reply and the conversation moves on without a ripple. Nor does she say anything when they have her doing the most menial jobs. She fetches teas and coffees, empties bins, mops up spills. Having typed the names and addresses on the envelopes, she stuffs in bills or letters by the hundred.

One day, she's sent to re-organise the large stationery cupboard down the corridor. She hefts in the great boxes she's been given, empties the shelves, cleans then re-stacks them. It takes her all afternoon. She thinks it's odd, no one disturbing her the whole time, but she's glad they don't. It's quite satisfying doing it properly, and she almost enjoys it. But when she emerges, dirty and tired, she finds the office empty, and it turns out everyone else is at the opening of refurbished displays at the Guildhall Museum, enjoying music and light refreshments. Why do they have to be so mean? she wonders. It's not as if I cause them any trouble. I'm always on the outside looking in. That's just how it is.

One thing that cheers her up is finding character descriptions that fit the people around her from the books she reads. There is Jane, who is always saying 'make an effort' to the lads she supervises. Eileen can't suppress a smile whenever she hears her use the phrase. She calls her Louisa Chick after the character in Charles Dickens' *Dombey and Son*.

Then there is Paul, the senior clerk from the floor above, who has a sort of swollen appearance like the German traveller in *Little Dorrit*. *Plethoric* describes him perfectly. He sports suits with waistcoats and a bright tie pulled up into a plump curve below his collar. A matching fluffed handkerchief peeks from his breast pocket. His shirt cuffs sport pearl and gold-coloured links.

Having never previously spoken to her, Paul startles her one day, appearing suddenly in the stationery cupboard - which she now thinks of as hers - when she's searching for foolscap envelopes. He closes the door and leans on it, waiting. The packet of envelopes in one hand, she turns nervously, puzzled. He doesn't move aside.

He says, 'Oh, you don't need to rush away. Leeny, isn't it? Take your time.'

She holds up the packet as if to say, these are needed.

He takes the envelopes and puts them down, smiling. 'Pretty blouse.' He flicks the collar.

She blushes.

'You're a quiet one. I like that.'

Eileen's palms are suddenly sweating. She wants to tell him she has to leave but all she can do is mumble.

'Nice hair.'

Is he mocking her? She feels she's scarlet. She tries to push past him.

'I've been watching you. You like me, don't you?' He grasps her shoulder. 'I've seen it. Now's your chance.'

She realises he's going to kiss her. She sees his open mouth, the lower lip fatter than the upper, drops of spittle visible on it, the tip of his tongue moving, and she shudders. She squirms sideways and hits her elbow hard on a shelf, gasps with the pain.

He growls, angry, and holds her firm. There's a rattle of the doorknob, someone is outside, trying to come in.

'Bit crowded in here!' he calls. 'Won't be a minute.' She's pinned down by his left hand. Her eyes tightly closed, she feels him lift her skirt, and he roughly grabs her knickers, pulls at them, tugging hard, tearing the fabric. He hauls again until the whole ripped garment is in his hand. She can hardly bear to open her eyes.

'All ready for next time!' he hisses. He holds her tattered knickers up to his nose, sniffs and smirks. Then he stuffs them out of sight in a pocket, and lets her go. He opens the door and walks out, whistling softly through his teeth, carrying a packet of staples. Maureen enters, a knowing smile on her face. Eileen looks at her briefly and registers her expression. Then she pushes past her and bolts for the toilets.

Her fists pressed into her squeezed-shut eyes, Eileen sits hunched on the toilet lid, behind the locked cubicle door, and sobs.

She keeps seeing his flabby, wet mouth, feels his rough hand between her thighs. She can't move, her heart pounding, her palms clammy, her legs trembling. Then, beads of sweat on her forehead, the back of her neck prickling, a wave of nausea engulfs her. She slides to the tacky floor and succeeds in opening the toilet lid before she's sick. She retches until there's nothing left but a bitter taste. She wipes a string of mucus from her mouth. The stink of the toilet bowl makes her retch again and she daren't move away.

She is thankful no one comes.

She has no idea how long it is before she can get up from the floor. By then she isn't thinking about what happened. She's scarcely thinking of anything. She's acutely aware that she is naked under her skirt. She swivels it round to look at the back and sees the wet patch she dreaded was there. There's only toilet paper, but she tries desperately to clean herself where his hand has been.

Eileen looks in the mirror at her bloated face, shiny with tears. She waits until the quiet tells her the office is empty before she emerges. Her coat, when she retrieves it, covers the wet patch. She doesn't want to sit on her soiled skirt, or have to talk to anyone, so she walks home rather than take the bus. That makes her very late. But it gives her time to compose herself.

'Oh, just in time,' Ena says. She's not looking at Eileen. 'I wondered where you'd got to. I'm almost ready to put dinner on the table.'

'I need to go to the bathroom. You start. Don't wait for me.' She goes upstairs and shuts herself in to wash herself. She rinses her skirt and hides it, washes herself again, dresses. Her meal is cold when she comes down but she's not hungry anyway. She says she has a stomach ache and goes to bed. Though not to sleep.

She's shivering.

What if someone hadn't knocked?

I can't stop him.

I couldn't tell anyone, couldn't say the words.

He'd just deny it anyway.

*What if no one had come?*

She can't get warm. She feels so ashamed and guilty. She isn't going to tell Ena anything.

The next day she must appear very unwell because Ena doesn't hesitate to go down the road to the phone box, to let them know at work.

Eileen's off for a long time. 'Post-viral debility', the doctor's note says.

She sleeps a lot. She wakes to a tangled mess of sheets and blankets. She goes for short walks and returns home exhausted. She asks herself: What am I going to do? I can't go back. I can't face him again.

One day she feels well enough to go on a small outing to the next town. She stops to read the cards in the Post Office window. One says, *'Typist needed in an established solicitor's office.'* There's a phone number. She finds some coins, goes inside and dials before she has time to change her mind.

The voice is familiar and when Eileen says her name, the woman replies, 'Oh, hello Eileen. This is Beatrix Roberts. You remember? We were nearly neighbours.'

Eileen says 'Oh… The job… I…'

'Where are you phoning from?'

Eileen tells her.

'That's just around the corner. Come round.'

And she does.

Mrs Roberts once lived down a bit from Ena's house, before she moved to a bungalow a few streets away after her husband died. Eileen has known her forever. She's the solicitor's secretary, plump, pink-cheeked, pleasant. Eileen has to do a typing test. Mrs Roberts tells her she's got the job.

Eileen tells Ena that she happened to see the advert and enquired. Ena doesn't query that. She gives Eileen a junkshop find, a pencil sharpener embedded in a lump of wood carved into the shape of a mouse. Mr James, the solicitor, takes to calling her 'mouse', but in a kindly way. The money's a bit better. She and Ena are even able to buy a second-hand television.

The work at the solicitor's is predictable and, with practice, not too difficult. The place is much nicer. A small office, pale green walls, venetian blinds, deep windowsills. Eileen has a desk under a window. She can see a tree. Beatrix, who doesn't want to be called Mrs Roberts, gives her a plant for the windowsill, an African violet. Eileen has her own desk lamp, her own drawer with a key, is responsible for her own typewriter. In the drawer she keeps a stapler and staples, a hole punch, treasury tags, a notepad, pencils and a rubber; everything to hand. For the first time she feels happy going to work.

She spends her days typing long, opaque legal documents. Mr James doesn't say anything when Eileen occasionally finds plainer forms of expression. She enjoys quietly making the words that little bit easier to read. Each document needs several carbon copies, and she can type accurately if not fast, so her work is appreciated. She doesn't really mind when whole pages have to be retyped to accommodate a tiny change. She rarely has to answer the telephone, which suits her. At lunchtimes she goes to the park and eats a sandwich she has brought from home, and wanders for a while.

She travels to work on the bus and, although that part can be a torment, she's always welcomed when she arrives. Beatrix and she take turns to make the tea. Mr James might bring home-made biscuits, baked by his wife. It's comfortable here.

Ena, working fewer hours now, has Eileen's tea ready when she reaches home. A bit of ham, boiled with lentils, carrots and celery. Or sausages with mashed potato, followed by apple pie and custard or maybe semolina with a dollop of jam. Eileen cooks at the weekends, experimenting with recipes from her mother's magazines. They eat well, with the help of Eileen's improved income. They each have their favourite TV programmes. Ena likes *Coronation Street*, though she minds that Ena Sharples is so ugly. They watch *The Black and White Minstrel Show*. They don't like

*Songs of Praise.* Eileen likes *Dixon of Dock Green*, he seems so kindly, and they both enjoy *This is Your Life*. Eileen is happier than she's been for ages, since before Mary went.

The weather turns very cold just before Christmas 1962. It starts snowing properly on Boxing Day, and it seems as if it will never stop. Huge drifts pile up, the roads are impassable, and the buses stop running. Ena struggles to make it to the Co-Op, but Eileen can't get to work at all. In the new year they show pictures on the TV news of the sea frozen over. In places, the weight of snow and ice on copper telephone wires stretches them so they reach the ground. No one has ever known such a winter, the coldest since 1740, Eileen hears.

Tucked in the corner by the Aga by day, Eileen reads Rene Gardi's book about a journey across the Sahara. At night she piles all the bedding there is, and her coat, on her bed. The heap is heavy enough she has to wake in the night to turn over. But even in the bitter cold she feels content.

And when the snow eventually melts after weeks and weeks, she's glad to return to her quiet job.

# FIFTEEN
# EILEEN TAKES THE BUS TO WORK
## 1964

The regular bus driver, Frank, is a big, stocky man with a fleshy face, a double chin and a thick roll of fat at the back of his neck. As the bus pulls in, Eileen avoids looking at him, isolated in his cabin at the front. She steps on the platform at the back, moves down to find somewhere to sit. If she can, she tucks herself into a seat by the window, to gaze out through the mud-splashed glass. On cold, wet days, when the windows fog up, she wipes the pane with her handkerchief so she can see, even though dirt comes off with the condensation.

If the bus is running early, Frank has to park at the stop outside the Social Club. The bus must wait there until the scheduled departure time. He emerges from his cab to stretch his legs. Eileen dreads his trips into the interior of the bus, him jolly and loud, chatting with everyone.

'Mrs Bolt, you're looking pretty in your daisy headscarf. Off to meet your fancy man?'

She smiles reluctantly. 'Just a bit of shopping in the market.'

'General, so dapper today. A red cravat. How daring.' The 'general' is an old, stiff man with a stick, who doesn't know what to say to this banter, sniffs and looks away, embarrassed.

Some encourage Frank.

Jenny Lunn prods his solid belly. 'My, you look prosperous these days.'

'It's the wife,' he pleads. 'She's pregnant and I'm eating extra, to keep her company.'

'Triplets is it, then?'

They roar.

He moves down the aisle, grinning, showing his irregular teeth. Eileen is repulsed by their yellow-grey colour. Like old tombstones. Horrible.

'Lena, my love, we must stop meeting like this, or people will talk.' Leaning over towards her he says, in a loud whisper, 'Behind the Scout Hut, tonight at seven,' and then he laughs and laughs, showering spit.

She cringes. Frank's forays are particularly distressing if she hasn't found a window seat, because then he touches her. His chubby, damp hands have dark, curling hairs across the knuckles and dirt under the nails, which are thick and stained orange. He rests a hand on her shoulder and then moves it subtly upwards, to caress the side of her neck. She sits hunched and frozen, hardly breathing, her skin prickling. When he takes his great paw away, he laughs and laughs.

A skinny redhead called Roy gives out the tickets, his face scarred from acne, his nails bitten down and his fingertips pink and raw in cold weather. His uniform hangs awkwardly from his spare frame. He is polite, nervous. He doesn't take part when Frank comes to harangue the passengers, but stands looking away, fidgeting with his ticket machine and chewing his fingers.

Frank sometimes picks on Roy. 'Roy, lad, how's that luscious blond you've been dating? I can see why she picked you, you look so sexy in your uniform!'

Roy is scarlet, head down and mumbling.

'And those delicate hands...'

Mrs Lunn interrupts, 'That's enough of that coarse talk. Shame on you,' but she's chuckling with Frank.

The lewd talk makes Eileen squirm.

In the middle of August, the Monday after her birthday, a

drunk gets on at the market and falls into the seat next to Eileen, his legs sprawled across the gangway. His arm lands in her lap and he grasps her thigh. She lets out an involuntary squeal and presses herself into the corner, but he turns to her, breath stinking, and grabs her leg harder, pushing his face right into hers. She crams herself back into the corner, paralysed with horror.

Roy appears behind him, coughs and says, 'You need to behave, sir. This is a public conveyance. I...' He gets no further.

The man heaves himself erect, grabs Roy's jacket front and pushes him hard. Roy staggers back and the man follows, thrusting him towards the open rear of the bus. Eileen, cowering in her seat, turns to see the drunk man battering Roy against the ends of the seats and the uprights as he shoves him along the aisle of the bus. At the step down to the platform, Roy loses his footing. The bus rounds a corner and he falls out onto the kerb. Someone presses the bell repeatedly until Frank slows. Half the passengers are on their feet. When the bus stops, the drunk staggers off and flees.

'Moved fast enough considering his state,' a man growls, amidst a storm of shocked protests.

Eileen remains in her seat, shaking, tears running down her face, unable to move in the midst of the hubbub.

In a while, a woman comes to perch beside her. She talks quietly. 'Roy's hurt,' she tells Eileen, 'but he's not too bad. Curled up on the pavement, he was, couldn't get up, bruised and clutching his arm. I think it might be broken. And there's a mess of blood in his hair, he must have hit his head. But he's going to be alright. Someone's been to the house over there and called an ambulance, and the police.'

Eileen accepts a tissue and mops her face. She can't stop shaking.

Everyone has to wait while the police ask their questions. Eileen gives the constable her name and address. That's all she can manage. She hears other people describing what happened. No one can remember much about the man, not even the colour of his hair or what he was wearing. For Eileen it's just a horrible blur.

The kind lady has stayed nearby, and she eventually persuades Eileen to try and stand. She has no memory of how she gets home. All she can tell Ena is, 'A man on the bus grabbed me.'
'What? Did he hurt you?'
'No, not me. Pushed Roy off the bus. While it was moving.'
'Oh, my word!'
Eileen can't eat supper. She takes a cup of hot milk up to bed. She sleeps but has a dreadful dream. Of a dog, trapped in a fenced corner, being beaten with a stick.

She's off work for a week. When she goes back, she hears that Roy does have a broken arm and won't be coming back until it's mended. There's a temporary conductor to work his shifts, a cheerful Irishman called Callum. He's tall, lean but muscular, with a mop of dark, curly hair. Eileen hasn't met an Irishman before. She's more timid than ever getting on the bus again after what happened. But he sings as he dispenses the tickets, a lilting, lovely tune she doesn't know, and he smiles. His eyes sparkle, dark-centred and green, with a dozen smile-wrinkles each side. She finds herself smiling back, despite herself.

# SIXTEEN
# EILEEN'S FLUSTERED BY ROY

In mid-October, on a Monday morning, Roy is back on the bus. As she takes her ticket, Eileen hesitates, flustered. She sits, as usual, under the window, but as the bus sets off, she finds herself staring at Roy, inadvertently catching his attention. Roy returns her gaze. It's as if he hasn't seen her properly before. She glances at her reflection in the window. Pale grey eyes, a small, straight nose, eyebrows forming narrow curves. Her lips are pale, unpainted. She sees her mouth is slightly open, showing her even teeth, the tip of a pink tongue. She closes it, glancing back involuntarily. Roy hasn't looked away. She blushes and ducks her head. She remembers that she hasn't thanked him for defending her, perhaps that's why he's looking at her like this. She's grateful to him, but she can't find a way to say it. She's too distracted by other thoughts.

The next day, as she fumbles for her ticket, they face each other again. He looks as though he's expecting her to speak, and he wants her to say something, but she can't. She looks down and turns away to seat herself.

On Wednesday Roy says, as he takes her money, 'D-did you miss me, then?'

She's startled. She stutters too. 'I... I was... What happened to Callum?' Her face feels hot.

'Who's Callum?' Roy asks.

Mrs Lunn answers, 'He's the lad who took your place while you were off. Irish. You'll have noticed him if he's still at the depot. Cheerful, he is. Sings.'

Roy says, 'No. No one like that. Must have moved on.'

Eileen turns away. Her thoughts are in turmoil.

Ireland, Callum had said, where the difference between night and day is that you can't see the rain. He'd made her laugh.

He'd told stories. 'Come here til I tell yer,' he said, patting the grass bank where he'd settled. 'Yer man there, Frank, was in the pub with me mate Padrick. There's this big dog at Padrick's feet.' He sketched the shape of a dog in the air, his supple fingers curling round the imaginary ears. 'Frank asks, "Does your dog bite?" And Padrick says, "Sure, he doesna." Frank bends down to stroke the dog and it nearly rips his arm off. "I thought you said your dog didn't bite!" sez Frank, furious. "I did, so. That's not my dog."'

Callum said the Irish had no respect for anything or anyone. He certainly had none for Frank. The thought of her torturer getting himself bitten makes her smile. She surfaces, looks up to see Roy smiling back at her. Of course, he couldn't know she was miles away, thinking of someone else.

But that's how the ice is broken. She's miserable, but Roy doesn't seem to see that. He's nice to her, which helps. He speaks a word or two to her each day after that. Towards the end of October, he asks Eileen if she's planning to go to the bonfire. The village has one each year, in the field behind the pub, with a small display of fireworks. The publican makes a bit of extra money selling sausage baps and drinks. She is going, she tells him, she goes with her mother.

On the night, Eileen is surprised to find Roy waiting for them by the gate. He says, 'Hello there, can I get you ladies a drink?'

People turn and look.

Ena frowns at him, suspicious, doesn't recognise him out of uniform, until Eileen introduces them. Ena agrees to a Babycham, Eileen has orange juice and Roy a pint of shandy.

Ena chats. 'This is a first. My Eileen is so quiet I didn't think she knew any young men, and here she is introducing me to one!'

Eileen says, 'It was Roy was attacked by that drunk man who so scared me. He's the one got pushed off the bus. Broke his arm and had to have stitches in his head. He's not that long back at work.' She sees Roy looking at her in amazement. She realises she's managed four whole sentences.

Roy is standing tall, looking proud of himself. He says, 'Oh, it wasn't so bad. I thought he was going to hurt Eileen…' He looks at her, perhaps hoping for something, but her eyes fall to his knees. Brown corduroy. She can't say any more. She only looks up to see the rockets. Ena keeps a conversation going, moaning about the proposed changes to the bus timetable, the complaints from her neighbour about the need for a shelter at the bus stop, October being particularly wet and windy.

Roy says, smiling, 'I don't know about all that, I just give out the tickets.' He turns a little away from her, towards Eileen.

Ena, please think of something more to say, Eileen silently begs.

'Isn't it time that ripped seat on the bus was properly repaired?' Ena asks.

Roy shrugs. 'S'pose so.'


As the fire dies down and people begin to disperse, Roy offers to buy another drink, but Eileen shakes her head and Ena excuses them, saying she's getting chilled. Eileen glances back as they walk away and sees Roy's sad gaze following them. I've still not thanked him properly, she thinks.


The next time Frank swaggers down the interior of the bus, Roy places himself, nonchalantly, at the end of her seat.

Frank minds. 'You're in the way', he says, 'My sweetheart and I need some time together.'

Roy holds his ground. He scowls at Frank; he's trying to look tough. Eileen can see the speeding pulse flicker at his temple. Unexpectedly, Frank desists. Eileen waits for a mocking jibe, but none comes.

Instead, Eileen hears Frank say quietly, 'You fancy that girl, don't you? Best of luck there. You'd have to take it very slow. That one's easily frit,' as he moves away.

Please don't let it be true, Eileen thinks, Roy can't be interested in me.

But maybe it is true. Each day he talks to her whether she replies or not. He seems cheerful and friendly, and doesn't push. And she feels her confidence with him slowly increase.

'Morning Eileen. Wet, isn't it? Always more crowded when it's wet. I thought that dog was going to get trodden on.'

As Eileen and the other passengers board, he stands across the end of an empty pair of seats, so that there's a corner spot for her.

'Thank you,' she says softly. Somehow, gradually, she is getting used to his familiarity. Though other events are making her increasingly anxious.

He beams when she thanks him and always finds something to say in reply. 'I see the lights have gone up already.'

She nods.

Next day, 'Getting colder now; ice on the puddles. Mind you don't slip.'

Then, 'I might see you at the carols outside the church?'

She shakes her head at this, tells him, 'We don't go to church.'

She doesn't want to meet him away from the bus, but she realises from what he says that he does. She feels flutterings of alarm, tries to calm herself. I can just keep quiet, she thinks, say no, it'll be fine, no need to panic. Then one market day Ena boards the bus with her and greets Roy cheerfully.

At the back, two women are discussing the New Year dance.

Roy asks Ena, does she dance?

She smiles. 'No, I'm past that kind of thing. Eileen learnt to dance at school.' She looks firmly at her daughter.

Eileen remembers the awful practice sessions, the waltz, the foxtrot, girls paired up clumsily.

'Would you like to come to the dance with me?' Roy asks Eileen.

Before she has a chance to draw breath, Ena says, 'I'm sure she'd love to!'

Eileen feels a muscle twitching at the side of one eye, sudden sweat in her scalp, she twists her handkerchief so tight that the hem tears. She takes trembling breaths, looks up to see that neither Ena nor Roy have noticed. She has to say 'No'. She must. But she can't speak.

She does go. She can't think of a way out; she'd have to talk to him, explain. But how could she explain? She can't even talk to Ena about what's worrying her.

On the day, Ena insists she make an effort. Eileen wears her tartan dress with the velvet collar, a pearl necklace, and heeled shoes Ena lends her, though they bother her, she's hardly ever worn heels. Her lips are coated in red lipstick. She can't stop herself touching them, it's as if they hurt. She knew she would feel self-conscious and nervous. But with all that's overtaking her, it's worse than that. Her thoughts are a complete mess, fighting for space.

The dance is held in the church hall, where they have the jumble sales. A barn-like, draughty place, rather dilapidated. The vicar's two children are manning the door, taking tickets and directing people to where the coats can be left, in heaps on trestle tables. There are tired Christmas decorations: tinsel, paper chains and balloons, some of them limp now. The light is dull and, at the same time, harsh. Eileen feels people are staring at her. She shivers as she looks about, hunches her shoulders and wraps her coat more tightly, just as Roy moves to help her out of it. She asks herself, what made me think I could do this? She feels quite sick.

Roy looks awkward and uncomfortable in a slightly shiny suit, a white shirt and a diagonally striped tie in orange and purple. He must have had his hair cut, and he's slicked it down. There's a spot of paper stuck to his chin where he's cut himself shaving. He smiles hesitantly at her. She accepts, without a word, the orange juice he offers; she can scarcely sip it. She doesn't raise her eyes to his face. She hears him take noisy gulps of his beer.

They stand with their backs to the wall. Roy, sounding nervous, says, 'They used to have live music, I believe. I've not been before. A band. Swing, rhythm and blues. Even jazz one time, though that didn't go down well, I heard.' He pauses.

She can't reply.

He sighs. He says, 'Last year, they had a man spinning records as well, a "disc jockey". Like on *Top of the Pops*? People really liked that, so this time there's only a DJ.'

Eileen manages a nod.

'The vicar was keen. Wanted to encourage the youngsters into "wholesome activities". But, on the bus, I've heard a lot of older people complaining.'

They listen while the long-haired chap with the records makes a big fuss over Steve Lock. 'Our own talent – our village pop star – first single out!' He plays it twice in succession.

Roy says, 'Lock's not really from round here. It's just he's recently married a woman from the village.'

Eileen thinks Roy must hear all the gossip. But then her thoughts return to her own worries. She knows he'll expect her to dance. They listen to the Dave Clark Five's 'Glad All Over'. Next is 'Rag Doll' by the Four Seasons and Roy wordlessly leads her onto the floor. Her knees threaten to let her down. She knows the song, cringes at the words.

'Hand me down
When she was just a kid her clothes were hand-me-downs
Hand me down
They always laughed at her when she came into town...'

She is stiff in his arms, she can't help it, almost pushing him from her, and she has to turn her head away so forcefully her neck hurts. When the track finishes, they return to the edge of the floor. She knows Roy's done nothing to deserve it, but she just wants to run. The Beatles, 'I Want to Hold Your Hand'. She's going to cry. It's no good. She says, 'I'm sorry. I can't.' And she leaves.

. . .

Every weekday after that, on the bus, she can't face him or speak to him. She wants him to leave her alone, though she hates to have to be unkind, he hasn't done anything wrong. Out of the corner of her eye she can see how dejected he looks. He doesn't ask why. She couldn't begin to tell him, she still hasn't told Ena.

Eileen hears Frank say, 'Leave it. You're wasting your time.'

# SEVENTEEN
# EILEEN EATS HER LUNCH IN THE PARK
## 1965

Winter, slanting pale sunlight, the paths smothered in wet, brown leaves. Eileen smiles, watching the man's dog. They're often in the park, the man and his dog, when she has her lunch. Sooty loves the leaves, rootles among them as they lie in wet heaps, rolls in them where they're scattered loose and muddy on the grass. His owner, camera slung round his neck as always, walks on, looking about, ignoring the tyke. Until he finds something horrid.

'Sooty! Come here!' The animal looks up then returns to excitedly ripping apart a brown paper carrier bag, scattering the contents. The photographer strides over, grabs his collar, scolding him. 'You hooligan mutt. Leave it! Leave it!'

Bedlingtons have smiley faces, which adds to the impression that Sooty loves misbehaving. Eileen likes watching him.

She comes to the park each day to eat her lunch. The weather's cold enough, now, that she has to keep her gloves on while she nibbles her sandwich. On such a chilly day, she likes to breathe in the cool air, blow it out, and watch as the moist plume disperses.

The big changes in her life have her consciously noticing what's altered since yesterday, what's remained the same. Today, the tracery of branches is a sharp dancing silhouette against the racing clouds and the glimpses of blue. Most of the puddles have dried, leaving little rounded beaches of gravel. Those that remain sometimes have shards of ice criss-crossing them, though not today. The flock of crisp packets, wind-blown, has settled into a pile of leaves. A grey gum mass persists on the back of the post supporting the litter bin; it's been there since the summer. She contemplates removing it, thinks of the sensation on her fingers, and again she leaves it.

Eileen knows the man's wife died some time back. She hears him sigh and say to the animal, 'At least you get me out of the house.' She's seen that he's quite disciplined, always hunting for subjects to photograph, so she understands when he adds, 'All the gems I'd have missed in the foulest weather if it weren't for you.'

She jumps when he addresses her, gesturing at the empty half of the seat. 'May I...?'

Startled, Eileen just looks at her feet.

He sits despite her silence. 'You're here most days, aren't you?'

She shrinks inside her coat collar. Why would he pay her any attention? Sooty arrives and sniffs politely at her shoes. She makes herself relax. He never jumps up at her, doesn't muddy her with his scratchy feet, like he does with other people.

'I like him,' she says. 'He looks like a lamb.'

'People think he's a poodle. He's much nicer than a poodle.'

'Mmm.' She makes an effort. 'Have you taken any pictures today?'

'A few. I've a commission for a series of tree paintings. I need two more designs.'

She looks at him, frowning slightly.

He explains. 'I'm an artist, I design cards and sell them from a shop in town. That's usually what the photos are about. I quite like painting for cards.'

She can imagine that.

'I prefer doing portraits, though. Much more interesting and challenging. Though not much demand. I always like an excuse to portray a face. Wondered if I could photograph you for a portrait?'

She can feel the blush race up her neck and face to her scalp, sweat on her palms. 'Oh no... I couldn't...'

'You sure? "Woman on the park bench"? This is your favourite spot, isn't it?'

She's alarmed to hear that he's been observing her. Though she thinks he can't have noticed that much, with her wrapped in her winter coat.

'Don't worry, I won't if you don't want me to. And I thought you'd say no, you're obviously a private kind of person. Just thought I'd ask.'

'Mmm.'

Fortunately, he changes the subject. 'No book today, I see. Probably too cold to sit here for that long. Oh, now what's he found?'

As he departs to drag the dog away from his latest discovery, she realises she's been holding herself rigid.

She takes deep breaths and stretches her shoulders. She needn't worry about the man disturbing her again, she thinks. She won't be here much more. With her stomach swelling.

The same questions that have been pestering her are back again. Ena. What'll she say when she finds out? Throw me out of the house? How'd I manage? She's been pushing such thoughts aside for weeks, but she can't hide from them indefinitely. 'I don't care what others think,' she tells herself.

She thinks: I never imagined I'd have a normal life, a husband and a family. I always saw myself on the edge of things, watching others from the fringe. But with a baby, that won't matter. I'll love and care for it – something will work out – and I really don't care what people think. They're not important. I'm used to it, anyway.

In a tiny corner of her mind, she thinks of how it happened. How lovely he was, how enchanting. He touched her ears, breathed in the smell of her hair, called her *banphrionsa*. Said it meant 'princess'. Made her feel beautiful. She remembers with a blush how she didn't realise what they were doing until it was done. In her memory he seems like a beguiling phantom, a will-of-the-wisp. She thinks, when they ask me who it was, I won't tell them.

'Hold thy tongue,' she remembers reading. 'Do not sully his memory with common gossip.'

The question of finding him and telling him was dismissed as soon as it arrived: he wouldn't want her as a wife. She couldn't be his wife.

# EIGHTEEN
## EILEEN SHOCKS ENA

Ena is washing clothes in the twin-tub when Eileen arrives home from work that spring Friday. Down the hall, the kitchen door is open, she's heaving sheets from the washer into the spin dryer with the big wooden tongs. The air is full of steam and the smell of detergent.

'In the kitchen,' she calls.

Eileen joins her, still in her heavy coat.

Ena glances at her. 'You look chilled. Make us a cuppa, get yourself warm.'

Eileen puts the kettle on the gas.

'This'll make you laugh,' Ena chuckles. 'I had a run-in over you with that new woman, Mrs Walker, in the shop. She said, "Your Eileen's looking bonny. Anyone would think she's in the family way."'

Eileen stiffens, nearly dropping the teapot.

'I told her what for. Cheeky madam.'

Eileen slumps into the chair by the table, suddenly finding it difficult to breathe.

'Eileen? Are you alright?' Ena throws the tongs into the sink, rounds the washer. 'Here, let me get your coat off. You've turned quite pale.'

Eileen stands again, unsteady, knowing what's coming. Ena's face: initial concern, then, as the covering layer is peeled away, shock and disbelief. Ena looks at her properly and sees her expanded belly for the first time. Winter's thick clothes have disguised what now, in the middle of spring, is obvious. Eileen is seven months pregnant.

'Eileen! I don't... I can't... Eileen!'

'I didn't know how to tell you,' Eileen mumbles quietly.

'It can't be true! You wouldn't know how!'

Eileen looks up at her briefly. Her expression gives the lie to that.

The whistle on the kettle blows, building to a scream, unheeded by either woman until, eventually, Ena turns off the gas.

'You've made a fool of me!' Ena is scarlet, her damp hair stuck to her forehead, burly arms across her chest, clasping and unclasping her hands.

Eileen stands motionless, not really listening. She's relieved. Over and over, she's rehearsed how to tell her mother, and now Ena knows. She's hugely relieved. Eileen straightens her shoulders, gazes to one side. She wonders again at the fact that she cannot feel ashamed, though she knows she's supposed to. There's nothing she can say.

She makes them tea.

Ena rails and she rails.

There's nothing Eileen can say.


It isn't until the following day that some of Ena's anger is replaced by concern.

'Were you raped? Why didn't you tell me? Talk to me!'

'No. I wasn't raped.' Eileen can give no explanation. She has thought, every day, about the baby's father, how he captivated and delighted her and then disappeared. She's not angry with him. He was wonderful to her. And now she has his baby. No one will persuade her to talk about him. They'd say things that wouldn't be nice.

'I warned you! I told you...!'

Eileen lifts the iron off the sheet where Ena has left it, in her distraction, and she takes over the ironing.

'I haven't seen you sick. You've not been throwing up?'

Eileen shakes her head.

'I can't believe this. You don't know any men. Except that ginger-topped bus conductor, Roy...'

Of course, he's the only lad Ena's ever seen her with, but still. Eileen can't help smiling crookedly at that idea.

Ena shrugs. 'Does that look mean it isn't Roy?' His name doesn't come up again.

In fact they hardly speak through the rest of the weekend, moving carefully round each other, avoiding having to touch. Until the Sunday evening. They're in the kitchen again. Ena roasted a chicken for lunch and Eileen is stripping the remaining meat from the carcass, to put in the larder meat safe for Monday. She's making soup from the bones, a handful of red lentils and the left-over vegetables. She notices grubby cobwebs bridging the gap between the gas stove and the sink and thinks she should give the cooking area a good scrub.

Ena is ironing pillowcases. In the narrow space, they have bumped each other a couple of times. Ena puts the iron on its back and coughs. She says, 'Eileen, there are some things I simply have to know.'

Ena only calls her by her name when it's serious. Well, it is serious, Eileen knows that. She does her best to answer the questions. But she will say not a single word about the father. Seven months. She wants to keep the baby.

'But how?' Ena beseeches. 'You know what people will say! Everyone will disapprove. How can you keep it?'

Eileen understands the truth of what Ena is saying, but it makes no sense to her. She already loves the child with a pride and joy she cannot express, and she recognises no reason to be ashamed. She does not contemplate anything other than caring for her baby, even though she half expects Ena to say that she must leave home, find somewhere else to live, some way of making a living. She has no idea how she would cope then. It would just have to work out, somehow.

Eileen hasn't seen a doctor. When she suspected there was a baby growing, she couldn't see herself saying to the man in the surgery, 'I think I might be pregnant.' As the weeks went by and she became certain, it was even more difficult: 'I'm six months pregnant...' Ena persuades her to go, and accompanies her. At the surgery, to her relief, it's Ena who answers most of the questions.

'She won't say who the father is, so don't waste your time asking her.'

Walking home, Ena says, 'I've been thinking.' She puts her arm round her daughter and crunches her to her side. 'Eileen, you've been the centre of my life since your father left. It's going to stay that way. I know I asked, but I don't need to know who it was. I'll help. Whatever's needed.'

'I don't have to leave home?'

'No. No. We'll stick together. Manage somehow.'

Eileen takes Ena's hand, beaming. If her mother has decided to support her and the baby, everything will be fine.

A new peace descends on her, her unspoken fretting and worrying replaced by optimism. She can look forwards, plan properly. She has read that hormones make expectant women placid. Now she learns what that means.

And Ena begins a cheerful campaign to support her daughter, to prepare for the baby, and to face out the nasty gossip.

When Freda asks, Ena says, 'Don't worry, she's not planning to set up in competition with the Virgin Mary.'

Freda doesn't speak to her for ages.

Ena buys baby clothes and equipment from the local jumble sale. She tells Eileen, 'I just stared them out. I said, "Lovely weather we've been having." And, "Aren't the daffs lasting well." I could hear them muttering among themselves, but they didn't dare say anything to me out loud.'

. . .

A Monday morning, Eileen has steeled herself, she can't put it off any longer. She stands in front of Beatrix's desk, hasn't even put her bag down or removed her coat. Beatrix looks up at her enquiringly.

Eileen says, 'Beatrix, I'm sorry. I'm going to have to leave.'

Beatrix's face crumples. She looks confused.

Eileen realises the kind woman thinks she's done something wrong, to make her want to go. 'Oh, no,' she says, 'It's not you. Or Mr James.'

Beatrix seems relieved but still puzzled.

'It's me.' Eileen takes off her coat, turns to put it on the hook, self-consciously smoothing her baby bulge with a hand.

A gasp.

'You've been so good to me.' A tear slips down Eileen's cheek.

Beatrix is stunned. She gets up, walks round the desk and folds Eileen into an embrace. 'Oh, my dear...'

'I should have told you before. Kept putting it off. But now I can't manage much longer. I thought, maybe the end of the week? I'm really sorry it's such short notice.'

Beatrix releases her. 'We'll cope,' she says quietly, taking out a lace-edged handkerchief to dry Eileen's face, 'Are you alright?'

Eileen nods, smiling shyly.

On the Friday, Beatrix gives her a toy rabbit and Mr James shakes her hand sadly, saying, 'Thank you for all your hard work. We'll miss you.'

She hesitates to accept the envelope, stuffed with money, he thrusts into her grasp.

He says, 'Think of all you'll need,' and puts his hands behind his back.

He's right. It will be very welcome.

Eileen can't see the office as she leaves for the last time, her eyes blurred. She's clutching the rabbit and the African violet Beatrix pressed on her at the last minute.

Beatrix calls after her, 'You take care of yourself. And come and visit, will you? Bring the baby. Please?'

The last month, at home, is filled with cleaning, sewing, knitting and painting. Ena has already created a wool blanket with squares made up from her bag of leftovers. Eileen pores over a pattern for bootees; she's not tried anything so fiddly before. They come out slightly different sizes, making Ena laugh. Together, they paint a crib Ena found in a junk shop.

'Poor thing. It'll think it's living in the jungle.' Ena chuckles as Eileen puts wobbly parrots on the ends, copied from an advert in a Sunday colour supplement. Red, yellow and green against the lemon painted wood.

Are these proper labour pains? She simply doesn't know. But the clenching spasms are much worse than the muscle cramps, the bad period pain she was told about. They are awful. Though Ena had warned her. She said, 'That tale the midwives spin is nothing short of a lie. It'll feel as though your insides are being torn apart. You just have to hang on to the thought that women survive it. Some even do it over and over. You will get through it.'

Eileen does what she's never done before and gets herself to the phone box to call a taxi. The money Mr James gave her is proving so useful. The taxi driver takes one look and knows what to do, where to go. As she sits in the back, suffering over every bump, round every corner, she's telling herself she will get through this.

Thank goodness her waters don't break until she's in the labour ward.

A midwife examines her and coldly says, 'Of course it hurts, you silly woman, you're in labour.'

She will know there's no husband, and disapprove. But at least she's told Eileen that this is it.

'If you'd thought of this earlier, you wouldn't be in this pickle. Your mother must be mortified.'

'Can you phone her for me, please? Let her know. She's at work.' The woman scowls but does as she's asked.

Ena arrives, all bustle and concern, proving the midwife wrong. And, somehow, getting her to be less hostile.

Eileen soon stops caring. The pains come stronger. Twisting, tearing, terrible pains. In between, she tells herself she must be through the worst. But she isn't. She stops caring who sees or hears her. She stops caring that all the parts of her body are on display. That her bladder and bowels are no longer in her control. Sweat runs in her eyes. Her hair is plastered to her face. The agony wipes everything else away.

Suddenly, the midwife looms over her. 'Eileen, you're ready. It's time. Listen to me. I need you to push.'

Ena's hand is crushing hers.

'I can't…!'

'Yes, you can.' There's a new encouragement in her voice. And in Ena's.

'No strength…'

'You're ready. Here it comes! Push now!'

And somehow she does.

Pain follows pain. Pushing. Panting.

And the baby arrives in a final rush.

Puce and smeared in gore, Eileen sees her child for the first time, through the tears pouring down her face. It's a girl. Who yells furiously.

'She's a lusty one.'

The baby is placed gently on Eileen's exhausted body. She is flooded with love for her.

It's Thursday 3rd June 1965. Ena tells Eileen that the first American space walk from Gemini IV was on the evening news, on the wireless. She's looking adoringly at the baby. 'Even though I think star signs mean nothing, that makes her doubly a Gemini.' She turns to look at Eileen, tears in her eyes. 'I am so proud of you,' she says.

. . .

The baby is registered as Alice Mallory, father unknown.

# NINETEEN
## EILEEN AND ALICE ARE AT THE VILLAGE BAZAAR
### 1966

The village hall is decked with paper chains, balloons and fairy lights for the Christmas bazaar. The tree has paper poinsettia flowers studded over it, an angel on the top. Stalls are dressed in red and green crêpe paper, a crib in the corner. Christmas carols play from tinny loudspeakers. It's crowded, the atmosphere hot and noisy. Eileen was hoping to find a Christmas present for Ena but is now wondering if this was a good idea. Alice is hanging onto Eileen's coat, looking uncertainly around, dragging her feet. Eileen holds her hand firmly.

Jars of jam, knitted tea cosies, hand-made cards shedding glitter; nothing that catches Eileen's eye. She's fingering a scarf, Alice now chattering and showing her rabbit, Henry, to a silent little girl in a pushchair, when she hears the father of the child say, 'I don't know much about these things, but shouldn't she be walking and talking by now? Eighteen months? And she's... sort of sluggish?'

He's talking to the new district nurse. Eileen doesn't know her name. She has her back slightly turned as if she might prefer to get on with buying her Christmas presents.

The woman says, 'Don't fret. Every child is different. I expect she's just not rushing it. Of course, if you're worried you can always make an appointment to see Doctor Daniels?'

'No, no. Doesn't do to be impatient with children, does it?'

She nods, smiling kindly, and moves away.

Eileen knows the little girl and her mother, Barbara Jenkins. Maggie was born the week before Alice. Eileen hasn't seen Mr Jenkins, Stuart, out with his daughter before. He's a stocky chap, she remembers him from school, he was already plump then. His hair is cut as if he's in the army. He's wearing trousers with a firm crease, a shirt and knitted tie under a V-necked sweater and a tweed jacket. An accountant, she's often seen him in a suit. Eileen wonders if the tie is Barbara's idea. He usually dresses so conservatively.

The girl looks dazed in all the racket, but content just to sit – Alice would be fighting to get out. Alice grasps the back of the pushchair to nudge Maggie to and fro, to and fro, smiling to herself. Maggie seems to like the rocking movement. When Stuart notices the bumping, he turns, scowling a little. Eileen smiles apologetically, disengages Alice's hand, beams at her small tantrum and turns to lead her daughter away. Just in time, she spots that Alice has dropped Henry and is clutching a soft, patchwork ball she must have filched from Maggie.

'Sorry,' she mutters as she returns it.

Too noisy; too crowded. Alice suddenly looks about to cry. 'Let's go home to grandma, have some tea,' Eileen tells her.

# TWENTY
# STUART HAS TO ACCEPT THE TRUTH
## 1967

Stuart came upon *The Common Sense Book of Baby and Child Care*, by Dr Benjamin Spock, in the library. He'd heard people talk about it and took a look. The descriptions of a growing child didn't seem right. He kept going back to the library and re-reading sections, unable to grasp what they told him. But by the next summer, when Maggie was two, he knew she was somewhat behind in her development. He and Barbara still hadn't discussed it. He tried, but somehow the conversation always got diverted. He wondered if Barbara also suspected but couldn't face the thought. He'd found himself getting angry at the prospect, if he was right, of having to tell people. He felt ashamed. Trapped. He knew his life wasn't destined to be a Cinzano advert, but he didn't want to be the saintly parent of a subnormal child. He wanted some joy.

They were at the doctor's surgery because Maggie had been stung by a horse fly on her face, which had swollen so badly one eye was closed. Stuart thought the doctor was bound to notice something.

Dr Daniels was gently prising the eye open. 'It's usually just the soft tissue that's swollen, but if I can, I want to see her eye, make sure it's alright.'

Maggie was grunting, trying to push him away with her fists, her nose running.

He wiped her with a tissue and had another attempt. 'I think the eye's fine.'

He had her sitting on the desk in front of him and he leant back, holding her in both hands, to take a good look.

Stuart glanced sideways at his wife.

She was pleased to hear the eye was alright.

He waited.

'Has she seen a dentist yet?' the doctor asked.

What had that got to do with the matter in hand?

Barbara said, 'Not yet. Should she have?'

'Well... Um. It's just her teeth seem an unusual shape.'

Barbara's forehead wrinkled in puzzlement. She put a hand out towards her daughter.

'What do you mean – unusual?' Stuart asked, on her behalf.

'Sorry, probably nothing. But can I ask some questions?'

They both nodded.

Dr Daniels went through it all. Speech – none. Walking – no. Standing – no. Potty training – nothing.

Stuart wished, now, he'd forced the issue with Barbara, since her face told him she'd convinced herself there was no real problem at all. She sat stiffly upright, ashen, her lips pressed firmly shut. Her hands were clutching Maggie's arm.

'I think we should have her properly assessed by a paediatrician. I'll make a referral.'

His wife looked quite numb.

And what did the comment about Maggie's teeth signify?


There were tests, assessments and consultations. They were told Maggie was developing slowly.

Stuart asked, 'She'll catch up? Later? Is that what you mean?'

'Well,' the doctor said. He seemed to be taking pains to be patient. 'She's behind on her milestones.'

What did that mean?

'And when the developmental delay is as great as this... It tells us... She might not reach the level of achievement of most children.'

Stuart could remember only fragments of what came after that. The words *congenital anomalies* kept coming back to him later. But afterwards, at last, he and Barbara talked about it.

'Are they saying she's retarded?' Stuart asked, immediately regretting the word when he saw his wife's reaction.

There was a silence. 'My beautiful girl,' she said eventually. 'I knew she was a bit behind, maybe wasn't going to be the brightest.'

So, she had considered it.

'But I was waiting for her to talk, see what she said.' She looked Stuart square in the face. 'Won't she ever talk? Or walk?'

He thought she was going to cry but she didn't. Somehow that made it worse. 'They haven't said that. At least, I don't think they have. All those medical words...'

'Can we ask, next time?' she said.

'We can try.'

At the next visit, he asked for the specialist to spell it out. It was a young woman, a 'registrar'. She talked with them for several minutes, mostly looking at Barbara, holding her hand across the desk. Among all the other things, the fact that her teeth hadn't grown normally was a sign that the problems were deep-rooted in Maggie's nature. Barbara emerged with tears in her eyes but smiling because of the positive things she'd heard.

Stuart couldn't tell her he was enraged. How dare that *girl* say such things? Those weasel words *congenital anomalies* again. She'd said it meant Maggie was born with problems that no amount of care could overcome. Born with them, implying she had got all this from her parents. From him. Even if she hadn't said as much.

Three weeks later, Barbara had gone to the shop, and he found himself shouting at Maggie. 'I'm not the one to blame! I won't have it!'

Why us? This isn't what we anticipated. Saddled with... He prodded her hard enough to make her gasp. I've done nothing to deserve this. He pinched her plump arm, and she squealed. There was bright red mark.

Oh, God, he thought. Will it have faded before Barbara gets back? I should have pinched her on a place that was out of sight. But then he smacked his hand fiercely. What an awful thing to think! 'Mustn't do that again,' he told himself loudly.

He knew he'd want to.

He dried her face roughly. 'It'll be like Down syndrome. The mother that's the cause.' He took a deep breath. 'I mustn't ever say that to Babs.'

# TWENTY-ONE
# BARBARA'S SURPRISED BY A NEW FRIENDSHIP
## 1968

Barbara Jenkins watched pretty, bright, two-year-old Alice stamp a circle around Maggie. Her daughter had dark eyes that never quite looked focused, a snub nose, dark curly hair. She was wearing her usual grin, displaying her oddly shaped teeth and fat gums. Mentally subnormal. Retarded. Backward. All the terms horrible. Maggie had still not uttered a word and was showing no inclination to walk. In fact she scarcely attempted to crawl, sitting squat on her fat bottom, as now, docilely gazing about her. At least she could sit, and she could also use her hands for simple things. She could grab and hold. Maybe she might learn to feed herself.

Alice was blossoming. Such a pretty face; bright eyes, blond hair scooped into pigtails, tied with pink ribbon. She was a sunny, lively child. She was singing tunelessly but more or less in time to 'I Can See for Miles' by The Who, playing on the radio. Watching the two little ones together was almost unbearable. Though Alice was so sweet with Maggie. Today she'd tucked her current favourite toy beside Maggie on the seat. A furry white teddy Alice called Pippa. Eileen had made it for her last Christmas after a baby polar bear was born in London Zoo. Pictures of him were everywhere at the time. He was named Pipaluk, which apparently meant 'the little one'.

How did it start, the two girls playing together? Barbara wondered. Maybe as far back as the visit to the GP's surgery for four-month vaccinations? She was sitting next to Eileen in the crowded waiting room, their girls in prams. Alice was propped up in that ancient contraption of Eileen's, looking with curiosity at Maggie. Maggie was in the splendid, two-tone Silver Cross Stuart had bought. It was waiting for her when she got home from hospital. He'd had it kept at the shop until then. At four months old Maggie couldn't hold up her head. Alice was able to lean out and stretch across to grasp Maggie's hand, holding it for long enough that Barbara said, 'Look at them, isn't that sweet.'

Eileen had smiled.

Barbara had recognised how different the babies were.

Later on, when they met in the street, Alice always seemed pleased to see Maggie; she waved and beamed.

One day, after Alice had started walking, Maggie in her pushchair, they bumped into each other at the Jenkins' gate, and Barbara invited them in. Eileen hesitated, and it was Alice who decided, waving imperiously at her mother. And, suddenly, there they were, Alice entertaining herself around Maggie on the carpet in the living room, taking possession of the toys that Maggie ignored, and playing with Maggie herself, giving her little pats. Eileen drinking tea.

Barbara remembered, when Alice was born, there was a lot of nasty talk.

'She's no right to look so happy. No morals that woman. God knows how the child will turn out.'

'Eileen takes after her heathen mother.'

'Conceived under a gooseberry bush, never mind found there. Or up against the back wall of the pub, more like.'

Lots of speculation about who the father was. Barbara looked at Alice. A bit like Eileen, but like no one else she knew.

In those early days, even when Eileen didn't hear the jibes, she'd have been hard pressed to miss the looks. But she didn't seem to care. Just abandoned herself, in her quiet way, to loving her daughter. Not bothered that no one befriended her. Used to it, perhaps.

Barbara found that was how it was for her too, when people realised about Maggie. They behaved as if Maggie's condition was infectious, avoiding both of them. It couldn't be infectious, of course, and they must've known that, if they thought about it. Barbara had not expected to be so isolated. She'd had several women friends. Perhaps if they hadn't moved with Stuart's work? Her old school friends were too far away now. But no point in thinking about what couldn't be changed. And Stuart was really patient and helpful. She sighed.

That day when the girls first played together, Barbara was feeling particularly in need of company. She'd received a long letter from her cousin about her Billy's achievements. Several funny anecdotes. The cousin wrote a good story. But no one wanted to hear about Maggie's feeble progress. Eileen was different. She was completely accepting. The visit was so nice that Barbara contrived more invitations. She was careful to keep them casual.

Now, she wouldn't have said that she and Eileen were friends exactly. They didn't talk much except about their girls, certainly didn't exchange other confidences, but Eileen was just there, smiling, being nice. No one else was. And here she was, Eileen, come to take Alice home.

'Your coat,' Eileen said gently to her daughter.

Alice retrieved it from the sofa, pulled it across the floor by one sleeve and beamed, talking baby talk to it. She refused help putting it on. The coat, created by Eileen, was a wonder. The fabric had a large pattern of zoo animals on it. Eileen had made little stuffed baby versions, which were attached to their mothers by ribbons, or peeked out of pockets. There was a kangaroo with a pocket where her pouch would be, a stuffed joey looking out. There was an ostrich with a line of plump yellow chicks suspended on a stout thread beside it. A monkey hung upside-down by its tail from the collar. The coat was a work of art.

Alice wouldn't put on the gloves that were attached to a string threaded through the coat's sleeves. Squirming, she reluctantly accepted her hat. Before she set off, she patted all the pockets, a recent ritual. She pointed at the neighbour's spaniel and said something Barbara didn't catch. Barbara watched as Alice and Eileen walked, toddler paced, down the street hand in hand, with Eileen humming. They swung their joined hands in time with the tune. Eileen skipped as she hummed, looking ridiculous and happy.

## TWENTY-TWO
## EILEEN GETS ALICE THROUGH THE MEASLES
### 1969

In the summer, all the young children in the village catch the measles, one after the other. Those who haven't already had it, that is, or had the new vaccine. Eileen wishes she'd had Alice vaccinated, like Barbara did with Maggie. The mite is coughing, miserable and then delirious. Her temperature climbs alarmingly past one hundred and four. The doctor comes and advises cooling sponge baths, frightening both Eileen and Ena with the possibility that, if her temperature goes any higher, Alice might have a fit. He insists the curtains are closed so that bright light doesn't damage Alice's eyes. Eileen had no idea measles could be so serious. Feeling so very guilty, she does everything he advises.

For two awful days and nights, Eileen sits beside her daughter. Somehow she makes herself calm. She bathes Alice's forehead with a cool facecloth, talks to her, sings to her. Tucks her in when she shivers, fans her when she flings the covers aside, her face flushed bright pink. Constant sips of water, constant encouragement.

'I remember when you had the chickenpox. I think you were ten,' Ena tells Eileen. 'There was no one to help out, I still had the chores to do. I had to leave you to it for the most part. I only took a couple of days off work – I didn't dare take more. I couldn't afford to.' Ena grimaces then smiles. 'As you got better you got bored with stopping in bed. A neighbour complained at seeing you in your nightie in the front garden.'

Eileen remembers the telling off Ena gave her.

Ena says, once Alice is on the mend, 'You have done well. I've been impressed. You've been worried sick, I know you have, but Alice wouldn't have known, you've seemed so confident.'

Eileen doesn't remember Ena ever saying such a thing to her. She is too overwhelmed to reply. She thinks about the last week. How did I cope? she asks herself. I've been thinking only about Alice, only about what she might need, making myself be calm – for her. It's not confidence exactly. It's just knowing that there is simply nothing more important.

Alice, in her nightie, peers round Eileen's bedroom door and says, 'Mummy, can I go in the garden? I think there's a bird's nest in the hedge.'

'Let me take your temperature first, then we'll see.' Eileen doesn't mean to sound cross. It's such a relief to hear her chattering. 'Come here so I can give you a hug.'

Alice clambers up into Eileen's bed for a snuggle.

Ena puts her head round the door and smiles, 'Looks like I'll be getting the breakfast. Don't either of you go anywhere. You both need to rest.'

Next thing Eileen knows, Ena is waking them up. They're still curled together in the warm bed.

Alice is so much better.

'I'll get the tea,' Ena says later. 'You spend time with her, take her for a walk, perhaps?' She peers out of the window. 'Maybe not, it's coming on to rain. You know I do like being a grandma. Helping you have time for the sorts of things I couldn't manage when you were little. Makes up for it a bit.'

Eileen gives her a long hug. 'You've always looked after me really well,' she says.

She turns to her daughter. 'Alice, are you well enough for us to make biscuits?'

As they wait for the biscuits to cool so that the promised pink icing can go on, Eileen takes Alice into the dripping garden. She can see Ena, peeling potatoes, watching through the kitchen window.

'Let me guess,' Ena says when they come in. 'You were showing her something. A plant or a bird, or some kind of bug. Is it the wrong time of year for tadpoles in the pond? All those things you learnt as a girl, tucked in a corner with a book while I was busy.'

Alice grabs Ena's leg. 'Ladybirds,' she says, 'Eating greenfly!' She mimes gross munching.

Once Alice is fully well again, Ena suggests they all go up to town on the bus. They walk from the bus station to Abbey Park. Ena has a bag of stale bread for Alice to feed to the ducks. She and Eileen stand watching, the little girl's face wreathed in smiles.

Ena tells Eileen, 'I remember bringing you here once when you were small. Traumatic, it was. There were geese and they frightened you. They strutted about like bully boys, snatching the crusts. Then one came and hissed so loudly in your face, you burst into tears. Look at Alice though. Not a bit worried!'

When the crumbs have all gone and the ducks have swum away, Ena bustles them along to the next thing – the model railway. Alice's eyes sparkle with excitement. Eileen helps her climb on and sits herself behind, holding her tight. though she's not sure she should trust the little train. Ena had told Eileen she would ride too, but now she shakes her head. 'I'm too tired. I'll just watch,' she says and sits down on the platform bench. She does look weary, but proud and happy.

After the ride, they have tea in the café. Scones with jam, and an ice cream for Alice. She shrieks with delight. A lovely day. That Eileen hopes Alice will remember.

## TWENTY-THREE
## EILEEN WORRIES WHEN ALICE STARTS SCHOOL
### 1970

For Alice's fifth birthday, 3rd June, Eileen makes a cake that looks like a bird's nest. She's put shredded coconut on the sides and around the top, making a nest for twelve sugared chocolate eggs and a fluffy chick she saved from Easter. She carefully puts one of Alice's presents, a knitted hat with a felt top made to look like a hen's head, over the clutch of eggs. Eileen and Ena laugh as Alice lifts the hat off and puts it back on the cake, giggling. It's a while before Eileen can persuade her daughter that the cake might be cut.

Ena had suggested they get a pet for Alice, maybe something undemanding, like a tortoise. Eileen was sure Alice would like one, but it would wander off or die. She doesn't want Alice to be losing things she loves. That was why she'd made the hen hat. A pretend creature is safe.

Alice likes the hat, and the picture books she's given, but pushes away the school uniform, making a face. She's not fooled by the pretty wrapping paper.

'Don't want to go to school,' she wails. 'I won't know anybody.'

Maggie won't be there, thinks Eileen.

Ena says, 'You have to Ally, it's the law. But you can come home and have your lunch with me. I'll not be far away.'

Alice still looks reluctant.

Ena says quietly, 'I'm planning to be at home more, I can't go on working the

hours I do. I'm getting too old for it. I'm going to talk to Himself about cutting down.'

Eileen looks at Ena. It's the first time she's heard her mention that she's feeling the strain. For four years, since Eileen went back to work for Mr James, she and Ena have dove-tailed their hours. They've managed. Mr James and Beatrix - Trixie she's told Eileen to call her - are so kind. They even let her bring Alice with her, on the odd occasion that Ena's unwell. All that time, Ena's been doing split shifts: the early morning hours stocking the shelves, late afternoon manning the till. Home with Alice in between.

Now she thinks about it, Ena does seem tired. Eileen watches and sees her mother stop at the corner of the stairs to catch her breath, and then again at the top, holding onto the newel post. 'Are you alright?' she asks.

'It's nothing, just my age,' Ena insists.

Eileen has only one thing on her mind, though. How will Alice cope at school?


For Alice's first day of school, Eileen arranges to start work late. She delivers Alice to the playground and then she watches her through the railings. Other mothers are there, looking anxious and proud, or distracted and tired. They are all giving sidelong looks at the only man there, with long hair and flared trousers, carrying a transistor radio, blaring tinny tunes. One of them is a song Alice likes, 'Magic Bus'.

Alice has forgotten she didn't want to go. All dressed up in her uniform, she is beaming at other children. Much more confident than I was at her age, Eileen thinks. A tall, skinny girl bends down to tie her shoelace, but seems to struggle. Alice walks over to her, cocking her head and smiling. She must have offered to help because the skinny one, wiping her eyes on her sleeve, stands up and puts the foot forward. Alice kneels. Eileen can imagine the look of concentration on her daughter's face. The girls are soon both grinning. They wander off in conversation, too far away to be heard. When the bell goes and all the children are called inside, the two girls go in together. Are they holding hands? Neither of them even glances back to the fence.

Eileen stands there for a while before she can tear herself away. She knows she'll be thinking of Alice all day, just waiting to see her again.

At teatime, Alice is buzzing with excitement, talking of what they did in class and at playtime.

'Miss Edwards is *so* pretty. She's got a hanky with a rose. In the corner, I saw it. It was pink. She wiped my face.'

'Who's she, sweetheart?' Ena asks.

'My teacher,' says Alice with her mouth full, in a tone that says: everyone should know that.

Ena grins at Eileen.

'Brenda's got long, long plaits with stripey ribbons.'

'Who's this Brenda, then, sweetheart?' Ena asks.

'She sat next to me. We had milk in little, little bottles. One just for me.'

So different from how I was at that age, Eileen thinks. She's amazed and relieved.

## TWENTY-FOUR
## EILEEN'S MOTHER IS POORLY

One warm day, Eileen notices that Ena's ankles are swollen. Ena makes a joke of them. 'Puffy legs, ankles bulging out instead of in, fat feet. Getting past it. Like in that Reg Cartwright picture: the old ladies with round feet stuffed into stretched, ancient shoes.' She laughs and changes the subject.

But when the weather cools, Ena's ankles don't improve. 'They ache a bit,' she admits. 'Just let me prop them up for a while.'

Eileen pushes the pouf in front of Ena's chair.

'Don't like to look at them like this,' she says crossly and covers them with the blanket Eileen made when she was learning to knit, out of leftover wool in different colours that never looked quite right.

The weeks go by, and Ena is coughing. When did that start? It's hard to pinpoint it. She's breathless on the stairs. Eileen tries to stop herself watching, but she can't.

Ena scowls at her. 'Don't fuss. You wait till you get to my age.'

Then a neighbour's cat scratches her leg and, after the trickle of blood stops, Eileen watches a slow, continuous ooze of clear fluid that runs down her mother's leg and makes her foot sticky in its slipper. Eileen's not seen that happen to anyone before.

Ena says, 'Don't be silly, it's nothing. Don't fuss. It'll heal.' Eileen can't help but worry.

Then one day, when she comes home, she finds Ena collapsed in the armchair neither of them like, the one with wooden legs and arms and an orange chenille fabric. She's staring blankly ahead.

'What is it?' Eileen asks. 'What's happened? Are you alright?'

Ena turns her head away, pushes herself up in the chair. There's a pause. 'I went to the doctor's,' she says.

'Oh.' Eileen's palms are suddenly moist. She wipes her hands on her sleeves.

'He was very thorough. Listened with his stethoscope, looked at my legs. He made me take my shoes and stockings off. He tutted at my feet, made dents in them by pressing with his thumb.' She smiles wanly, looking down at them.

Eileen watches her, her hands gripping her elbows to stop them shaking.

'He said I have leaking heart valves.'

There's a silence. What is a valve? It sounds frightening.

'My symptoms, he said, are due to "heart failure".' Ena picks up a piece of paper from the side table. 'He gave me a prescription. I haven't had the energy to take it to the chemist. Just came straight home.'

She must be feeling worse than I thought, Eileen realises, to go to the doctor at all. She wants to comfort her, but she can't think what to say.

'I was worried it was cancer,' Ena says.

Eileen nods. 'It's good that it's not.'

Ena grimaces. 'I asked him,' she says reluctantly. 'Heart failure? Did it mean my heart was dying? He said, "I wouldn't put it quite like that"...' She gazes out of the window.

What a terrible thing for Ena to hear. Eileen shivers. What a dreadful thing for him to have said.

'He told me the tablets would help.'

Eileen goes to her mother, drops to her knees and puts her arms around her. Heads together, they stay like that, saying nothing. Eileen hears her mother's breaths, coming more quickly than hers. She manages not to cry.

Ena gives her a little shake, 'Come on now. Alice'll be coming in. Get the kettle on for us.'

Ena reduces her working hours. Eileen takes over the digging in the garden, though Ena hates no longer being able to do it herself.

When she goes back for a check-up, the doctor talks about an operation.

Ena tells Eileen, 'I said to him, I don't need an operation. I'm not that bad. The tablets are doing a good job. I'd never have an operation, anyway.'

Eileen doesn't know if that's a good thing or not.

Some weeks later, Sunday, they are in the garden, admiring the snowdrops pushing through the wet leaf litter. Ena is talking about making a cabbage pie and stops mid-sentence. She gasps and staggers, clutching for the clothes prop, which isn't enough to support her. She falls, dragging the washing line down with her. Eileen rushes to help but fails to catch her in time. On the path, Ena lies in the weeds, her left arm bent under her and her mouth lop-sided, looking appalled.

Alice looks up and screams. Eileen only just stops herself screaming too. She tries to get her mother up, but Ena can't help, can't even speak. Her eyes implore but Eileen doesn't know what to do. Her heart is racing.

Alice, peering over Eileen's shoulder, says, 'She's gone crooked.' She sounds as if she's about to cry.

But that helps Eileen. 'Go find someone,' she says. 'Gramma needs an ambulance. Hospital.'

Alice scampers off, comes back with Freda from next door. Freda has a telephone and hurries back to make the call. When the ambulance arrives, Eileen goes with Ena, persuading Alice to stay with Freda.

They keep Ena in, 'for observation', though she's moving and complaining by the time she reaches a bed on a ward. No one explains anything. Eileen has to wrench herself away to go home to Alice. On the bus, she sits hunched up and shaking. What was it? It looked for a while as if she'd had a stroke. And that wouldn't just go away, would it?

Eileen learns what's wrong from a bright and enthusiastic medical student, a girl. Eileen is sitting at Ena's bedside as the lass shows the boy with whom she's paired some little purple marks under Ena's nails, the changed shape of her thumbnail, the 'residual signs of stroke'.

'It's classic SBE,' she says. 'We're so lucky!'

Ena's half asleep, hopefully can't hear any of this.

Eileen is worried enough for a burst of courage. She interrupts to ask what that means.

'Sub-acute bacterial endocarditis,' the girl recites. 'Will have come from the root abscess.'

Eileen stares at her. Ena had a terrible toothache a few weeks ago and the dentist did something that hurt a lot. Is that what she means?

'It's infection of a damaged heart valve. Came from the dental work – typical for SBE, that is.'

Why is this girl talking as if her mother isn't there? But she needs to understand. 'So is it like a boil, it'll burst and get better?'

'Not really. The infection causes more damage to the valve, and you get debris shed into the circulation, blocking small blood vessels downstream. That's what the purple spots in the skin are. And that's what happened in her brain, and caused the little stroke that brought her in.' She turns to her colleague to say, 'There'll be damage to the kidneys. I bet she'll have blood in her urine.' She seems so absorbed and excited.

Eileen knows what a valve is now. She looked it up in the library. Valves control the flow of fluid. There are all different kinds. She'd wondered how the names were chosen. 'Poppet' –

her dad had called her that – made her smile a bit, and 'butterfly'. Infection of a damaged heart valve. She imagines an autumn leaf losing its shape, disintegrating, shedding fragments into the wind.

'Can it be mended?'

The student replies, 'Actually, it's difficult…' She looks at Eileen's face and realises what she's said. The pair leave and minutes later a nurse takes their place. Rather than talk about what's wrong with Ena, she's just kind. Eileen can sense that, as her mind glazes over.

Ena comes home better, but not well enough to return to work. 'Not all bad, though,' she says, 'me taken sick like this. It's got me out of having to cope with this decimalisation business.'

She can still keep an eye on Alice while Eileen is out. Then one evening, she suddenly has bad trouble breathing. Eileen rushes out of the house to the telephone box and calls an ambulance. Ena is re-admitted to hospital.

It's the beginning of a sad, exhausting pattern of spells in hospital, periods at home, and each time Ena is less well than before.

Trixie tells Eileen, 'Don't fret, get yourself off home to Alice.' But they're short of money, Eileen needs to work now Ena can't. She doesn't want to ask Ena if she has any savings. Eileen has none to speak of. Perhaps she shouldn't have spent every spare penny on Alice.

Eileen is only five minutes late. Alice is back from school, on the step, calling out through the front door, 'Gramma, don't cry. Mummy'll be here soon. Don't cry Gramma.' She turns, so pleased to see Eileen, and says, 'There was a bump. She said a rude word.'

Ena has slipped and fallen and is lying close behind the door. She can't get up. Eileen goes round to get in the back of the house. Poor Ena has one elbow and both knees bruised and scraped. Lucky it wasn't worse.

Eileen can't bear the thought that something like that might happen again. She goes to work the next day only to tell them she has to stop. She has no idea what she'll do for money. With Alice being her only child, she doesn't even get a family allowance.

'I've loved working here,' she says sadly, 'But I can't manage anymore.'

Mr James says they'll find someone to fill in, short term. See how things work out.

That's kind.

## TWENTY-FIVE
## EILEEN'S MOTHER DIES
### 1971

Stuart is pushing Maggie down the street in her big buggy. He stops, jovial as usual. 'Good morning, Eileen. Alice at school? How's the world treating…?'

Eileen glances up, sees the concern on his face.

'Ena's no better? You look fatigued.'

Eileen shakes her head. 'No better, no…' She can feel tears welling up.

'I'll come round and visit, shall I?'

'Well…' Why would he want to do that? Ena scarcely knows him. But Eileen's too tired to argue.

He says, 'I'll just deposit Maggie at home.'

Thankfully, he refuses a cup of tea, just chats for a few minutes, getting a thin smile from Ena. But he returns the next morning, says he's contacted the doctor to arrange for a nurse to come in, to help with caring for Ena. He's found a wheelchair and a commode they can borrow. Eileen hadn't any idea such things were possible. She feels nervous at the thought of a stranger coming in. And how will Ena react?

The district nurse who mostly comes is a woman called

Siobhan. She's firm and kind, and Ena doesn't mind her. All that fierce independence, Eileen thinks. Gone.

Siobhan is matter of fact. 'You can't lift her on your own, and if you try, you'll hurt the both of you. So here's what we'll do...' She wipes and turns Ena, and tucks sheets in. She sings Irish folk songs in her sweet voice. Eileen recognises some of them and tears well into her eyes.

The smiling face, on the bus, all those years ago.

'There, now,' says Siobhan softly, catching sight of her.

Eileen rubs her face on her sleeve. 'It's alright. I'd forgotten how lovely those songs are.'

Sometimes Ena is better and chats away, giving her old, irreverent slant on things. She says she isn't at all sure about life after death, 'On balance, I hope there isn't any.'

'Oh yes?' Eileen says, though she knows the reason.

'If you think about it, it would be so crowded,' Ena says. 'I like a bit of company, but that would be too much.'

Eileen smooths the bedspread.

'Why do people think there's a life after death if they believe in God, but not if they don't? Why can't there be life after death and no God, or a God and no afterlife?'

Eileen has heard all this before. She smiles wistfully, remembering how cross their devout neighbour, Freda, was at such profane ideas.

Eileen's too sad and tired for laughter. Each day Ena is less her feisty self, her wry humour fading. She is departing. Eileen already misses her so much. She tries to appear cheerful for Alice's sake.

One time, Ena tells Eileen, 'This is my last summer, unless I'm much mistaken. I'd like to see the flowers, spend time in the garden. Talk to Siobhan and get her to help. I know it'll tire me, but what does that matter? I want to feel the sun on my cheek and the breeze under my collar. I could get wet in the rain, I'd like that.'

Eileen swallows back her misery and smiles.

Siobhan pats her shoulder when Eileen tells her, and they manoeuvre Ena into the sunshine. The trip outside is possible only the once.

Siobhan speaks to Eileen about what she might tell Alice. 'I know it's hard, but it will help her if you can talk to her about what's happening to her grandma.'

'I don't know that I can.'

'When bad things happened, my mother could never talk about them with me and me brothers. And what did we do? We worked out a story for ourselves. She'd have been horrified; what we made up was often much worse than the truth.'

Eileen remembered she'd thought her father was dead, the day he left them.

'I know you're not religious, and nor am I now. That makes it easier to my mind.'

'You think I should just tell her?'

'Yes. And tell her clearly, say the proper words. When the time comes, don't confuse her with "passed on", "gone to sleep", "lost".'

'What do I say if she asks where she's gone?'

'A good question, one to be prepared for. What would you like to tell her?'

'Oh. "I don't know", is the truth. But maybe, "She'll be with us in our memories."'

Eyes sparkling in sympathy, Siobhan hugs her quickly, giving Eileen no time to shy away.

Stuart visits, sometimes taking Alice home with him for her to have tea with Maggie. Alice returns with tales of cakes with silver bobbles or chocolate sprinkles on them, iced gem biscuits and sugared almonds. She might bring a little screw of paper home with something. Eileen hasn't been able to see Barbara, her only friend, in ages. Stuart isn't really a friend. When they were at school, him two years younger, he was picked on because he was already fat. That's probably why she noticed him. And now he talks in that formal, distant way. If she didn't know his age, she would have thought he was much older. No, he isn't a friend, for all his helpfulness.

Ena says to him, one visit, her voice with a new huskiness to it, 'I've been thinking about my funeral. Cremation, I think. I don't want to be put in a churchyard.'

Eileen has to sit down.

'I know I won't be there to be bothered by it, but I don't want the usual religious rubbish. There must be alternatives, do you know what's possible? Can you find out?'

He says, 'Certainly I can,' but he looks away.

Eileen puts out her hand to touch her mother.

Ena feebly swats the hand away. 'Find a piece of paper and write things down for me.' She lists the music she would like, including the theme from *Coronation Street*.

Stuart looks shocked.

'A bit of a dirge, I know,' Ena says, 'but it's for that horrid part when the coffin disappears into the furnace. I don't think anything could make that pleasant to watch, but maybe a chuckle's just possible.'

Eileen shakes her head. She can't conceive of life without her mother. She thinks, suddenly, of her lost friend, Mary, who she's not seen in all these years. How has Mary's life turned out?

Of course, Eileen does have Alice. Beautiful, sunny, always-surprising Alice. Who brings her a recovering long-tailed tit she's found, dazed from hitting the kitchen window. It weighs almost nothing.

Ena dies in October. Stuart arrives, the following morning. Siobhan must have told him. He sits opposite Eileen at the kitchen table, fiddling with a biro, clicking it in and out. Eileen doesn't have any words, and it seems nor does he. She reaches across and puts a hand over his, to stop the movement. He jumps. His hand is as clammy as hers, though his doesn't tremble. She registers fleetingly that she has avoided touching him before. He lets the pen fall, looks up at her shamefaced. He probably didn't realise he was fidgeting so.

She says, 'I'm glad it's over. She wanted to go, she was ready to go.'

His eyes widen. He squeezes her fingers hesitantly.

She stares down at the embroidered flowers on the tablecloth. She says very quietly, her voice wavering, 'I have already missed her so much, I can scarcely miss her more. She has loved and supported me my whole life, even when I made it so difficult. And she has loved my Alice.'

Stuart moves his hand a little and she remembers that he's there. He's leaning forwards, peering at her, his big face at her eye level.

'I owe her so much, and she's gone and I'm glad. She needed to go.'

Stuart coughs, passes his large handkerchief across his damp face. 'I thought you might need some help.' He sits up. 'With the practicalities.'

She lifts her head and his face comes back into focus. 'Yes,' she says, 'yes, thank you. Of course. There must be things I have to do…'


In the following days, it's like swimming through weeds. Condolences are offered by villagers Eileen hardly knows; she can't reply. It makes no sense. She can't get to grips with what's needed. Stuart guides her through, helps with the arrangements. Suddenly, the day arrives. As Ena wanted, there's no religion in the crematorium service. Eileen drifts through it, seeing people as if through gauze. Roy is there, at the back. That's kind of him. He doesn't come to the wake, where villagers noisily invade their sitting room. The Co-op manager has provided lemonade. Sausage rolls. Stuart has left Barbara at home minding Maggie. He is smiling, saying 'How are we today?' to everyone. Eileen wants them all to leave.

. . .

In the weeks after the funeral, she finds herself wandering through the small cottage, touching things. She picks up and smells the hand-stitched, lace-edged sachet of lavender that lived underneath Ena's pillow; she wonders what she should do with the bottles of tablets.

Six-year-old Alice trails behind her, tugging the hem of her dress, talking to her. 'Will Gramma still have birthdays?' she asks.

'Mmm. We won't see her, though. I don't think we should do presents. We could have a cake if you like?'

'She likes your chocolate one.'

'With the orange icing? That'd be nice. And we could grow flowers for her.' Eileen strokes the leaves of the white cyclamen on the kitchen windowsill. It has flowered for Ena every year. She would leave the pot on its side, by the back door, looking dead for months, then bring it in when leaves started to reappear. She'd water it, and it would revive and grow. Every time, Eileen would think how remarkable it was.

She could re-pot it, putting Ena's ashes under the soil.

'Gramma likes flowers,' Alice says.


Ena's union rep appeared months back. He'd heard about her illness. He said, 'I thought the Union, USDAW, might help. We've a convalescent fund. She's worked so long for the Co-op, always a sensible voice at the meetings, I'm sure she'll qualify.'

The money is a godsend. Not that Ena would have called it that.

Eventually, that and Ena's meagre savings are gone. Like Ena, Eileen takes a job at the Co-op. Except these days it's in the new, ugly, flat-roofed building, next door to where the old one stood. It's self-service now, with wire baskets for the customers and tills by the door. Blue savings stamps for the dividend. She gets to go home for lunch, when they close. She'd be paid a bit more if she were there after six, or on a Saturday, but she mostly contrives hours that fit in with Alice's school time. Barbara helps out with Alice, and even Freda does occasionally, when Eileen's desperate.

She can't face sorting out Ena's possessions, until the day Alice brings her the trinket box.

She holds it up, saying, 'Mummy may I look? Gramma used to let me touch her pretty things.'

Eileen squats down to give her a hug and they open it together. Alice is clearly familiar with all the bits and pieces. A broken jet necklace. A pretty garnet ring. It was Ena's engagement ring. Eileen threads a narrow ribbon through it, to hang it round Alice's neck, telling her where it came from.

Alice's wears it with a huge smile.

There's an old piece of crumpled lace that held together Ena's wedding bouquet. 'Would Henry like this?' she asks her daughter. 'Would your rabbit look smart in a bow tie?'

'Yes, please. I can tie it.'

Eileen had forgotten about the two battered blocks of glass that Ena's father brought back from the Great War; he'd been called up towards the end. They are prisms, from a trench periscope.

Pointing at them, Alice says, 'Gramma made rainbows for me.'

'I remember that,' Eileen tells her, 'from when I was little. We need to wait until late in the day. Meantime, could you help with Gramma's clothes? I can't put it off forever.'

Ena was taller, altogether bigger than Eileen, so the clothes that are good enough will go to a jumble sale. Eileen collects them in the laundry basket. She lets Alice choose which handkerchiefs and which padded hangers she would like. Eileen keeps a pair of shoes for herself; Ena had small feet. Sorting out her things proves not that big a job after all.

As the sun goes down, Eileen finds a place to perch the prisms to catch the light, on the bar across the middle of the sash window in the front room. Alice sits and waits as Eileen gets their meal. From the kitchen she hears her daughter's delighted squeal.

'Rainbows, Mummy! Rainbows. Come and see!'

# TWENTY-SIX
# BARBARA HAS CANCER
## 1972

The spring of 1972 began in March with a fortnight of balmy weather. The winds were light, the sun shone with some warmth at last, and the trees blossomed. Yellow spring flowers brought hope, though not to Barbara Jenkins.

On the morning after an operation to remove a breast lump, the surgeon visited briefly, said the drain could come out and she could go home.

'Drain?' Barbara said, visualising the grating in the gutter outside her front gate.

He pointed to a tube emerging from under a dressing on her side, inserted into a glass bottle that was sitting on the floor. She had been trying to ignore it. She felt a wave of revulsion.

He said, 'I'll see you in my clinic in a fortnight. I should have the report from the tissue analysis.'

Tissue, she thought. Crisp, thin white paper to wrap a silk blouse or a delicate porcelain cup. She knew that wasn't what he meant.

He said, 'We can't be certain it's okay until we have the tissue report. It could be alright, but there are things that can't be seen or felt at the time of surgery, that show up when it's looked at under a microscope, and sometimes treatment is necessary.'

There was something in his tone of voice, or perhaps the way he didn't look at her as he said this, that made her wonder: does he say this to everyone? Or is he warning me that he suspects it's serious? Though it can't be, I'm thirty-two, far too young.

The drain removal was disgusting. The nurse cut a coarse, black, holding stitch, put a pad of gauze over the skin there, pulled steadily on the tube and it slid out. Without really hurting, it was true. Barbara shouldn't have looked, but she did. The drain was made of stiff, transparent plastic, about a quarter of an inch in diameter and perforated with a pattern of holes towards the tip, which had been inside her body. A purple and honey-coloured drool ran in wet strings down the channel and out of some of the holes. She felt cold, saliva pooled in her mouth and the back of her neck prickled. She tried not to gag. The nurse deftly collected together the ghastly mess and put it into a yellow plastic bag marked 'clinical waste'. Shuddering, Barbara wondered what else would go into a 'clinical waste' bag.

The nurse said, 'I don't want to rush you, but we do need your bed for another patient. Can your husband be here to collect you before lunch?'

It wasn't said unkindly. She felt wobbly after the drain removal, a little faint and sick, but she said nothing, realising she should be gone, keen not to be a nuisance. She was sitting in the Day Room when Stuart came promptly to collect her at twelve.

He was always so good with people in need, confident, but he didn't seem to know how to be with her. He didn't hug her or even look directly at her. He took her overnight bag and they walked out together, not touching, down the corridor and round a few corners. At a sign that said 'Radioisotopes' they stopped. Each absorbed in their own thoughts, neither taking notice of the direction boards, they didn't recognise where they were.

Stuart asked at the 'Radioisotopes' reception desk and the woman smiled.

'I thought you seemed lost. All the corridors look the same, don't they? Go down to the end there,' she pointed, 'Turn right, and you'll see a blue line on the floor. Follow it and it'll take you to the main entrance.'

Off-white corridors, with lines of plaster missing where something had gouged it away, fluorescent strip lighting. A notice board with details of staff vacancies. A shop with sweets, cigarettes, get-well cards, newspapers. Wilting flowers. Left-over Easter eggs. A bowl of tired apples.

Outside, in the rain, Stuart couldn't at first remember where he'd parked the car. Barbara joined Maggie on the back seat and put the arm on her good side around her for a long hug. When they eventually got home, Stuart seemed as exhausted as she was.

At the follow-up appointment the surgeon asked how Barbara was, nodded to Stuart and then said, 'I have the tissue report,' he paused, 'I'm afraid it's not good news. The lump was a nasty after all, so we need to talk about treatment.'

Barbara's mind went blank and she heard only fragments of the rest of his speech.

Surgery... New treatment from the States, but he wasn't convinced... Wednesday week... He asked, 'Do you have any questions?'

She couldn't speak.

He turned to Stuart, who shook his head. Barbara looked at him. How cowed and pathetic he seemed; just like she felt.

Later, at home, the word 'cancer' wasn't said. They spoke about the practical details, things they hadn't thought to ask. When would the operation be, had he said? How long would she be in hospital? Would Stuart be allowed to bring Maggie to visit?

He said, 'I expect they'll send a letter,' and went in the kitchen to make a pot of tea.

Maggie sat staring at her, moaning softly. She always knew when Barbara was unhappy.

There was a deep ache in Barbara's guts. Her vision flickered. The tip of her left middle finger was numb. There was trouble everywhere. She wanted to scream at Stuart, 'I'm dying! Can't you see that?' She wanted to shout at him, to tell him how angry she was, how afraid. But she didn't. Maggie would get upset.

When the letter came, she had to read it several times before she was sure what it said, and then couldn't recall the details. Except that she should wear no jewellery. She fingered the single diamond hung on a fine chain round her neck. Stuart gave it to her for their fifth anniversary. She'd have to leave it at home. She felt she was disappearing.

On the day, the young doctor who went through all the questions, gave her a consent form to sign.

She read it and said, 'I don't know what this means.' She pointed, 'What does that say?'

The doctor looked uncomfortable; he was just a boy. He told her, 'Mastectomy. Excision of the breast. It's the standard treatment.' As if she was supposed to know that.

She was to have her breast removed? They still did that? Why, when she knew she had cancer, was having an operation for it, had she not thought to ask what they were planning to do?

Barbara was conscious that she was lying on a bed in a long ward and, although she couldn't see them because there were curtains round, other patients, visitors, anyone, could hear. Despite that, she said, 'Is there a big raw area where my breast was?'

He abandoned her to go and find help.

The more senior man who came told her, 'You have a line of stitches from here to here.' He pointed to her breastbone and a spot below her armpit, handing her the consent form, which she signed. She had to. Let them do what was needed. No point in questioning it.

. . .

Barbara lay on her bed wearing a thin cotton gown, tied loosely at the back. People around her were joking about last weekend's football fiasco – there were men as well as women on the ward. She heard medical words: gallbladder, hernia, trigger finger. A man was discussing the news, something about Bloody Sunday, then the miners' strike. Everything was grim. Not that she cared.

How would Maggie be while she was away? Would Stuart cope? She hoped he'd be able to go on helping Eileen with Alice, she hadn't actually asked him about that. She'd got in a supply of the tinned spaghetti both girls liked. She thought Eileen wouldn't visit her while she was in hospital. Two buses; too difficult. And Eileen probably wouldn't realise how pleased Barbara would be to see her.

Her worried thoughts were interrupted by a nurse saying she should visit the toilet. Barbara walked down to the bathrooms wearing no make-up or nail varnish, a shabby beige hospital wrap over the flimsy gown, her shoes with no tights. She hated how she must look.

Two lads were waiting, when she got back, with a trolley for her.

The older one gave her a sympathetic grin and said, 'Coming for a ride on my chariot, love?' The dressing gown had to be discarded but he made sure she wasn't exposed as she clambered clumsily aboard.

Barbara's recovery after the operation was 'uncomplicated', she was told, but she felt awful. Everything was different. She couldn't look at her body and she couldn't talk to Stuart. He must have realised she was miserable, since he was constantly making jollying comments. He meant well, but they didn't help.

She wanted to say, 'I'm not interested in a bloody walk in the sunshine!' Instead she told him, 'I think we should have a new bathroom mirror. I hate that one, I've never liked it, get rid of it. When I've the energy, we'll go out together and get a nice one.' He unscrewed it and put it in the loft, took to shaving awkwardly at the kitchen sink, with a hand mirror propped against the windowsill. She didn't tell him she bathed in the dark. She hoped things would get easier.

Then the chemotherapy started, with the vomiting, and her hair falling out in clumps. Thank goodness the mirror was gone.

Maggie seemed to understand her misery. She was quieter than usual. Gave her mother little pushes and pats. It helped that Eileen had brought Alice to visit Maggie, though Barbara hadn't often been able to join them. She gathered that Alice had schoolfriends whose mothers had kept an eye on her after school, until Eileen finished in the shop. It must have been hard for Eileen since Ena died.

At the hospital again, when the drug treatment and the radiotherapy finally came to an end, she saw the mastectomy nurse, a cheerful, older woman with curly hair and vivid makeup, wearing a royal blue uniform. In a room not much bigger than a cupboard, Mrs Booth displayed the selection of breast prostheses, to tuck in Barbara's bra so that, clothed, she'd look normal. They were obscene. Salmon-pink and heavy, plasticky to touch, in shapes she could not have guessed.

She never showed Stuart what she wore. At night she reverted to long, buttoned-up winceyette nightdresses, like she wore as a child, so Stuart didn't see her chest. Or the rest of her.

He didn't ask her about how she felt or what she thought about what had happened. But he did try to make life easier for her in practical ways. When her shoulder was stiff after the surgery, he started doing the laundry and hanging it out, then carried on doing it. He did the vacuuming, saying she shouldn't lift the Hoover. She found she didn't have the energy about the house that she had before. She concentrated on Maggie.

She needed to be okay for the next five years. They said she was to come for outpatient visits until then. So that must mean she was cured if she could stay well that long. She pushed aside the awful thought that she might not be there for her daughter.

. . .

Months later, Barbara saw the same nurse, Mrs Booth, to try a new prosthesis shape.

'I know it won't make much difference. I don't suppose anyone but me will notice anyway. I can't bear him to look at me. Grotesque.' She hadn't expected to say such a thing.

The nurse looked at her thoughtfully, head tilted, and asked, 'Are you able to be intimate with him?'

Barbara had to think about what she might mean. 'Oh,' she replied. 'No. I couldn't let him touch me. Not naked, I couldn't.' Mrs Booth, she imagined, must think that was wrong. 'We hug...' She visualised them hugging, fully clothed, her taking care that the prosthesis was always shielded by her arm so that he couldn't feel it. In truth, they rarely even hugged.

'Have you thought about breast reconstruction?' Mrs Booth asked her.

Barbara released her held breath. She never wanted to talk about sex. Not with Stuart, nor Eileen, certainly not with a stranger. Never.

'It's more surgery, of course, but it would give you a reasonable breast shape, you wouldn't need to wear things like this anymore. And you could come to feel more confident with your body, with your husband?'

Barbara looked at the leaflet Mrs Booth handed her, with its diagrams and pictures. 'No,' she said, 'I don't think so. It's too late now. I wouldn't want another operation.'

'You might want to think about it for a bit? Take the leaflet home? Discuss it with him?'

Barbara shook her head and blurted out, 'We didn't have sex before, so we're not going to now.'

Mrs Booth's face hardly changed. She said, 'D'you want to talk about that?'

Barbara thought about it. 'You know our daughter's disabled?' Mrs Booth nodded.

'Well, we've not had sex since our Maggie was diagnosed,

that's years ago. 1967, when she was two. I couldn't. How Maggie was, I just couldn't. They told me it wasn't my fault, but it didn't help. I felt that... that part of me was corrupt. And I daren't risk becoming pregnant again.'

Mrs Booth looked as though she didn't fully understand, but she didn't pry. Barbara watched, up-side down, as the nurse wrote carefully in her notes. 'No sex since daughter diagnosed. Declines reconstruction.'

# TWENTY-SEVEN
## EILEEN CAN'T FIND ALICE

Saturday afternoon, a week after Alice's seventh birthday, and Eileen's cross with her. Alice can be quite stubborn, and she doesn't want to go down to the shop. There are a few things for the weekend that Eileen forgot yesterday. But Alice is determined to stay in the garden.

'I'm busy, Mummy,' she says. 'I'm teaching.' She waves her stuffed rabbit in the air. 'He needs to learn about slugs and snails.'

Eileen smiles, despite her annoyance. Alice is a beautiful child. Pale, smooth, almost translucent skin. A floppy fringe, the rest of her fair hair scooped back in bunches with yellow ribbons, revealing her pretty, perfect ears, their shape just like her father's. Her bright, clear, dark grey eyes catch the sunlight. She grins confidently at her mother, showing her even, pearly teeth.

Eileen tells herself that other women leave their children, age seven like Alice, and the Co-op is only just down the road. She sighs and picks up her bag. She gives her daughter a kiss and tells her, 'You be good, now. I won't be long,' and goes.

In the shop Jack, behind the till, wants to tell her about the antics of the current Saturday girl, who, he says, is, 'having a fag out the back'.

Eileen listens distractedly, thrusts her money at him muttering, 'Can't stop. Sorry.' On the way back Freda, weeding her next-door front garden, says something, but it turns out she's just talking to herself. Eileen hardly pauses.

When she reaches home, she puts away her shopping, calling for Alice. No response. She goes out into the back garden. No Alice. Her rabbit is lying on the back path. Eileen's puzzled now, becoming alarmed, tries to keep calm. She'll be hiding, teasing me, she thinks, and looks in Alice's usual hiding places, then everywhere else. Alice is nowhere to be found. A chill grips Eileen. She checks the whole house and garden again, hurrying, stumbling, feeling sweat prickle the back of her neck. She goes down the front path, intending to run along the street to search, but can't decide which way to go. A car almost runs her over when she stumbles into the road. It's a light blue Ford Anglia driven by a man she hasn't seen around before; she stares after it paralysed by the thought of Alice getting run over. Or worse.

Eileen rushes back into the house, afraid to leave the place where Alice should be. 'Where are you?' she mutters. 'Where have you gone?' She scurries frantically from the open front door through the hall and the kitchen to the back garden again, turning back the way she came, crying Alice's name and moaning, 'No, no, no!'

## TWENTY-EIGHT
## FREDA LEARNS THAT ALICE HAS DISAPPEARED

Freda was complaining to herself as she worked in her garden. 'These hostas look terrible. Almost nothing left.' A shadow fell across the plants and she looked up to see that Eileen had stopped next to the low garden wall. She was looking confused. She had a bag of groceries; must have been to the shop.

'With all the slugs,' Freda said. 'Almost nothing left.'

'Thrushes eat them,' Eileen replied.

Did Eileen think the birds ate the plants? Freda coughed and returned to her weeding. She hated slugs. Nasty, slimy, disgusting black things. Must get more pellets. She wanted her hostas to look nice.

Some little time later, a horrid wailing sound made Freda pause again. Maybe Mrs Judd's radio. The Saturday afternoon play? It came again, louder. An awful sound, Freda thought. Time to go indoors; she put her garden tools together. Where was the noise coming from? It didn't really sound like the radio, now that she listened properly. She stood up, brushed the dirt off her hands, and saw Eileen. She was on the pavement outside her front gate, twisting from side to side, lifting each foot in turn, looking as if she was about to run, one way then the other. And it was her making the terrible moaning sound. Eileen turned back to her house and disappeared.

She could be very strange, Freda thought. She considered just retreating indoors, ignoring whatever was happening. Her conscience wouldn't let her. She put her things down and reluctantly followed Eileen.

The front door was open. Freda stepped inside, hesitant, muttering, 'Sorry. Wouldn't normally walk in like this.' She found Eileen. Freda had never seen anyone more distraught. Her face was all contorted. And Eileen must have run her fingers through her hair, again and again; it was standing up in a bizarre frizz.

'What's happened?' Freda asked.

Eileen seemed unable to produce proper words, was mouthing and whimpering. Then Freda grasped what she was trying to say. Alice was missing. Freda gave a sharp intake of breath. She thought, oh, the poor thing. It can't be. As if there wasn't enough bad had happened in this house.

Freda moved to try and soothe Eileen but couldn't. She couldn't even get near her, the woman was so frenzied, rushing from room to room, up and down the hall. Then abruptly stopping, rooted to the spot. And it was as if she'd gone deaf, taking no notice of what Freda said. Mrs Judd, Eileen's other neighbour, round the corner, put her head in the door, must have heard the crying.

'Eileen can't find Alice,' Freda explained. 'She's beside herself with worry.'

'I'll go get people to help.'


Mrs Judd got her son Tim to assemble his Scout friends and organise a thorough search.

Bless them, Freda thought, just lads, but they know what to do. Eileen's awful shrieking made her clench her teeth. Her jaw ached.

Coming back, Mrs Judd stared at Eileen, now on the floor, keening, her head in an armchair. She said quietly, 'She's hysterical. Not surprising. There's nothing worse could have happened to her.' Mrs Judd leant against the wall, watching Eileen, her hands over her ears.

Freda couldn't think what to do either.

More people collected. Some tried to talk to Eileen, to calm her.

'Have you tried the coal hole? My Jimmy used to love the coal hole at her age.'

Eileen turned towards the speaker, her eyes black with fear.

'Where have you looked? I'm sure she'll not have gone far. Such a good girl, your Alice.'

A pleading look at Mrs Judd, who ushered people out.

She said to Eileen, 'It'll be fine. We're sure to find her any minute.' Though she didn't sound convinced.

Eileen wasn't listening anyway. Her face now had a distant, blank look. It's as if she's gone deaf, Freda thought again.

Mrs Judd said, 'I'll make a cup of tea.' She stepped over to Freda and quietly added, 'I'm sure she'll be right as rain the moment Alice turns up.'

'I hope that's soon.' Freda silently prayed to St Jude, for those in desperate straits. Though should it have been St Anthony?

Eileen couldn't even hold the cup she was given. It slipped from her grasp and spilled across the floor. She turned away, sliding a hand through the warm pool, oblivious.

Mrs Judd went home to call the police, leaving Freda hovering unhappily. Poor Eileen curled herself up, face pressed into the seat cushion, her hands wrapped around her head. One fist was clenching a toy rabbit.

## TWENTY-NINE
## EILEEN LOSES HER MIND

Police and questions. Mrs Judd answers them. Eileen can hardly move her mouth to make a sound. She is in a chair. Someone has propped her up. She feels herself shuddering, bereft of words. The house is full of horror.

The policemen leave, and in the quiet she manages to say, 'Please go.'

The room empties.

Though there's no peace. She tries to calm herself by doing ordinary things, but she can't. Everything is wrong. She holds a mug in both hands, unable to recall how to make tea. Her hands are stiff. Her steps are small and erratic, and she catches her feet. She stands, staring into space. Her heart races. She sees Alice's empty chair, and she sobs.

I must find Alice. I have to search every corner. Not just here, but outside. The garden, the street, the fields, everywhere. She walks and walks, looking behind dustbins, in sheds, under hedges. People shout at her. Some come with her to search for a while. She mutters a thank you when she remembers. The light fades through dusk to dark. She finds herself sitting on the seat by the War Memorial. I can't give up. But I can't see.

Tears run down her face as she makes for home. Is that still what it's called?

. . .

Eileen turns away from the black window, curls herself up in an armchair, eyes closed. Nightmare scenes flood her mind, she can't push them away.

After a long time, she goes upstairs and finds her way to her bedroom. She passes Alice's closed door. But she sees the room beyond the door as if it has been bombed. The outer wall is gone, the floor broken and canted, covered in shattered glass, shards of furniture, toys half buried in rubble. The picture of a balloon that hangs on the wall above Alice's bed is tilted and dirty. Eileen doesn't open the door, doesn't dare. Was there an explosion? She takes deep breaths. Tries to think clearly. No explosion. But something terrible has happened to take Alice away. She stumbles into her own room.

Eileen can't stop herself crying in the night. She thinks of Freda, disturbed by her noise. But she can't stop herself howling. Her thoughts a jumble, a morass. When they briefly straighten, she remembers what has happened and is plunged back into devastation. She doesn't sleep. Staring with her eyes shut, she has appalling dreams. Trying to fight her way out she becomes knotted into a tangled, sweat-soaked sheet. She abandons her bed and stands, barefoot at the window, staring out into the darkness. In the early light before dawn, a robin sings from the cherry tree. In mockery.

Somehow it is morning. Eileen stumbles downstairs and out to search the wet garden again. Drizzle settles in her hair and eventually soaks through her nightie. Her muddy, cold feet finally register, and she goes back inside.

Freda is at Eileen's front door, calling her name. She says she is on her way to church. It must be Sunday. She will pray, Freda calls. Eileen can't reply. She finds herself in different parts of the house, with no memory of how she got there. And tomorrow she's due at work.

. . .

Eileen doesn't know the day or time, and there's a banging that doesn't stop. Then the front door is being unlocked. She hears Freda's voice saying 'Eileen?', and there's another woman.

A hand touches her. Eileen screams, thrashing out. She is petrified.

Someone prays. Eileen screams again. Her mind is full of terrible, frightening images. Storm and huge clouds and... She opens her eyes but struggles to focus, and she cannot move. Her body won't move. The stranger – she's all in dark blue – draws Freda away.

Eileen is scarcely aware of any time passing. Her mind is full of a roaring sound, like a hailstorm tearing through forest. There are lulls in which she catches fragments of talk. She recognises Dr Pettigrew, speaking quietly; she can't listen. Except she hears when he says 'Alice'. She shakes violently.

He takes her arm and hurts her. She thrashes and shrieks, lights flashing. She feels hands pressing her down. More pain. Eileen hears her heart pounding, she heaves for breath, terrified. She hears herself shouting, wailing, whimpering. Silence and dark.

# THIRTY
## FREDA HAS TO HELP

Freda wished she didn't live next door to the Mallorys. A long time ago, but she still remembers how awful it was before Eileen's father left. She wanted nothing to do with that sort of thing. But she called the police when the sobbing at night didn't stop, Eileen failed to emerge in daylight, and the milk piled up on the step.

She let the lady bobby in with her emergency key, calling out, 'It's me, Freda from next door.'

They found Eileen, looking stiff with fear, folded in a corner of the sofa, her eyes tight shut. She screamed when the policewoman touched her.

'The poor lamb, she's crazed by it,' Freda said, and started to pray. 'Our father, which art in heaven...'

Eileen screamed again.

Freda waited, as asked, while the policewoman fetched the doctor. She kept her distance, didn't move or make a sound, in case Eileen reared up and attacked her. When Dr Pettigrew went to give Eileen an injection, she shrieked and fought, it was horrible. The needle broke, and blood spattered across the pale cushion he'd pushed under her arm. Shocking. The sudden smell told Freda that Eileen had wet herself.

The doctor beckoned Freda and the constable near. Freda just wanted to go home, but she moved in – he obviously needed their help. The two women stood over Eileen, who'd knotted herself tightly, eyes squeezed shut, hands facing palms outwards as if to push something away. He mimed what he wanted them to do. At his signal, they took hold of her. Freda had not touched her neighbour before. Their grasp had Eileen fight so hard they could scarcely hold her. Her eyelids fluttered, her eyes rolled up to reveal the whites, as if she was possessed. Freda wished again she didn't have to be there. An injection into the flesh of Eileen's arm and it was done.

They all three relaxed as they stood slightly apart from her, watching her slight body unravel and fall limp.

'Let's not try to carry her upstairs,' he advised.

He pushed a cushion under Eileen's head and Freda fetched bedding from upstairs and tucked it around her. She brushed the grit off Eileen's bare feet with her hand.

'Feet are cold,' she said, and went to find socks.

Freda hadn't noticed until then that Eileen was in her nightdress, though it was the middle of the day. And the nightie was damp. No wonder she was so cold. Eileen lay slack, breathing slowly, snoring slightly in the quiet.

Dr Pettigrew said, 'She clearly can't be left alone.'

Freda muttered, 'I can't stay. I scarcely slept the last few nights as it is.'

He replied calmly, 'Of course you can't. But if you can wait for a bit, while I organise someone?' He murmured to himself, 'She may need more sedation, later.'

Freda sat nervously, the room warming when the sun came round. A fat bluebottle battered itself against the window. Freda hated bluebottles. Outside she could see a truss of roses, the air behind them shimmering up from the pavement. She wanted to go, to be out of all this nastiness. Was it St Jude, the patron saint of hopeless causes?

The next day a nurse knocked on Freda's door. 'Just to let you know, your neighbour's no better. I can't even get her to drink plain water. The doctor's been again, says she's getting dehydrated. Weather's not helping. She won't do. He's having her admitted.'
    'The Royal then,' Freda said.
    'No. Carlton Hayes,' the woman replied, grimacing.
    The loony bin! Freda was horrified. The shame of it. She closed the door muttering the 'Our Father'.

Everyone joined in the searches, but Alice could not be found. No clue, no explanation. Freda prayed, but as time passed, she couldn't imagine any good coming out of the events, and she wasn't sure what she might be praying for. Eileen, she heard, was too ill to know, her mind locked shut.

# THIRTY-ONE
# STUART IS INTERVIEWED BY THE POLICE

Maggie sat, squat, on the thick carpet, her pudgy legs in the odd frog position she favoured. She was whining and scratching her forearm. Stuart hadn't been able to cheer her up or distract her. The arrival of a uniformed police officer made her even more grizzly.

The man had come to interview Stuart, who knew someone would arrive. After all, he knew Alice well. He could tell them about how caring Eileen was, how bright and sensible the child.

The officer seemed bothered by Maggie's presence and the noise she was making. He hunched sideways, his back half-turned away from the girl.

'Sorry,' Stuart grimaced, 'but I have to keep her to hand. My wife's out and I can't leave her, especially when she's like this. Something must have upset her.' She's been like this for a while, he thought.

The officer scowled. He took out his notebook and pencil and, after a few preliminaries, he asked, 'When did you last see Alice Mallory?'

Stuart had explained things to the police before, on behalf of villagers. He felt confident as he answered. 'That Saturday. Eileen brought her round in the morning and came back to fetch her for her lunch.' He nodded towards Maggie, noticing anew how miserable she looked. 'They played outside for a while.' He recalled, when he fetched them in at midday, seeing that Alice had been collecting little things for Maggie from around the garden. She'd made a small pile. The skeleton of a leaf, a red stone, a selection of seed pods. 'She's always nice with Maggie,' he added. The man had no interest in this. 'Were you alone with Alice at all?'

Stuart was startled by the question. 'I don't know... Well, no. We've known her so long it's difficult to think.' He saw the officer's cold look.

'Are you in the habit of spending time alone with Alice?'

'Well, no, not really.' Stuart straightened himself in the chair and mopped his suddenly damp face with his handkerchief. 'I don't think I was alone with Alice. She was playing with Maggie, like I said. My wife was in and out.'

'Though you might have been just with Alice and your daughter, say, when your wife was in the kitchen, getting your meal?'

'Yes, but...' What was he suggesting?

'And your daughter, as I understand it, can't tell us anything?'

Maggie was swollen-eyed, her nose running, snot smeared across her face and sleeve. The policeman looked with distaste at her, then back at Stuart, his eyes hard.

Stuart felt sick. His stomach heaved. He didn't know if his face showed his emotions, but he was aware of a host of unpleasant images. Abruptly, he found himself shouting, waving his arms. 'She's Maggie's only friend! My wife and I have known her since she was born! If you think...' He spluttered to a halt, his face hot. He'd knocked a book off the table. A strand of hair fell across one eye. He tugged it back, wishing he hadn't lost his temper.

The man raised an eyebrow, licked his stub of pencil and laboriously wrote a note.

Stuart squirmed, heard the chair seat groan under his weight. He wiped his sweaty palms on his trousers.

The officer was stony faced. 'You need to calm down, sir. These are questions I have to ask. I don't think anything.'

Stuart slumped, gazing at Maggie. She fell silent. She had

scratched her arm raw, and tiny beads of blood stood out on her skin. He sighed, thinking he should do something about the bleeding, wondering what the man was going to ask next.

A key turned in the front door. By the time his wife reached the room he had blown his nose and sat up straight, but he knew she only had to glance at him to appreciate his wretchedness.

Stuart looked at Barbara, framed in the doorway. It must have been raining outside, there were droplets of water on her head and shoulders, catching the light. He hadn't noticed there'd been a shower. Her familiar, slightly heavy features. He took in her straight, mousey hair, a wig to mimic her usual appearance, cut level with her jaw. She wasn't graceful, not tall, and she was stocky, though nowhere near as large as he. But she stood straight, in her tidy, plain clothes. She had a calm, kind, purposeful air, he thought. Despite all she was going through. She created the impression of competence. Just the sight of her made him feel better.

Barbara smiled brightly at the officer. 'You must be here to ask us about Alice. We were expecting a visit. Can I get you a cup of tea?' She spoke gently to Maggie and scolded her sympathetically for her sore arm, fetched a soft pad to tape over the scratches and found a pink felt-tipped pen to draw a daisy on it. Maggie, still dripping tears, snot and now saliva, smiled wanly and fell quiet.

Stuart was encouraged to see that the officer's demeanour had changed a little. Maybe his suspicions were softened by Barbara's solicitous courtesy.

Barbara went out to the kitchen and the man continued. 'Can you give me an account of what you were doing that day?'

Stuart collected himself. 'Not much to tell,' he said. 'Eileen came for Alice before lunch and, a bit later, Barbara went out and I took Maggie for a walk.'

The tea came with biscuits. Maggie drank milk out of her baby's beaker, dribbling it down her bib as always. Barbara didn't fuss, just cleaned her face and hands when she'd finished. Maggie still needed as much help as a toddler, even now she was seven.

Stuart told Barbara, 'He asked was I ever alone with Alice, or just Alice and Maggie? Of course I am.'

She turned to the man. 'Are you suggesting my husband was somehow responsible for Alice's disappearance?' She considered briefly but didn't wait for a reply. She said, 'My husband has always helped with Maggie and, when Alice visits, he's often with them, whether I'm there or not. I might come and go but I have never walked in on anything untoward. I appreciate that you expect me to defend him, and will need to ask others. The whole village will have seen them together. Ask anyone. You will find no reports of any suspicious or inappropriate behaviour.'

The policeman was paying her attention. He grunted.

Stuart blew his nose again and pulled his tie straight.

Barbara continued. 'My husband is well known in this parish. He's an accountant and he helps people with their money problems. He volunteers for the Citizens Advice Bureau. And he's been involved in the staff training for the change from Purchase Tax to VAT. Haven't you, my dear?' She smiled at Stuart. 'He helps many of the residents with a variety of practical problems.'

The officer was writing again, pressing the pencil lead hard into the paper. But he looked less belligerent.

Barbara waited until he stopped. 'My husband is a man of integrity. Those who know him will vouch for his good character. You will find no evidence against him.'

Standing there, speaking quietly but firmly, Barbara looked much taller than her five foot two. The implications of the questions Stuart had been asked were horrifying. But might what she said be enough to allay suspicion? What a good woman she was, Stuart thought.


And Barbara must have been proved right because the police didn't bother him like that again. And Stuart was reassured to hear that any man who'd had contact with Alice was questioned much as he was. In the following weeks, as he did his walks around the village with Maggie, he heard the tales. When he asked, 'How's the world treating you?' people told him what'd been said.

The school caretaker confessed to being reduced to tears. 'They came just two days after my wife heard her father had died. A lovely man, he was. I just broke down.'

Young Jack, who worked in the Co-op, was questioned twice. 'I'd told them, the first time, if I'm not at work I'm with my mother. You know how she is. How she depends on me.' Somehow, they'd heard he'd written a letter of sympathy to Eileen, seemed to take that as evidence of guilt.

The one male teacher at the junior school, a weedy, solitary chap over whom a cloud descended, felt persecuted. He told Stuart, 'I was away from the village all that day, on a trek with the ramblers, but still they harass me.'

Women were also interviewed, and not only to corroborate the men's claims. One who came under scrutiny was another schoolteacher, a stout mannish woman who lived with a friend. She got very angry and protested to Stuart, 'Just because I live with Esther doesn't mean I'm a pervert! Wasting time on bigotry when they should be concentrating on finding the girl.'

Betty Scott and her postman husband were suspected of stealing the child. Stuart knew about Betty's problems in carrying a baby to term, and how depressed she was after her fourth miscarriage. They'd nowhere where Alice might be secreted. The interrogation didn't help Betty at all.

Stuart thought about his wife's account of him. A good, helpful person was what she'd described. It was, perhaps, high time he did more. Maybe become a parish councillor; he knew they were short of members. It would mean meetings in the evening and would otherwise occupy him. He wouldn't have as much time to spend with Maggie. But that would be alright, once Barbara's treatment was finished. He always felt uncomfortable, out in public with Maggie, and Barbara wasn't bothered. He could leave his daughter with his wife again. That would be welcome.

People were asked about Alice's father. Who was he? Might he be involved? Stuart had another visit from an officer to see what he might know.

'No one seems to have any idea who the father is,' the man said. 'The next-door neighbour...' The officer paused to check his notes.

'That'd be Freda Bailey?' Stuart offered.

'That's right,' the man said. 'She said Eileen Mallory wouldn't say.'

Stuart remembered a long-ago conversation with Mrs Judd. She'd told him, 'None of us have ever seen a single proper boyfriend. She's kept to herself, always. It's a complete mystery how she became pregnant. And her so happy with it, too. Alice doesn't look like anyone I've met. Such a pretty child...'

Yes indeed, Stuart thought. He told the officer, 'That's correct. I believe not even Eileen's mother knew. She's no longer with us. Passed on last year.'

'And Eileen Mallory's too ill to interview,' the man said ruefully.

Stuart knew she'd been admitted to the psychiatric hospital. Should he visit? He was rather afraid of what he might have to see.

Maybe visit when she's back home.

## THIRTY-TWO
## BARBARA GRIEVES FOR EILEEN

'What do you think can have happened to Alice? No, don't answer that. I just can't face the thought.' Barbara was sitting in her chair by the grate, holding her knitting. The pattern wasn't complicated, but she kept making mistakes.

Stuart didn't look up. 'No. Well. Terrible.'

'I wrote Eileen a letter. Took three goes before I could bear to sign it. There just aren't words for this kind of thing.'

'No indeed.'

He was fiddling with something. He might be as upset as she was. It was hard to tell. Didn't talk about it. But men never did, did they?

She wished she could go and see Eileen, they were friends after all, weren't they? But she couldn't. Couldn't face that place. Barbara had never known anyone before who had to be admitted to a mental institution. She'd heard Eileen had been screaming and fighting before they took her away. They didn't still use straitjackets, did they? Drugs instead, perhaps. How horrible. She must be very ill, she maybe couldn't even talk. A complete breakdown, people said. Whatever that meant. Alice was everything to Eileen. She would be completely crushed by this. How do you recover from such horror? Permanently damaged. Barbara looked at Maggie and shuddered.

What would she have done if someone had taken Maggie away? In between the treatments, she couldn't leave her daughter for long. Maggie had to choose now to have a bad spell, didn't she? No. That was unfair. Maggie didn't get to choose anything much. Had she even registered that Alice wasn't visiting? Maybe she had. Maybe that was why she was in a state.

Stuart had moved to the window, was staring blankly out. He was upset too, wasn't he?

## THIRTY-THREE
## EILEEN'S IN HOSPITAL

Eileen doesn't remember much of the first months she was in hospital. Or perhaps she does, but she can't think about them. They are locked away behind a thick door. She can't bear to open it. Dreams keep coming, though. Awful dreams.

Alice, stick thin and ghastly pale, is in a cellar. She is so weak she can scarcely breathe. She is silently dying. Eileen is transfixed by the conviction that she has done this, she alone is responsible. The simple, hideous scene lasts for interminable time.

A different dream. She must choose how Alice dies. She sees her suffering the awful alternatives.

Poison.

Stabbing – pink loops of bowel shed from her belly for the little girl to see.

Hanged.

Drowned on a ducking stool.

Burnt at the stake on a bonfire, surrounded by revellers. Eileen sees Alice's clothes turn to ash, her little, naked body exposed. Her skin blisters and blackens. Her hair, briefly, a crackling torch. Sometimes her agony is voiced, sometimes she is silent and only the writhing of her small, rope-bound body expresses her pain.

Rape.

In the night, Eileen hears herself scream and knows why, even before she wakes.

What happened during those months? There is mostly fog, but Eileen can picture disjointed moments, like fragments of a mostly forgotten nightmare. She hadn't been able to think at all, her mind was not there. Looking back now, she knows this. Her surroundings, the people, had been the colour of stone. Someone told her, after, that she didn't speak for weeks, then when she did, it made no sense. 'Collapsed thunder chair.' She remembers being asked what that meant and having no answer. People talking, she remembers. Being afraid of everyone. Terrified. Curled into the corner of a sofa, wanting to hide. Then, once, standing, trembling, while a small woman wiped tears from her face. They've told her that there was a mark on her forehead where she had repeatedly pressed it against the wall.

She could scarcely drink and they had cajoled her. A child's beaker. 'It's only water,' but it had tasted bad. The voice was persistent, telling her she must drink, and she had tried her best.

They've told her she didn't eat for ages, that she said the food was bitter.

'Don't spit it out,' they said. 'You have to eat. Take your time. Don't spit it out.' But she hadn't been able to swallow anything solid, would hide a chewed wad in her cheek, trying not to retch.

She remembers soups and sickeningly sweet milky drinks that made her stomach heave.

She would count out loud. She'd always found counting calming, for some reason. But she would lose track of the numbers and have to start again. Each time, she'd be scared, convinced of an awful retribution.

One day that stood out for her in her memory of that time, a young man came. By then, she could sometimes see colour. She remembers he was wearing light blue. He gave her children's building blocks. She took them and sat on the floor, stacking them up in small towers, counting the bricks. Each time she started anew, at the bottom of a pile, the re-starting was less frightening. But if she built the tower too high it would fall. And she would be unable to breathe, drenched in sweat.

He helped. He would say, 'Is that big enough, now?'

She remembers that the blocks and the counting had been the beginning of her mind coming back. Like a thin shaft of sunlight between thick clouds. The blocks were red, blue and yellow. She could tell colours again.

'Eileen, love, I've found a couple or three more blocks for you, though they're a funny colour. Mauve, is it? Purple? Any road up, they're there if you want them.'

And she was given different drinks to taste. 'Try this, careful it's hot. It's not tea, I know tea tastes foul. It's lemon and ginger. Try it. Or there's mint.'

She could taste toast again. And eat it. And people helped. She was brought toast and jam. Toast and marmalade. Egg on toast.

Buttered toast sprinkled with cinnamon and brown sugar.

Like Mary's mother had made for her once as a treat, when she was small.

She wipes tears from her face.


One day Eileen wakes in the morning and notices a spider at the base of the wall, under the window. She sees the window. She gets up and opens the cream-coloured blinds. There are splashes of rain on the glass, blurring the outdoor scene of greens and browns and grey. Bright buds on the bushes. It must be early spring. She realises she has been here for a long time, she's been living in this room. The walls are plain, painted pale green. The window and door frames are white. The door is varnished wood, with a small window at head height. There is a fluorescent strip light in the ceiling. This is a hospital room, she knows. And she can see it. She washes and dresses.

She finds a nurse and says, 'Clothes?'

The nurse looks at the trousers, held up by a drawstring, and the loose top that Eileen is wearing. 'You'd like something else to wear?'

Eileen nods.

'Can't blame you. Let's see what you've got in your locker.'

There isn't much in Eileen's cupboard, just the night-clothes she came in with.

'We'll need to do better than this,' the nurse says, 'What's your favourite colour?'

'Blue,' Eileen replies.

'Sky blue, royal blue, navy blue?'

After a long pause Eileen says, 'Sky blue.'

'Okay, I'll see what I can do.'

Sometimes, she still can't sleep at night and can't stay awake in the day. The air might be too thick. Or she can't bear the texture of meat again. Sometimes colour disappears once more, leaving only a grey photograph of war. A sound alarms her: screeching trolley wheels or a cackle. But now the worst stretches are shorter and less crippling. Though unpredictable. She knows the structure of her small world can collapse and bury her without warning. But she is learning how to cope, how to protect herself, become less fragile.

She counts. Often, she counts the same things over and over. On bad days she reaches high numbers. They are perilous.

On good days she can think of things beyond the room she is in. She can remember her daughter, that she disappeared, and go on breathing.


The slight male nurse – his name is Jeremy – suggests she might like to knit.

'Forgotten how,' she replies.

'I can show you,' he says. 'My dad taught me, he was in the

Navy. You might like it. Specially if you did it before. Things to count: stitches, rows, colours. It's soothing, if you like it.'

She does like it. He starts her off with big needles and thick wool and soon she is making a long, striped scarf. She gets upset if the number of stitches changes. But she stops dropping them. People bring her yarn. Different, bright colours. In the big pocket of a borrowed pinny, she carries the work with her. She roams the corridors with the needles sticking out.

One day she's stopped. 'Sorry sweetheart. Someone might take that to hurt themselves.'

She doesn't want to do tassels; Jeremy does them for her. On the third scarf the colours are coordinated. Her fourth scarf is really nice, she thinks. It's in Christmas tones, as a present for him. Though maybe it isn't Christmas.


She hears herself say whole sentences. 'Please may I go outside?'

She is able to talk a little to the medical staff. She tells one of the doctors about a recurring dream she's had since a child.

'I dream I'm at school and ink covers everything and everyone. I can taste and smell it. I need to go to the toilet but I can't find it in the blackness. I wet myself. I can't find my friend either. I wake and remember I don't have one.'

He just smiles at her and looks puzzled.

She has another dream. It is simple. A foal is being nuzzled by its mother. They are in a grassy field with a fence of posts and wooden horizontal bars, the top bars notched where horses have chewed them. There are trees in the background and a blue sky; the sun is shining. The scene continues, unchanged. But Eileen has a steadily increasing sense of dread, which builds and builds until she wakes. She is terrified. There is sometimes a different ending. The scene shifts, like in a film, to a distant view of a car, a Ford Anglia, with the sloping back windscreen, stopped on a road, one gangly foal's leg visible lying across the white lines in the middle. Eileen wakes in horror.

She doesn't talk about the worst dreams. She can't.

. . .

She doesn't recognise anyone except Jeremy at first. After a bit, though, she sees there's a big cleaning lady, she doesn't know her name. Then a young woman visiting her brother talks to her. She is called Nicola, works in a travel agent's, brings sunny pictures of boats and beaches.

Eileen thinks the staff are looking at her differently. A man is brought in to meet her. Ian. He smiles and takes her hand to shake it. She looks at his hand, confused. He doesn't say much, that first time, just walks with her in the grounds. He is some kind of nurse, they tell her, though he doesn't wear a uniform. Dark trousers and jacket, zipped up over a light blue polo shirt. Her favourite colour. Tall. Tousled hair. Kind eyes. He works mainly outside the hospital, he says. She hears him talking to Jeremy, asking about her. She is used to this, people talking about how she behaves, but he also asks Jeremy about what she likes.

A few days later he comes again, bringing a tiny bunch of violets. 'My father-in-law picked them for you.' The next time he brings a jigsaw puzzle with a picture of a Victorian cottage and garden. They start it together. He talks about what is happening in her village. It seems so far away. A foreign land, like in the brochures Nicola leaves behind.

'Is it sunny there?' she asks.

'Do you want to go see?' he replies.

She sits down in a heap. Could that happen? She nods.


When Eileen returns to her house for the first time, she doesn't speak. She wanders from room to room, touching the dusty furniture. She stops outside the bedroom that has a paper picture of a pink rabbit stuck on the door. Tears roll down her face. She turns away.

Ian talks quietly to her, gently persuades her back downstairs. 'It's bound to be hard. Especially the first time. Breathe. Let's make a cup of tea. I've brought some milk.'

He finds cups. She fills the kettle from the tap. Then stops and looks at it. What should she do now?

He shows her. 'One step at a time. You're alright.'

There are cobwebs at the windows. She stares out, through the grime, at the garden. A bramble pushes out from the overgrown hedge and waves in the breeze, to almost reach the windowsill. She can just see the buds of new growth at the tip. The path is hidden under dead leaves, old foxglove spikes, rotting nasturtium sprawl. The whole garden is full of dead stalks from last year, but she can see new plants pushing up between. Yellow primroses are in bloom. And daffodils. The beautiful blue grape hyacinth.

'You're smiling,' Ian says.

She turns to look at him.

He says, 'The flowers are… hopeful?'

She nods.

## THIRTY-FOUR
## EILEEN GOES HOME
### 1973

Ian takes Eileen home once a week. The third trip, they go out for a walk. To the post-box (though she has no letter to post). Freda comes out of her house to say hello. 'Good to see you back, after all this time,' she says. 'It must be so strange for you.' Eileen nods. It is very strange.

Next time, Ian takes her down to the shop for a few things. She can't choose. 'I don't know what...' she says, gazing at a shelf of washing powders, shifting her weight from foot to foot.

'What did you have before?' he asks.

She manages to collect a few purchases. At the till, she stares blankly at the unfamiliar person.

Ian says, 'May I?' and takes her purse to find the money.

Another day, they go to the library. She chooses *Pride and Prejudice*. She knows it almost by heart. It will be safe.

The seventh visit, when they arrive, he says, 'This time, I'm going to leave you here for the day. I think you'll be alright on your own. I'll be back at teatime. What were you planning to do this visit?'

It hadn't occurred to Eileen that she might be there alone. They've been slowly putting the place back to rights together. She straightens herself. 'The windows,' she says. 'Clean the windows, so I can see the garden. See the birds. They like it, how it's got, all overgrown. A blue tit's nest by the kitchen window.'

He walks over and peers out. 'Those blue and yellow jobs, with faces like pansies?'

She smiles at him.

When he's gone, though, she's lost. Wandering. Touching things. For hours. But she doesn't want to let him down and eventually finds the Windowlene they bought, and a cloth. She only has the energy for the kitchen panes. She puts together the tea things and waits for when he returns. Elbows propped up on the windowsill, watching the comings and goings of the tits. Beaks crammed with caterpillars.

Three trips later, she has her few things with her, and she stays at home.

Her own bed.


Ian visits the following morning. 'You're up and dressed already. How you doing? Did you sleep alright? I forgot to say, I've arranged for meals on wheels. To get you started.'

'I did sleep. I didn't think I would.'

He comes every day for a while. Always asks, 'How you doing?' Always tells her when to expect him next. Helps her keep track of time.


'Still got enough tablets?'

She shows him her dosette box.


'What are those pretty red things by the door?'

'Camellias. Always been there,' she replies.


'Did you remember to pay the rates bill?'

She has put that in the kitchen drawer. She pulls it out.

'Why don't we do that while I'm here.'

'You been able to do much?'
He doesn't fuss that the cottage is grubby. 'Darned my cardigan.' She shows him the repair. As she put it on that morning, she found the buttons were in the wrong holes. Had put that right since he was coming.

Eileen attends a day centre for a while, collected from her home by a volunteer. Ian persuaded her to try it. He appears there out of the blue. She's sitting in a corner.
'Have you not found anyone to talk to?' he asks.
Eileen shakes her head. She doesn't like to see him disappointed, but she can't help it. She's just waiting to go home. 'I'm better on my own,' she says.
'Though it's good for you to get out of the house.'
'I'd rather walk.'
He looks at her sideways.
Perhaps he thinks she'd get lost. 'I can find my way alright. Lived here my whole life.'
'Course you have.'

As summer sets in, she is usually outside when he arrives, in the garden from first light on dry days.
'You must have spent ages out here. You've tidied the whole stretch along under the hedge! Shall I make us some tea?'
She nods.
He pauses before he goes in. 'Your system is a mystery to me,' he says. 'You've left all those buttercups.' He tilts his head at her.
What's wrong with buttercups?
He shrugs and smiles, 'I suppose a weed is only a plant where you don't want it.'
Freda, next door, digs out all the wildflowers. Eileen can't

understand that. She likes things that seed themselves to make patches of colour. Doesn't matter what they are. Dandelions and wild daisies flower alongside pansies and wallflowers. She uproots a clump here and there and takes them to the compost heap, to make room for things that bloom later. She loves identifying seedlings, so she can keep the ones she wants. Honesty. Violas. That summer a huge thistle grows.

'You never buy seeds or plants?' Ian asks.

She shakes her head.

He brings her some. 'These are leftovers from my father-in-law's allotment,' he says. 'Thought you might like them. Any you don't want can go on the compost heap. These seeds are hollyhocks. You don't have any. But maybe you don't like them?'

Runner beans appear among the aquilegia and climb into her apple tree. Courgette stems thread through love-in-the-mist and buttercups. A bed of strawberries appears. The hollyhocks grow tall against her south-facing wall, the flowers dark red or cream. Bees love them.

She is talking to Freda one time when she turns to see him there. He will have heard her saying, 'No church. No praying. Not for me.'

Freda leaves in a huff.

Ian is beaming for some reason. 'Still not given up on making a Christian of you?'

'No. Don't think she ever will.'

'All credit to her, she goes on helping, though?'

He must have noticed, last time, the slice of home-made plum pie in the fridge, half a loaf of bread in a brown paper bag on the kitchen table. 'Even though she… disapproves. Yes.'

'At least someone close at hand is keeping an eye on you. Her and… Barbara, is it? I don't have to worry so much.' He grins at her.

He surely doesn't really worry.

· · ·

They're in the Co-op one day when a man, coming towards Eileen, drops the packet of biscuits he's just taken off the shelf. He squats to pick it up, but stays down, one knee on the floor, his eyes fixed on her. His hair is thin on top, a gingery brown, his nose freckled. Black-rimmed glasses. An anorak over a red check shirt, work trousers, and worn black shoes. 'Eileen?' he says.

She startles. Hardly anyone speaks to her. She looks at her feet, as they shift up and down in turn. She wants to run away but they won't take her.

Ian breaks the silence. 'Yes, it's Eileen. You seem to know her?'

'I do know her,' the man says. 'At least I did. Eileen, it's Roy.'

She gazes at him.

Roy stands up, moves forward and gently holds out a hand to her, touching just her fingertips.

So gentle.

Roy says, 'I heard what happened, and how ill it made you. I was so sorry. You're out and about now?'

Eileen says, 'Roy. From the bus.'

He smiles. 'I'm not on the buses any more. I work in a garage – went to tech and did exams and stuff. I hardly ever come by this way these days, since my mother passed away. I always thought of you when I visited her. Wondering if I'd bump into you.' He looks at Ian, then Eileen, then back to Ian. 'You a friend of hers?'

Ian hesitates, says, 'I hope I am. I've been helping her since she came home.'

Roy scratches his head, frowning. 'You're…?'

'A nurse,' replies Ian.

Roy's face relaxes. He stands up straight. 'How are you, Eileen? Since…'

She hopes she is smiling. 'Good to see you.'

Roy nods. He looks sad as he moves away. He turns back and waves goodbye to her once he's finished at the till.

Ian says quietly, 'You okay? You look a bit wobbly.'

She takes a breath, thinking what to say, composing herself. 'Long time ago. He was kind to me.'

He touches her shoulder.

Ian's kind, too.

A warm evening, towards the end of the second summer since she left the hospital, Eileen is sitting in the shade under her privet hedge and hears Freda talking to Ian. He must have just arrived.

'Here again,' Freda says.

'Like a bad penny,' he replies, cheerful as always.

'She manages now. But you're still not sure about her? She is strange, isn't she?'

'Oh, she's safe enough. I signed her off months ago.'

But he's still visiting. Eileen can feel her heart thumping.

'But you're still visiting,' Freda says.

'To be honest, she reminds me of my mother. Died a few years ago. It's as much for me as her. But I hope I'm a help to her sometimes.'

There's a pause.

He says, 'That incident when she grabbed a schoolgirl in the street? The kid must have looked like her daughter. Eileen called out Alice's name and properly frightened the child. A bit of a panic. The girl's mother phoned the police. Fortunately, I was here when a constable visited that evening. I told him the background, and no action was taken. And kids kept their distance after that, taunted her less, left her in peace. Which was good.'

Eileen realises that he no longer comes during the day. Evenings or weekends now. She hadn't noticed that.

He appears beside her, towering over her, and his smile falters. He says, 'I didn't realise you were out here. Should have thought.' His brow is crinkled.

He's wearing jeans and a tee shirt with a huge sunflower on it, his curls crammed under a baseball cap. How had she not seen things were different? 'You are so kind to me,' she says, reaching out a hand to him.

'Phew. I'm glad you're not cross.' He's grinning. 'Thing is, I like seeing you.'

. . .

One day, in a thin drizzle, the plants in her garden hazed with tiny water droplets, he arrives when she's indoors, reading.
'It's lovely and warm in here,' he says. 'You look a picture of peace, sitting in that pool of golden light from the lamp. I hadn't really registered how many books you have.' He gestures at the alcoves each side of the fireplace. 'The shelves, here, are stuffed with them. I don't remember seeing you reading a book before, either.'
She shows him Gilbert White's *The Natural History and Antiquities of Selborne*.
'Well,' he says. 'Wow.'

If she isn't in her garden or the house, he comes looking for her. He must know, now, where she will be. Pottering down the streets. Talking to herself. Counting the things that have lodged at the bottom of hedges. Counting litter, because that's what's there, as she looks down, avoiding seeing people's faces. The shiny, bright colours of crisp packets. The counting always a comfort.
She is less than forty, the first time she hears someone say, 'Mad old bat counting rubbish.'

# PART THREE

## THIRTY-FIVE
# SHARON ENJOYS WORKING WITH JANICE
### 2016

'I'm still not sure the play area will pass its inspection,' Janice told Sharon. 'Don't seem to be able to get anything done for worrying about it. And it's pointless, there's nothing more I can do, they're coming tomorrow.'

'That little boy who fell and scratched himself?' Sharon asked.

'Mmm. I can't find any sharp bits on the frame, but his mother's insisting.'

'Tricky.' Sharon moved to make them tea. 'Let me tell you something, maybe take your mind off it.'

Janice swivelled her chair away from her paper-strewn desk.

'This'll make you smile. I overheard three ladies talking about the drive to the hall. One said, "I don't do motorways and I don't like to drive in the rain. Or the dark. And I don't do right turns." No right turns! Think how difficult it must be to avoid right turns!'

'I'd have to think hard how to do that.' Janice was relaxing.

'Maybe a right turn at a roundabout would be okay. Oh, yes, and another lady – little, plump, fussy thing – asked for directions to a shop and was told something like, "You can get onto the ring road from yours? Well, you carry on until you come to the big left turn towards Rugby, and you take that…" The fussy woman interrupted, said, "Oh no, I can't do it like that. I have to count roundabouts." Wow. What counts as a roundabout? What about mini roundabouts? Those two-into-one jobs? It's a wonder some of them drive at all.'

'Well of course, some of them don't anymore.'

'True. Oh, and this was amazing. There was an elderly woman by the entrance the other day, just standing there, so I asked was she alright. She said she was fine, just waiting for her lift. Her friend was taking her to her sewing class. She couldn't drive herself, she said, because she was blind. Double wow. I couldn't stop myself. I said, "How can you sew, then?" And she told me. Turns out she was blind from some inherited retinal pigment thingy. Her father had it.'

'Sad.'

'Listen to this, though. She was tested when he was diagnosed, she was only twelve. So she knew, just twelve, that she'd lose her sight. But she didn't want to become like him. He just gave up, as his vision went, ended up sitting in the corner, moping. So, as a girl, she taught herself to do things with her eyes shut, in preparation. And now, completely blind, she can still do all sorts of things you wouldn't expect. Like make her own clothes. With help, but still, awesome.'

'That is impressive.' Janice was turning back to her work, her shoulders no longer scrunched up.

Sharon smiled and returned to the minutes of the last council meeting.

But by lunchtime Janice was fretting again.

'Why don't we go down to the park and have another look?' Sharon suggested. 'It's nice out there. We could take our sandwiches.'

Off they went, Sharon chattering to distract her. She talked about the U3A ladies who came to the hall for Zumba. 'They're all wrinkly and old, as you know. I've been making a study of the wrinkles.'

Janice looked sideways at her as if she was mad.

Sharon wasn't put off. 'There are nice ones, in a fan from the corner of the eye. From past smiles?'

Janice said, 'Like Prince Philip has. Except his go with squinting, being too vain to wear glasses.'

'Is that a fact? Anyway, then there's those vertical lines above the mouth, above thinned lips,' she grimaced. 'Go with hairy chins.'

Janice screwed up her nose. 'Yeuch, what is the matter with you? Sane people try not to look. You've been spending too much time on the wrong bits of YouTube.' But she chuckled.

'You've seen all that stuff about wrinkle treatments, then?' Sharon asked, miming slapping gunk over her face. 'I thought about us selling home-made avocado and frankincense face masks. We'd have enough customers. But, no, here's the thing. I remembered my Gran. She was the same clever, witty person underneath even when she was ancient. So I'm trying to imagine them when they were young and less off-putting.'

'Easier said than done.'

'Yeah. I mentioned it to Geoffrey and he said, "Our reaction to appearance is all about reproduction, looking for a suitable mate, it's hard-wired."'

'That's so what he would say.'

Sharon replied, serious now, 'Yes. But I think we've got to move on from that, half the population's over fifty these days.'

Janice nodded. Though she obviously thought this was all too weird.

'That blind lady I told you about wasn't a bit wrinkly to me. I think I'm getting addicted to LOL. Useful when there are so many in and out of the hall.'

Janice raised her eyebrows questioningly.

'New LOL. Little old ladies,' Sharon explained.

Janice laughed.

Sharon suddenly wondered if her mother would grow old. Actually, was her LOL fad partly because her mother was getting to look so crumbly?

. . .

They both went over the children's climbing frame, carefully stroking all the surfaces, and found nothing. But Janice did find a bent nail poking out of the nearby fence. She took a picture of it and went back, much more cheerful, to fetch a pair of pliers.

Stuart came into the office that afternoon, looking for the meeting minutes, which Sharon hadn't quite finished. Wondering what was so urgent, she emailed him her draft and he sat at the hot-desk computer to read it. She could see him out of the corner of her eye as she typed. He was huffing, he didn't like reading off computer screens. Sharon thought, looking at his balding head and paunch, older men could be every bit as unappealing as women. They could do with mirrors that showed the side view, so they could see the weight they carried at the front. Stuart really was so fat. She thought of the disappearing willie issue; he couldn't have seen his in ages. Revolting image. She tried to imagine him in his thirties but simply couldn't.

Stuart heaved himself up and came over. 'I couldn't quite remember what was said about the dog refuse bins, what I was supposed to be doing, but you've completed that section. Thank you.' He dragged a chair across.

Sharon's heart sank. There were dark, wet crescents on his shirt, under his arms. She could smell his sweat.

'Your mother had another fall, I gather,' he said, peering at her.

'Yes.' How did he hear about that? Nosy what'sit. 'She's fine. She was just a bit shaken.'

'I was thinking. Might she need a wheelchair at some point?'

Sharon sat up straight. He was just being helpful. She nodded. 'Mmm. Maybe.'

'It's just you perhaps didn't know that the Red Cross have a supply? If you needed one in a hurry.'

There were beads of moisture on his forehead, she had to stop herself drawing back, made herself smile politely at him. 'Thank you. No, I didn't know. That could be useful.' She did find it difficult to be around him.

He beamed back. 'I know the man who manages the chairs. Let me know and I'll introduce you.' With a grunt he got himself back on his feet and ambled out.

They'll have a website, Sharon thought. I won't need his help.

# THIRTY-SIX
# SHARON ON A LONG WALK WITH GEOFFREY

That Saturday dawned clear and bright. As Sharon dressed and packed her small rucksack, the pale blue of the earliest daylight hours was already deepening, the dawn chorus done. She met Geoffrey at the gate to the footpath, where the geocache box was hidden. They set off in comfortable silence, Sharon's thoughts on how much had changed for her. On the surface, her life was much the same as when they'd first walked together. She still lived with her Mum and worked in the parish council office. But as she looked out over the dew-spangled field and stepped deftly over a stile, her boot-clad foot anticipating the slight rock of the step, she smiled broadly.

Geoffrey saw, and grinned back. 'We seem to have a lovely day for it. If that's why you're beaming?'

'Yes, It's gorgeous. But actually I was thinking about how much has changed for me in the last year. Remember the first walk we had? I knew nothing about the environment. Everything we saw, you had something to say, that I didn't know about. You talked the whole time, and it was a revelation.'

'I wondered how you put up with it, me going on and on. I thought you'd be put off, but you weren't. You've almost forgotten I was your teacher now. It's good.' They were striding down a rough track between fields with grazing sheep, hedges either side, part of an ancient thoroughfare, she guessed. He said, 'You've come a long way...' Then, more quietly, 'How's your mother?'

'She's not too bad. She hasn't had another fall since that trip down the step. Things seem pretty stable at the moment. She keeps cheerful.'

'That's good.'

'Doesn't stop her planning ahead. We went the other day to look at wheelchairs at the Red Cross, though she's nowhere near needing one. Stuart put me onto them. They prefer to use theirs for short-term problems – broken legs and suchlike – but it was useful to talk to the man and for her to sit in some.'

Geoffrey had his head slightly tilted as he listened.

'There's more to it than I guessed. Should it be collapsible? What kind of tyres? All sorts of attachments to help carry things. Not to mention the colour. She was quite funny about the colour, talking about being too old for pink, not near enough to death for black, acid green too bilious.'

Geoffrey smiled.

'She said orange was an absolute no-no, she hated it. I didn't know that – amazing. We got talking about what we'll do when she gets more disabled.'

'Ahh.'

Sharon took a deep breath. 'She's facing it squarely, being really brave. She says she's determined not to have me at home looking after her, though we haven't worked out alternatives yet. I suppose it means day care, helpers visiting, perhaps residential care eventually. If she doesn't change her mind.' She heard the catch in her voice and stopped speaking, didn't look at Geoffrey. Her eyes were tearing up. Would she be able to do it, look after her mother full-time, if Lizzie did change her mind? She wasn't at all sure. She sniffed, recovered herself. 'A long way from that yet, and MS is so variable. Though she doesn't seem to have the benign version.'

He moved across and gave her a quick hug.

'Do that again,' she laughed. 'Physical contact's hard to come by.' She felt safe with him.

'You have to think of yourself as well, you know. I haven't seen a boyfriend…?'

'No boyfriend, no. What an olde worlde word. I'm not looking for one, so there's no interest. You know what it's like. If you're gagging for it, it can be like there's a neon sign on your head saying, "Come and get it," and men appear out of nowhere. The signs I'm putting out must be all negative, too much else going on. You? Liam OK?'

His face softened, 'Liam is very good indeed,' he said. 'He'll currently be fast asleep. Busy night at the restaurant.' He added wistfully, 'We don't get to see much of each other,' then grinned. 'Don't get the chance to get bored with each other's company.'

They continued without talking for a while, the day warming up, the first short-lived puffs of cloud drifting overhead in the lazy breeze. They paused to listen to a song-thrush, loudly shouting its territorial claim from the top of a tree, its neck stretched upwards. Skirting a tree-fringed pool, a moorhen startled. Sharon noticed the sunlight, reflected from the water, was illuminating the under-surface of the lower branches. It looked lovely.

She glanced sideways at him. 'Your mother called in to see mine the other day.' She knew about the gulf between Geoffrey and Mrs Johns, with her conservatism and her religious beliefs. Though he visited frequently and fixed and fettled around her house. 'Or maybe she was checking me out as a prospective daughter-in-law?'

Geoffrey grimaced.

She thought Mrs Johns didn't know about her son's partner. They lived just far enough away for her to have difficulty visiting. 'She means well, brought a pretty pot with a daisy-type thing. Though I do wish she wouldn't talk all the time about her "friend in Jesus". I see Lizzie curling up. And she had a bit of a go at me, with my job and no prospects of a husband.'

Geoffrey winced, he was about to protest. She put a hand on his arm to stop him interrupting.

'It set me thinking. She was saying how it wasn't natural for a young woman. The clock ticks and so on; I can't postpone having children indefinitely. She said that if I don't have kids, I'll regret it. I'll be "unfulfilled as a woman". She talked about childbearing and child rearing as being "the highest call for a woman".'

Geoffrey was grinding his teeth.

'And when I said I wasn't sure I agreed with her she said, "You can't understand it if you haven't experienced it, but when you hold your own baby in your arms, then you'll know. Then you'll understand what love really is, what life is for." She must really want you to have children.'

'I won't listen to that kind of talk. One of the many things she can make me really angry about, but there's no point in my arguing, she'll never understand. And I don't want to argue with her anyway. So I just stop her.'

Sharon wondered what he said to shut his mother up.

He paused before he continued. 'Thing is, it's wicked. Telling you you must have children, telling you you're not a proper woman without, and that weasel logic about how you can't imagine the joy and the fulfilment, you have to go ahead and procreate. And it devalues everything else a woman can achieve. You can become a High Court judge, but it counts for nothing if you're childless. Evil.' He was almost shouting now, arms thrusting in protest as he turned circles beside her, passionate, explosive with passion. 'We need women who can cope with not having children. That's what the world needs. Millions of them. There are far too many people in the world – what an understatement that is. Humans have to find a way to reverse population growth.'

'Hey... hey... I know.'

He didn't stop. 'That means fewer babies, women having fewer babies. Lots of women having none at all. If you don't actively want a child, you shouldn't have one. And that's not self-ish. Childless women should be seen as heroes, as wonderful, valuable people.'

She patted his arm as he swung round again. 'There, there. It's alright. I know. But it's good to hear you say it; makes me feel better. No one else says it, though. Why is that?'

'A huge elephant in the room, isn't it? I guess they're scared. What will the world be like for their progeny if the numbers keep increasing, the resources dwindling, the environment degrading? People get scared when they have really hard stuff to face, and they turn away.' Geoffrey was scuffing a trampled dandelion into pulp.

He really cared about this stuff. Sharon suspected most people wouldn't listen.

He continued. 'There was a strong reaction against what the Chinese did, limiting couples to one child. The psychological harm from single-child families. But nothing about what it would have been like if they hadn't done what they did.'

They were stopped on the track. He turned to face her, took her elbows in his hands. His eyes were unfocussed, directed over her shoulder, his expression sad. 'If you look at it logically, what can you do to reduce population? You can reduce fertility – births – and you can reduce length of life. Other than mass emigration to another planet, that's it. As to choosing for people to die younger if they want to, we're aeons away from being able to consider that properly.'

Sharon said slowly, 'Choosing to die. People think you're a monster if you talk about voluntary euthanasia, assisted dying, whatever you want to call it. But I think Lizzie might want it, when the time comes. I've thought about it.' She hesitated. 'I'd help her, even if it meant going to jail.' She thought, there, I've said it.

He seemed completely unfazed. 'That makes you a good, kind person, not a monster. We're kinder to animals. We're much kinder to animals.' He touched her cheek.

She was beginning to feel self-conscious.

He maybe noticed, since he turned to walk on, a little ahead of her, humming softly.

Two bird calls. Scanning the sky, she found them. A buzzard, mewing, glided serenely until the crow, screeching, came close. The raptor dropped a wing, feinted and dodged. The bigger bird seemed oddly tolerant as the black nuisance followed and harassed it.

Sharon caught Geoffrey up. There was more she wanted to say. 'I know there are lots of reasons why the law makes it so difficult for people. Trying to prevent murder, the religious business about life being sacred. Loads of stuff. But if the person isn't actually there any more because of dementia, or is suffering terribly...'

Geoffrey glanced at her. 'You're maybe too young to remember the elderly couple who committed suicide together on the overnight train from Scotland to London. People said, "How tragic." No one said, "Well done." But it wasn't tragic. They'd thought it through, made their decision and got on with it. The guard would have seen nastier scenes of a morning than two old people at peace, curled together like spoons. I want to be allowed to say when it's time for me to go.'

Sharon shook herself. Time to change the subject. But she couldn't resist a dig, 'Can I have a say too?'

And then he said, 'Ahh, look.' They'd come through a wood with tall trees and were now out in the open, the land ahead falling away down a steep slope, a broad valley revealed. In the bright sunlight and clear air, the view extended for twenty miles or more. The slope, covered with gorse brush and brambles, was alive with insects and birds. Geoffrey pointed. A small brownish bird was perched on a bare branch, looking alert and sprightly. It launched, turned an acrobatic manoeuvre and landed back. Through her binoculars Sharon could see it had an insect in its pointed beak, see its pale, flecked breast, though she already knew from the flight pattern that it was a spotted flycatcher. One of her favourites. Will have just migrated back, she thought.

. . .

This walk was to be the longest she'd ever done: twelve miles in a meandering circle, planned by Geoffrey to include woodland, water, views and history, paced for pleasure, which is why they'd started so early.

Geoffrey said, 'One of the girls in class said, "The thing with exercise is to do enough for a good shot of the smug hormones, but not so much as to make you pissy". Endorphins, she meant. She's right; let's have a rest.'

They sat for a few minutes to enjoy the view and drink some water, then set off again at a steady pace, aiming to eat their sandwiches at the castle, a bit over halfway.

Sharon wanted to ask Geoffrey about Stuart, about what happened last week. Which actually, now she considered it, probably began some while ago. She was trying to work out where to begin. Probably with the Maisie business. She could tell him about that for a start.

# THIRTY-SEVEN
# SHARON TALKS ABOUT MAISIE'S FALL

'Did you hear about Maisie Oates?' Sharon asked Geoffrey as they strode along.

'She's your neighbour, isn't she? No. What about her?'

'A couple of weeks ago. I was woken by something. A noise, I thought.' Sharon was drawn back into the drama of the story. 'Five am my clock said. Panicked a bit, thought it was Mum, but she was fine, fast asleep. Heard a thrush, looked out of the window and there was Maisie, face down on her rockery.'

'That's not good,' Geoffrey said.

'I grabbed my clothes, thinking she might be dead – I've not seen a dead body, you know. She was groaning as I got to her, so not dead. Groans maybe what woke me. She was cold, though, only in her nightie, just as well it'd been a warmish night. I covered her with my coat. But I couldn't rouse her. I'd left my mobile behind. I didn't want to leave her. What to do?'

'No one about?'

'Well, Stuart turned up. Had to be him, didn't it? Though what he was doing out at that time... I said could he stay with her, I wouldn't be long, dashed off, phoned for an ambulance. Grabbed my duvet to cover her.'

'Long to wait for the ambulance?'

'No, it was early morning and the paramedics were there in no time. She was coming to by then. They thought she'd broken her nose – it was bleeding. And they pointed out her wrist was all wonky. Actually, it turned out there wasn't much damage done, they only kept her in hospital a few days, then she went home with a bright blue plaster. But her confidence is really shot.'

'Ahh.'

'And I think she may actually be losing it. A few weeks before all this, she called to me over the fence, asking for a drop of milk for her breakfast. When I took some round, there she was, everything laid out: tablecloth, proper napkin, teapot, toast rack. She had this little milk jug with a cloth cover, weighted with coloured beads sewn round the edge. So sweet. But Kevin, that's her son, said he thought she'd run out of milk because she'd been watering the plants with it. And Lizzie's seen her in the street in her slippers, when, before, she was so neat and proper.'

'Not much you can do to help, I imagine.'

'No. Though Lizzie keeps a watch out for her. Lucky Kevin gave us his number when he did, after the milk business. I called him and he arrived with the ambulance. But I'm forgetting why I told you all this: Stuart. Always taking charge when there's a problem. But this time he didn't. Just gawped. And, though he waited with me for the ambulance, he hardly said a word. Not like him at all.'

'No.' Geoffrey shoved his hands in his pockets. 'I'd noticed something seemed wrong too. I asked him.'

'And?'

'It's his wife, Barbara. Her cancer's come back. Affecting her bones. I didn't know, but she had breast cancer back in the seventies, long since signed off follow-up, has been fine all this time. Stuart seems devastated. Though apparently, it's not unusual for it to show up again decades later.'

That explained it.

Neither of them could think of anything to say for a while.

. . .

They lunched as planned at Belvoir Castle, with the stunning view of the valley spread out below them. Geoffrey instructed her about clouds as they ate, prompted by a pair of buzzards calling as they cruised in circles overhead. By this time there were cumulus clouds dotted across the whole sky.

'See that curved section in the slope, shaped like a bowl? Hollows like that collect the sun's warmth, making a hot spot to trigger a bubble of warm air, which rises. It's called a thermal. You know the air cools steadily with height? The air at the top of a thermal's liable to be cold enough the moisture condenses out, making a cloud. Like that one,' and he pointed to a floating meringue, high up overhead.

The buzzards became tiny specks as they soared upwards, using the thermal's power to gain height, Geoffrey explained.

Later, he spotted a glider. Sharon hadn't seen one before. It was climbing under a thermal like the buzzards did. Swirling gracefully upwards on its incredibly long, white wings. Below the cloud, it straightened up and set off away from them. It flew so fast it seemed to simply evaporate.

Mid-afternoon, Geoffrey noticed a taller cloud upwind. 'You see that one that's gone higher than most, topped with a horizontal wispy bit? That's grown tall enough to reach the icing layer. It's frozen moisture making the slew at the top. The cloud will get seeded with ice crystals, making it rain.'

'Is this your convoluted way of saying "We're going to get wet"?'

He poked his tongue out at her. 'Look underneath it, those grey streaks? That's the start of the rain.' He was right, of course, and soon there were other towering clouds, and then they were getting soaked.

'Refreshing,' he said cheerfully as he put on the thin waterproof he'd stowed in his backpack. Sharon hadn't thought to bring one. Never mind, the shower didn't last long.

. . .

She was often surprised on her walks with Geoffrey. They climbed a bank and were suddenly stepping across a railway line. With a little sign giving the phone number for the Samaritans. Or there was a footbridge over the motorway, that she'd not noticed before, though she'd been on the road often enough. Geoffrey pointed out the cast iron mile markers by the canal. Bargemasters, he said, billed by the mile, in the days when the canals were major freight routes.

On a field path they came across an obelisk, engraved, 'Lottery Feb 21st 1886'. Intrigued, Sharon copied the inscription onto her phone and Googled it when she got home. Lottery was a horse, the first proper winner of the Grand National at Aintree, in 1839. The following year, within the span of a month, he ran in six steeplechases of over four miles, in widely separated parts of the country, winning at Leamington, Northampton, Cheltenham and Stratford. He was walked from each one to the next – there was no other way of transporting a horse in those days. In a career lasting eight seasons, he was so successful, special handicaps were devised to disadvantage him. The monument was erected in 1886, long after his death at the nearby stud farm where he spent his last years. Amazing.

She emailed the story to Geoffrey. It was brilliant to be able to tell him something he didn't already know.


Her mother called from the next room, 'Sharon, when you've got a minute? No rush.'

Lizzie had broken a nail and couldn't see well enough to trim it. Oh, well, back to real life.

# THIRTY-EIGHT
# SHARON HELPS WITH HER MOTHER'S PARTY

Saturday afternoon, Sharon was ironing, ear buds in, listening to music. Lizzie touched her on the arm, to get her attention. Sharon upended the iron and pulled a bud out.

'I've been thinking about my birthday,' her mother said.

Something in her tone of voice made Sharon switch the iron off.

'I know I said I didn't want a fuss, but you only get to be fifty once, so I'm thinking of a party after all. I'd need your help, of course. What d'you think?'

There hadn't been a party in their house since before her father died. 'I'm game,' Sharon said. 'What d'you fancy? Fireworks? Hire the village hall? Morris dancing?' Lizzie smiled, relaxed, but Sharon could see she'd been scheming. She waited.

'I made a list of people.' Lizzie had it in her hand and passed it over.

This conversation had been planned.

'I hoped you could invite a few of your friends and make it up to twenty-five or thirty? I thought we'd have room for that many if we used the conservatory – you'd have to clear it out, I'm afraid. A buffet in the sitting room, drinks in the kitchen, candles in the garden if we're lucky and it's dry?'

Sharon was skimming through the names.

'I know my fingers aren't much good now for cooking, but we could keep the food simple, get party packs from the supermarket, or Indian snacks. Pakoras, samosas, chutney, perhaps?'

Sharon sat down to read: a dozen friends from the village, Lizzie's sister and her husband and kids, two people from Lizzie's work who'd kept in touch over the years since she left. Two Sharon wouldn't have guessed: the nice man who came in to cut Lizzie's hair, and the older chap from the Co-op who, months ago, brought round a box of groceries when Sharon had flu. She thought who she might add. Janice and her husband, perhaps? Ought she to include Stuart, he'd been so helpful, and Barbara? Christine and Joan, her friends from school, who she hardly saw these days. Geoffrey and Liam? Would Geoffrey bring his partner to the village? Though Liam might be working.

'Looks good,' she said, 'I can add some youngsters, people with purple hair, so it's not all baldies and silver-tops.'

Lizzie made a crooked face at her. 'Silver top used to be a kind of milk.'

Sharon laughed. 'Whatever.' Though seeing Lizzie had developed a new spasm, she looked away. 'Your birthday's on a Monday. Do you want the do that day or the weekend before? Lunchtime or evening? I like the Indian food idea, though maybe we could do both. There are people who actually like pork pies and sausage rolls, I'm told.'

'That farm shop we visited does good pies,' Lizzie reminded her. 'We could do joke food from the olden days. You probably don't remember those dreadful hedgehogs of cheese and pineapple chunks on cocktail sticks? Jammy dodgers, fly cemeteries, fig rolls. Can you still get iced gems, d'you think? I used to love them, would bite the icing off.'

Sharon screwed up her face in mock disgust.

Lizzie wasn't discouraged. 'How about jelly and Instant Whip? I really liked the butterscotch flavour.'

'What on earth is Instant Whip?'

'Like Angel Delight only better.'

. . .

It would be the Sunday lunchtime, they decided, easier for those who had to travel, and those who worked. People would be able to wander in the garden in daylight. In the rain. No candles or fireworks, but pots of pansies everywhere. Lizzie could do those. Her hands could still manage plants. Sharon had noticed that she now used her knuckles to push potting compost into place. Lizzie said she'd almost no sensation in her fingertips.

The afternoon disappeared as they made plans. Sharon's session in the gym went out the window.

Later, over a mug of tea, Lizzie said, 'Another thing I wanted to talk to you about. Hope you don't mind.'

Here it comes, Sharon thought.

'I've changed my mind about my present.'

Sharon was right.

'I want a wheelchair. I think I'll soon need wheeling about.'

Sharon was stopped short. Her hands trembled. She sat on them.

It was a while since they'd been to the Red Cross to look, but it seemed Lizzie had made notes and had done some research on the internet.

'I know it's expensive,' Lizzie went on, 'and I don't want you to pay for all of it; I want to use my savings. But it's what I want. It's time. And I don't think I can propel myself. After the last bout, the strength in my arms hasn't come back enough. So it needs to be the type that you push.'

Sharon suspected her face betrayed her. But, with Lizzie's rubbish vision, perhaps she couldn't see that.

'I don't want to be stuck indoors all the time, you'll understand that. But I also don't want my getting out to be dependent on you, it wouldn't be fair.' She waved away Sharon's protest. 'You're too late. I've contacted the Scouts – I know Mr Lane from way back – and I'm going to be a regular job for a bob. An hour or two a week, and they'll take me wherever I want. Two lads together. Just as well I've not got fat, or I'd need the whole troupe.'

Sharon gazed at her, lost for words. She knew cheerful acceptance was characteristic of multiple sclerosis. Which was good. But it could be really difficult to take.

'Lizzie laughed again. 'Don't look at me in that tone of voice. It's okay. And I'm going to have flashing fairy lights on the wheels, so you'll have to smile. They do movement-activated coloured LEDs, like on children's trainers. What d'you say to that?'

Sharon shook her head and grinned despite herself.

On the morning of the party it rained depressingly until ten and then the sky cleared to a deep blue. The wet grass sparkled in the sunlight, and dried. The yellow and magenta pansies brightened. By late morning the house and garden were looking cheerful and welcoming.

Sharon found her mother sitting gazing at herself in her dressing table mirror, in the dining room that was now her bedroom. Seeing her every day, Sharon didn't often really look at her. She couldn't help but notice her today.

Lizzie's slim form was shrunken, very different from the strong woman of Sharon's childhood. She had on an old favourite Sharon dug out for her from the back of her wardrobe, a calf-length pink and grey dress in a flattering silky fabric. The glittery silver kitten-heeled pumps would be fine. Lizzie wouldn't be walking in them. Her jewellery was silver, too: chains with pearls or glass beads at intervals, one wound round her wrist, another trailing in great, long loops from her neck. Her wrinkled, pale skin, with its mauve blotches and dark blemishes, was hidden under foundation and Sharon had applied subtle, iridescent eye shadow for her. She swallowed carefully and said, 'Let me just smooth this out, I've left a couple of smudges… And now you look fabulous.'

'Take these shoes off me, will you? I want to walk,' Lizzie said. Pushing down with her hands she got slowly to her feet, took Sharon's arm, and they made their careful way out onto the patio.

Lizzie settled in a high, comfortable chair, the shoes back in place. 'I feel like a queen,' she declared, smiling.

Sharon's old friends, Christine and Joan, arrived early, together, with a chocolate fountain and a basket of marshmallows. Geoffrey brought his mother. Sharon beamed to see him hide his guitar in the garage. JJ's joined it and the pair of them went into a huddle over the amplifiers and speakers secreted there on Saturday while Sharon had taken her mother out in a taxi to collect crockery from the hire place. Sharon was introduced to Chris Moore, also in Gee and JJ's band, she remembered. JJ's Dad, Steve, appeared too, pulling a tatty shopping basket on wheels. A small electronic keyboard poked out of the top. He unloaded an extension reel and a collection of strange instruments: small percussion pieces, a harmonica, some kind of pipe, and a painted gourd that rattled.

Just as well they were able to use the garden, Sharon thought. There was a whole crowd coming.

A comfortable hubbub developed as people started on the food and drink. Sharon heard Geoffrey's mother lecturing Christine on child discipline, talking about the advantages of the teaching in Christian schools. Christine was deliberately leading her on, seemingly enjoying the predictability of her comments. Bad Christine, Sharon thought, but at least she was keeping the wretched woman away from Lizzie. Mr Lane arrived with six uniformed Scouts, so clean Sharon could imagine their mothers scrubbing them behind the ears that morning. Lane made a bee line for Lizzie in the garden and introduced the boys; they were due to start the wheelchair rota the following week. He set them to distribute food. Sharon then found him at her elbow.

He removed the plate of sausage rolls she was carrying, handed her an empty plate and a napkin and said, 'The boys have instructions to take over any job you might have to do. So if you pick up a jug to circulate, one of them will come and take it from you. Anything you need doing, just start and they'll get the message. No argument.' The doorbell rang and a freckled redhead, one sock collapsed at his ankle, ran to open it. Sharon grinned, delighted. Though she had a sudden vision of a boy following her into the toilet.

Stuart phoned to give apologies. He and his wife wouldn't be able to come, Barbara wasn't well enough.

At two o'clock, through the conservatory window, Sharon saw her mother look at her watch. Lizzie sent off her attending Scout, who brought Mr Lane to her. He squatted beside her chair, their heads together. He then came into the house to tell everyone to go outside because Lizzie wanted to make a speech. Sharon saw Geoffrey glance at her across the room. He must have seen her alarm, because he negotiated his way through the mob, took her arm solemnly in his, and escorted her outside for them to stand at the back of the crowd. He silently passed her a paper serviette.

'Tomorrow will be my fiftieth birthday,' Lizzie was saying, 'and I'm so glad you are all here with me to celebrate. I'm not going to be maudlin about my health, but it looks as though I won't be up to parties much longer. This MS is getting to be a real nuisance and I'll soon not be fit for human consumption. So I want you all to enjoy today with me. And I want to ask a favour. When I'm a complete wreck, please don't be strangers. I want you to be here, not so much for me – I'm sure I'll be well looked after – but for Sharon. She'll need the company. Give her some light relief.'

There was a hum of supportive muttering. Sharon tilted her head back, squeezing her eyes tight, trying to stop the tears from rolling down her face.

'And talking about light relief, have you seen the wheels on my chair?' She indicated the new wheelchair parked to one side and a Scout, who must have been briefed earlier, pushed it back and forth to demonstrate the flashing. 'Brilliant, don't you think? Cheers everyone. Thank you for coming.'

As Sharon blew her nose on the serviette, saying, 'Oh, Lizzie...' Geoffrey handed her another.

'How many d'you have, stashed away there?' she asked between blows.

'Twelve,' he replied.

She grimaced.

Her arm tucked in his, Geoffrey walked her down the path, away from the crowd. 'She's impressive,' he said. 'Most people don't have the confidence of Stephen Hawking, apparently comfortable in public despite his appearance.' Then he gave her something else to think about, 'You call her by her first name. If I called my mother Joan she'd have a fit. You must have called her Mum or Mummy when you were little?'

Sharon looked at him, squinting into sun. She could imagine Mrs Johns' reaction, she would see it as disrespect. 'I don't actually remember when it started,' she mused. 'I guess, as I got older, with no father there, we got more friendly. It seemed friendlier. Then, when she was ill, became disabled, and depended on me more... A bit of role reversal, perhaps? Anyway, she likes it, so that's okay.' She heard her defensive tone. Others had criticised.

'I like it too. I'm jealous,' he told her, giving her a nudge.

She couldn't think what to say to that.

Steve Lock waved at Geoffrey. 'Ready to go?' he called.

The music started. Sharon saw her mother's surprised smile. Excellent. Steve was the main man, co-ordinating the others. They started with nursery rhymes, rapidly moving on to tunes from the seventies and then the eighties. Janice sang Madonna's 'Like a Virgin' in a reedy voice, followed by Geoffrey with 'I Want to Know What Love is'. Sharon hadn't heard him sing before; he had a nice voice. Then JJ introduced a group of boys from the school, who'd been hiding in the garage. They did 'Everybody Wants to Rule the World'. Lovely harmonies. Got an enthusiastic round of applause.

'Tears for Fears, 1985,' hissed Geoffrey, returned to Sharon's side.

He's avoiding his mother, she thought.

Geoffrey told Sharon they'd picked songs mostly from around 1986, when Lizzie would have been twenty. People's strongest musical memories were formed at that sort of age, he said, 'The age of hope, idealism and romance.'

The selection seemed to work, with Lizzie swaying and tapping in time to the beat, mouthing some of the words and looking happy. By the time it came to 'Shout', many were joining in, the volume high, perhaps too high. Steve maybe thought so too, since he changed the pace to a softer, slower background, livened up by odd, entertaining cameos.

Two of the Scouts performed a folk song duet.

He persuaded half a dozen youngsters to play his peculiar percussion instruments and, after a bit of practice, they produced a quite creditable backing to 'Mony mony', making people laugh.

Late that afternoon, Eileen wandered in. Sharon had invited her but didn't think she'd come. A Scout found her a chair and brought her a plate of food and a beaker of juice. Eileen didn't speak but just sat watching shyly, a flicker of a nervous smile appearing at intervals.

# THIRTY-NINE
# THERE ARE DULL PARTS TO SHARON'S JOB

Throughout June, Sharon was busy at work. There was a lot going on, much of it rather tedious. Geoffrey presented his 'front gardens' report, doing his pontificating. She felt guilty that she was hardly able to listen. She didn't believe the councillors could possibly be taking it all in. Though he started well enough, it was just too long, too much.

'In 2005 there was a study in Ealing where over sixty volunteers assessed going on for eight thousand front gardens. And a Mori survey, commissioned by the RHS, the same year. The websites are listed at the bottom of the papers I've circulated, so you can look for yourselves if you want to. Mori showed the proportion of front gardens that were more than three quarters paved varied by region from 47 per cent in the Northeast to 14 per cent in London, 25 per cent here in the Midlands...'

There was a bumble bee battering itself against the far window.

'...avoid doing any gardening... Those with garages are more likely to park their car on hardstanding, not less... The Ealing group identified forty-three reasons why you shouldn't pave your front garden. I've condensed their list for you.'

That was a mercy.

'We can talk about any of the points.'

He stopped and people shuffled through the stapled pages he'd given out.

He said, 'You'll be aware that you now need planning permission for new paving of over five square metres, because of the risk of flooding from run-off. Not that people often know to apply for it. Or bother if they do.'

Mrs Hilary said, 'My son, when he moved, was advised by the estate agent to put in hard-standing, and they increased the asking price for the house when he did.'

Geoffrey replied, 'I don't suppose the estate agent mentioned the fact that when most of the street has done the same, property prices go back down again, because it all looks bare and unattractive. I've probably said that before. Then there are the effects on health of being surrounded by a sea of concrete. If you live in a leafy, grassy environment the studies show you're happier and at less risk of depression. Less heart and respiratory disease, even obesity.'

Someone scoffed, 'That's airy-fairy stuff. Maybe there's less depression and those other things in people who can afford posh houses and gardens with gardeners! I can't imagine there's any direct harm.'

'Well, actually there is. See, soil and plants absorb pollution and airborne particles, while concrete doesn't. Paving actually does contribute to respiratory problems.'

Sharon looked around the councillors and saw that several were fidgeting and Stuart Jenkins was picking at a hangnail.

Mrs Freestone said, 'It must be safer to get parked cars off the road.'

Geoffrey replied, 'You'd think so, wouldn't you? But it's not that simple.'

Of course it isn't.

'When the road's clear, people drive faster so the accidents cause more damage. And, reversing onto the road, residents' cars hit people, particularly little ones.'

Sharon's attention went again. She was looking at Mrs Hilary's nail varnish. The chairman didn't usually wear any, but today she had proper nail art, with tiny crescent moons and stuck-on crystal stars. Maybe it was her birthday.

Just as well Geoffrey would email her his report for the minutes. Sharon had missed several bits.

Someone must have said something to get him onto biodiversity. He was saying, 'Hard surfaces are a barren desert without the food and shelter wildlife needs to survive. That's self-evident. There's data, for example, to show the decline in sparrows is linked to increased paving...'

They covered subsidence, weather, noise pollution, antisocial behaviour, global warming, the lot. To Sharon's relief, Mrs Hilary eventually called a halt. 'It seems, on balance, that this trend for increased hard-standing creates problems.'

Around the meeting there were some nods and a yawn.

'You'll see Geoffrey has made some suggestions about what we might do, and you may come up with ideas yourselves. Janice, can we put it on the agenda for the next meeting, please?'

Yet another item carried over. What was the latest time a council meeting had finished?

Geoffrey was leaning back, looking round at his colleagues. Wondering if he'd wasted his time? Just as well they were moving on because there was an even bigger item next, the planning applications. Sharon had needed to learn a lot about planning so she could respond to the stream of queries. The process was long-winded, she rather hated it, so she found entertainment where she could. With the protest messages that came in – it wasn't all emails, some were letters, occasionally even hand-written ones – she guessed the age and background of the author. From things like the font choice, how many exclamation marks there were, and the text itself, of course. There was usually someone who knew the person and could tell her how wrong she was.

'That's Maisie Oates' younger sister, Flo. Lives in the Orchard residential home. Studied law, worked as a solicitor. Computer literate. That fooled you, didn't it?'

She was constantly amazed at educated people's spelling.

There was one planning application that was huge, and it had been discussed so many times that Sharon was thoroughly sick of it. Three hundred homes on what was now farmland, just outside the village boundary. To be accessed from a road that was already clogged each morning and evening. Plenty of objections had come in. Sharon wasn't surprised. It would make a real difference to the village... perhaps not all of it bad, though. A group of residents got together in opposition, focussing on the traffic. They'd done their own survey. At peak times, there was often a jam of twenty to thirty vehicles backed up behind a junction that formed a bottleneck, and delays of up to fifteen minutes, with entrances to side-roads blocked along the way. They argued that the estate could only make things worse. However, the formal traffic assessment determined that the planned road junction changes – a mini-roundabout where the estate road joined the main one, and a set of traffic lights at the bottleneck – should improve traffic flow. It was the leaden progress of all this that got to Sharon. But eventually the parish had decided to support the application, and the proposal was approved.

Some of the homes were to be smaller and cheaper and that helped a lot. The developer had also included several features that Geoffrey told Sharon he particularly liked, not least the relatively small amount of paving and gravel.

Well, he would approve of that, wouldn't he?

They were going to keep the line of mature trees along one edge, and plant at least two new ones for each house. A footpath and cycle way were drawn, at the far end alongside the stream, connecting with an existing bridleway. At the furthest point from the main road there would be a small park with a grove of silver birch trees and oaks, a fenced-off play area and a pond. The material scooped out from there would contribute to a bund, planted with hazel and hawthorn, screening the houses from the main road. These green features helped compensate for the fact that, on the other side of the village, the country park development had stalled, with one hold up after another. The latest was to do with a bridge over the disused railway line. It had been assessed as unsafe, but no one admitted to owning it; the deeds had gone missing, so repairs couldn't go ahead. Sharon couldn't believe you could lose the record of ownership of a thing like a bridge. Anyway, there was little prospect of the country park happening any time soon, which made a play area and a copse on the new estate especially attractive.

Jack Dawkins, the project manager, made himself known at the council offices at the planning stage and said he would visit at intervals during the build, maintain good lines of communication. Geoffrey's kind of age, he was personable and seemed straightforward. Once the work started, he appeared in the office most weeks, as promised. Cheerful and muscular, he wore jeans, a great tartan padded shirt, and muddy Rigger boots, his brown hair tousled.

Sharon heard him say to Janice, 'The boss has taken a particular interest in this one. I think he used to live round here yonks ago. He's unusually keen. Wants to make this a useful contribution to the community.'

As if he was paying back some debt. Maybe making up for past dodgy deals?

Dawkins went on, 'Perhaps he wants to do something good before he retires, for him to be remembered by. He's that kind of age. He's always interested in the bottom line, of course, but with this one it's also about affordability, environmental impact, quality experience and such like. Whatever his reasons, it looks like it could be better than most.'

Janice muttered to Sharon, out of his earshot, 'Not sure I believe all this. Sceptical from past experience. Though I admit there are some good features.'

Sharon thought of that massive, overgrown, dark garden being ripped out to make way for five large houses in place of one.

Residences with porches supported by columns, double garages and 'gardens' of ornate terracotta tubs dotted on half an acre of slate. It did look as if this one would be less posh, less cramped and bleak. Sharon quite liked Jack Dawkins. She rather hoped the estate would be as good as he said.

Around the time she started the job, there was all that health and safety fuss over plans for a lake in the country park. At least that stuff hadn't come up again.

# FORTY
## SHARON IS HORRIFIED

Sharon had learnt that a large construction project could be held up by all sorts of things. Great crested newts. Gas pipelines. Buried treasure. Things didn't necessarily just trundle along happily. Though this one did to begin with. Until they came to the pond. They scooped out a basin and lined it with clay. The outflow route was created, to take excess water back to the stream. All it needed was to dig the channel from the brook, which would fill the pool.

The day that work started on the inflow, Stuart came to the office to pick up some documents, with an agitated Maggie.

'I walked with her up to the site to see progress, but she got in such a state I had to bring her away,' he told Sharon.

Maggie's eyes were swollen, her lashes clumped. She whined like a toddler, despite her age. Maggie picked up papers and twisted them. Sharon had to retrieve some important ones. She settled the stocky woman in a chair with a bar of chocolate, some scrap paper and a fat, red felt-tip pen. Stuart looked grateful. Maggie calmed down after a while and he took her home.

It was quiet for a bit. Until Jack Dawkins arrived.

'Bloody hell! Oh, bloody, fucking hell.'

Sharon thought he hadn't seen her; she hadn't heard him swear like that before.

He was pale and sweaty, mopping his face with a large handkerchief. 'Christ almighty!'

Sharon coughed.

He jumped. 'Sorry, love. Shouldn't... Oh, bloody hell.'

'What's happened?'

He dropped himself into a seat and said, 'I'm,' but stopped. 'It's... Oh God...' He couldn't find the words. 'Bloody hell!'

Must be something awful. She made him a mug of tea as he sat there muttering.

He sipped and pulled himself together enough to talk properly.

'You know we're doing the pond? 'Course you do.'

Sharon waited.

'We'd cut down the trees on the section of bank where the inflow channel begins. I'd set Andy with the digger to get the roots out. And the reeds and stuff.' He stopped.

'And?'

A deep breath. 'The bottom of an old willow came out. There's this great tangle of roots comes away in a rush, mud splattered everywhere.' He was grey and shaky, mopping again. 'He's lifted the bucket and held it up for the water to drain. Takes a while for the mess to settle.' He wiped his eyes. 'Which is when I see this... This small... Well, it looks like the remains of an arm.'

Sharon had to sit down.

His voice had gone up a notch. 'The skeleton of a limb, anyway, poking out, shaking with the digger's engine.' He was almost in tears.

'Oh, no.'

'I kept telling myself it would be from an animal, a sheep or something. Or it could've been a toy, y'know, plastic? An animal. But the hand... It really looked like the little hand they showed on that history programme. I just yelled for Andy to stop. I think I screamed, in fact. Anyway, what with me rushing forward, waving, he got the message.'

If only she'd got herself a tea too. Her hands had gone cold, and she could do with something to hold onto.

'He got down from the cab. I don't think either of us wanted to go nearer but, of course, we had to. It didn't look plastic. And in the hollow, there was more. What looked like ribs and other bits? A skull. A wee skull. I thought I was going to throw up.'

Sharon felt herself go numb. She shivered. It sounded like a child. The thought of a dead child... The face of her cousin's youngest swam into view.

'I called the police, and they arrived pretty fast. '"Secured the area". Cordoned it off with their tape. They were covering the hole in the bank with a tent when I left.' He took a deep breath. 'They wouldn't have done that unless they thought it was human remains.'

They both fell silent.

Then he said, 'This'll screw up the timetable and no mistake.'

Sharon's mind was racing through the list of children she knew. Though it couldn't be a child...

'Janice not here?' he asked.

Sharon shook her head. Her tongue was stuck to the roof of her dry mouth.

He got out his mobile to phone.

Before going home and telling her mother what'd been happening, Sharon visited the site to see for herself. She couldn't get near. Strangers were standing about, chattering as if they were watching a soap. Pointing mobiles. How had they heard about it? There was little to see. She didn't stay long.

She walked back. Was it a human skeleton? If it was, it must be from a while back, could be ancient. Geoffrey would know how long it takes for a body to decompose down to just bones. The only local person she knew of who'd gone missing was Eileen's little Alice. Her pulse picked up speed, she could hear it thumping. People living in the village now, how many would even know about Alice?

. . .

These were human remains. The news leaked out quickly. Then no other information. Plenty of gossip, much of it making no sense. There was talk of an illegal abortion being hidden, but Sharon was sure that what Jack described would be from someone older. The driver of a truck full of illegal immigrants dumped a dead body. Gypsies stole a child.

In the Co-op Sharon heard someone joking about it. 'It'll be a midget from the circus, no-one bothered to look for, lost when they fired 'im out the cannon.' She had to go home without the butter she intended to buy.

People seemed not to think about Alice.

The beginnings of an answer came when the police visited Eileen. They wanted to interview her and asked did she want someone with her? Stuart offered. He said afterwards that Eileen could hardly speak at all. They told her the remains were from a child. A little girl, aged seven or eight. Who'd died probably decades ago. No bony injury; cause of death unknown. The formal words they used did nothing to soften the horror, Sharon thought. Eileen let them take samples from her for DNA testing.

The child was Alice. Sharon thought, who else could it have been? It made her feel sick to her stomach. What had happened? Had she slipped and drowned?

They'd never know.

Stuart and his wife volunteered to be there when the police visited Eileen again – Barbara was out and about, walking with a stick, she'd had some treatment to her back. Stuart was still upset afterwards, talking about how it went. 'There was a WPC in uniform and a chap in civvies looking sympathetic. Eileen just sat there very still as they told her. She didn't say anything. They're explaining about the DNA test, and I'm wondering if she even knows about DNA. But she does. When they've said their piece, she's still and silent, tears streaming down her cheeks. Then she says, "My Alice," over and over. Quaking.' He blew his nose. Janice put a hand on his arm.

He said, 'I hadn't thought before, but of course she'd be a suspect. At one point I thought they were actually going to ask her if she killed the girl.'

'Oh my God! But they didn't?'

'No. Fortunately.' He sighed. 'She stands, after a bit. Unsteady. Walks out into her garden. We waited but she didn't come back in. Barbara went to the kitchen door and Eileen was halfway down the path, looking out over the back gardens. She must have heard Babs because she turned and looked at her. She waved. Barbara was certain she meant for us to go, so we did. The police too. Though I think they may go back and see her again.' Stuart heaved another deep sigh.

Janice sat there with him. There was nothing to say.

## FORTY-ONE
## SHARON WALKS AGAIN WITH GEOFFREY

August, the weather hot and still, Sharon was trailing behind Geoffrey on a bridleway. 'I saw Eileen the other day,' she told him. 'I'd wondered how she was doing. She looked okay, I think. I hope.'

'There'll be a funeral at some point, I suppose,' he said, thoughtfully.

They paused by a badger sett.

'Looks like it's active,' Geoffrey said, indicating the new soil on top of the spoil heap, and the bedding. He pointed, 'Footprints over there.'

It had Sharon thinking about digging holes. She said, 'That reminds me. When they found Alice's body. Something odd happened that day. Stuart was up by the site, walking with Maggie, and Maggie got herself into a real state. He brought her into the office. She was moaning, ripping up my notes for the minutes.'

'Maybe she picked up on the atmosphere? People were pretty excited,' Geoffrey suggested.

'No. That's the thing. This was *before* the remains were found. As if she had a premonition.'

'Just a coincidence?'

'That's what I thought. But then, what if she actually knew that something bad had happened there? Could she have been there when Alice died? I remember hearing they were often together.'

Geoffrey looked at her. 'She never goes anywhere on her own, I don't suppose she ever did. Someone's always with her.'

'Okay, but could she have been there just with Alice? Children had more freedom then, I think.'

Geoffrey shrugged. 'Maggie couldn't tell us if she was.'

'Of course, if she was there with Alice and someone else, that person would also know what happened.'

Geoffrey raised an eyebrow.

'And has kept quiet all this time,' Sharon murmured as she moved on down the lane.

Sharon was flagging and even Geoffrey seemed weary, it was too warm and humid. They collapsed on a bank in the shade of a horse chestnut tree. Butterflies were everywhere; the air hummed and buzzed with insect life.

Looking up through the branches at the brown-blotched leaves, Geoffrey gestured at them and said, 'Look, you see that disease the chestnuts are getting, the brown leaves on this one? I heard my neighbour say he'll have their tree cut down, it looks so ugly. Over a hundred years old, it is. Huge. I want to point out that infestations are natural, and that he won't live to see any replacement grow to maturity. I haven't said it yet. He probably wouldn't plant a replacement anyway.'

'What makes the brown spots?' Sharon asked. 'Looks like a fungus.' Did he realise she was indulging him? She watched him go into teacher mode. She didn't mind when he did that. It was often interesting. And she could always tell him to shut up.

He smiled and said, 'I'm so glad you asked. Leaf miners: larvae of the moth *Cameraria ohridella*. If you look closely in a good light, you can sometimes see the little worm-like beasts squirming inside the leaf.'

'Tell me more. Go on, you know you want to.' Sharon grinned at him.

'First seen in London in 2002, they're everywhere now. They don't kill the tree, or even cause it much hardship, apparently.'

She was gazing up into the canopy, enjoying the dappled sunlight.

He changed the subject. 'Your asking reminds me, and you don't have to answer if you think I'm out of line. I imagine you didn't go to college or university because of your mother. You didn't feel you could leave her? But you're always fascinated by things, always curious. Have you thought of some kind of further education? Evening classes or OU perhaps?'

Sharon looked down at her hands, clasped loosely in her lap. 'I wasn't going to tell you yet. I was going to wait and see how I got on. But I'm already enrolled at the Open University. Science, technology and maths access module. I'm not sure yet, but maybe a degree after that. Natural sciences, biology, perhaps.'

'That's brilliant!' He wasn't quite crowing.

'Actually, I'm really enjoying it. I thought it might be beyond me, but not so far. First two modules have been really interesting. Got a new computer. Just learning all the IT stuff has already proved useful. I'm a bit nervous in group tutorials, how I match up with others.' She felt herself blush.

'Fun, though?'

She grimaced. 'Yeah, sort of.'

He must have realised it was time to stop asking. He said, 'Come on, let's get going.' Before they set off again, though, he gave her a big, encouraging hug.

# FORTY-TWO
## SHARON COPES
### 2016

'Fuck. Fuck! Fuck!!' Sharon yelled.

Big advantage to walking in the countryside on your own was you could say what you wanted, as loud as you wanted. Not that she did it that much, but today she'd just had to blow off steam.

Earlier, she'd gone to pick up the post from the mat. She walked back, opening what looked like a personal letter, unusual these days. It wasn't personal, of course, just one of those annoying supermarket promotion things. She caught her leg on the folded-up footrest of the wheelchair. On her shin, that really sensitive bit. Hurt like hell.

The pain was mostly gone now, it wasn't that making her swear. It was all the paraphernalia, everywhere. The wheelchair half-blocking the hallway. The kitchen gadgets that didn't allow Lizzie to open a jar anyway. Extra table lamps all over the place. More hand rails. Pills, empty pill packets, rumpled drug information sheets – with all of them listing horrible side effects, starting with sudden death and ending with an itchy arse. Well, okay, maybe not that specific an itch. Correction, pruritis. Where do they find these words? And then there was the bathroom… She wanted to scream, not just swear. She felt smothered by it all; buried. She had to let it out somehow. Though not with Lizzie.

'Argh!' she yelled.

The spaniel that appeared from round the hedge must have heard her. It stopped dead with that puzzled look they do. The owner was trailing well behind, luckily.

What could she do about all the irritations at home? Nothing. Nothing she wasn't already doing. Number one: making a study area in her bedroom for her course work. Thank God for the OU, keeping her busy of an evening, giving her a legitimate reason to disappear. She was determined to move on to the degree course.

Two: exercise. She'd got herself a gym membership and an exercise regimen. Not that she liked the gym – too many preeners – but the endorphins really helped.

The stash of alcohol made three. She tried not to use it too much. But she had started going down the pub 'to watch the women's football' on the big screen. She'd have to be careful with that one, her mother might spot when there were no games being broadcast.

Perhaps change her diet? No, it wouldn't work not to eat dinner with Lizzie. And shopping for special foods would only give her more chores. She groaned.

The slog up Juniper Hill took her into the full force of the wind. Rain had gone through earlier, leaving the air scrubbed sparkling clean. The view went on forever. She had to work to stand still in the blast. That was better. That was good. She'd survive.

Sharon was sort of used to difficult conversations with Lizzie by now. But that didn't prepare her for her mother's latest news.

Sharon was home from work, talking about what she'd do for their supper while Lizzie sat at the kitchen table, peering unhappily at a piece of paper. Her eyesight was rubbish these days.

'What've you got there? D'you want me to read it to you?'

Lizzie put the paper face down, 'No. It's fine. But I have something to tell you. I think you may be shocked, but don't be.'

Sharon hurriedly took the chair opposite, feeling her knees about to go.

'It's sooner than I thought, but only because the opportunity just happens to have come up. There's nothing with my health that I haven't told you. It's just there's a vacancy in an assisted living place near Melton, where you don't have to be ancient to apply. It's a sort of warden-controlled flat. The place is run by a trust set up by the Belvoir elderflower people.' She looked nervously at Sharon.

'You're not going to move out! You don't need to. We're doing fine!' It was the first Sharon had heard of this place.

Lizzie sighed. 'Yes, we are. But I told you I wanted to plan ahead, and this looks as if it would be perfect for me. Like with old folks' accommodation, there's a link with a nursing home for if and when you need it.'

'Lizzie!' Sharon wailed.

Lizzie gritted her teeth and spoke firmly. 'The other thing I said was that I wasn't prepared to blight the next years of your life. You need your own time and space, your own interests. We only get one go at living and I couldn't bear... You're too young.'

Sharon imagined herself in the house on her own and felt bleak. 'I can't rattle around here without you,' she said feebly, looking at her battered fingernails.

'No. Well.'

Sharon sat up. What was coming next?

Lizzie said quietly, 'I'd have to sell the house.'

'What?' Sharon gawped at her.

Now all the new properties in the village took on a different significance. But not for long. Sharon soon found they'd be beyond her, even though, with a bit of luck, Lizzie would be able to give her something towards a deposit. So it'd have to be a rental. She went to look at several places, ending up coming back a second time to some new flats at the other end of the village.

This was where the older buildings were; a Victorian workshop was being converted.

The apartments would be compact, but quite nice. A proper kitchen. She wasn't bothered that there wasn't a bath in the bathroom. A green space with trees outside, maintained by the council. Five minutes to the Co-op. Not too much traffic. The flat at the top would be the nicest, the rent not too steep. The woman said they should be finished within a few months. If Sharon wanted one and paid a deposit, she could choose the colour of the curtains. Dunelm, not John Lewis, but still, that was nice. Sold.

She thought she'd love the flat. So why, then, was she waking in the night in a lather? Worrying about Lizzie, of course. Though there was no need. She'd have a cleaner, and a nurse popping in. She'd be on her own a lot less than with Sharon at work half the time. And she'd have a panic button, couldn't possibly fall and not get help straight away. For all Sharon's self-confidence, perhaps some of the sweatiness was about how she herself would cope. Living on her own. No one to chat to, bounce ideas off. She knew lots of young people just wanted to get away from their parents. But she didn't. Lizzie was her best friend. But she had to leave her. Lizzie wasn't going to change her mind. And in the end, she moved out before her mother did, having insisted Lizzie wear an alarm from then on. A posh one, with automatic fall detection.

It was weird, living at the other end of the village from her mother – it took all winter for the house to sell, and for Lizzie's move to actually happen. Sharon kept thinking the Belvoir place would get snatched away but it wasn't. That was a relief. Having got out on her own, she soon realised she wouldn't want to go back to how it was. She just loved waking on a weekend morning, making a coffee and taking it back to bed. Deciding what she would do with her day. Even though she knew she would visit Lizzie, do Lizzie's shopping, sort out stuff for her. It just felt really different. And she was drinking less. Plus the men she bumped into seemed altogether more attractive. That bloke who'd spoken to her at the gym, for example, was fit in both senses.

# FORTY-THREE
## SHARON GOES TO ALICE'S INTERMENT
### 2017

Sharon was surprised at how long it was before Alice's interment happened. What more could they learn from just bones? And Eileen wasn't as passive as she expected. Which upset Stuart, who'd taken on the organisation of the funeral.

He said to Janice, 'I just proceeded with the arrangements, like I did when Ena died. I thought I knew what she would want.'

'But you didn't?'

'When I told her, she was almost angry. I've not seen her like that before. I had to take her to the funeral directors so she could make alterations.' He looked peeved.

Stuart might reasonably have expected Eileen to be too upset to cope. But surely it was her right to say what she wanted. It was good that she could.

'At least I got one thing right: no religion. She accepted the lay lady officiating and the non-denominational part of the graveyard. Though she changed the plot. To one at the edge, under a beech tree. "Where the squirrels will visit," she said.'

She'd agreed to the chapel in the cemetery as the official location, but insisted that neither she, nor Alice's remains, would enter it. '"Outdoors," she said, "even if it's raining."'

A wicker coffin. 'More like a basket than a proper one,' Stuart said disapprovingly. 'And she wanted Alice's stuffed rabbit to go in.'

She's kept it all these years.

'Would it be alright if I went along?' Sharon asked. Eileen rarely spoke to her, but Sharon always kept an eye out for her. She wanted to be there.

Stuart seemed surprised. 'There's nothing to stop you, I suppose. Eileen does know who you are,' he said uncertainly.

On the day, there were no hymns, no readings, no eulogy. A nursery rhyme, 'Golden Slumbers'. It brought tears to Sharon's eyes. And two folksongs. Played on a Music Cube supplied by Geoffrey when Stuart, in desperation, asked for his help. The wickerwork box, so small, must have been made specially. She wondered who did it. A photograph was propped amongst spring wildflowers on the top. Sharon saw that they were growing in a shallow tub. Someone said Eileen had made it months back, planning for this day all through the winter.

A small group of people had assembled in the wan sunshine. Freda, from next door to Eileen, looking absolutely ancient. Mrs Judd, not quite so old, and her son. Stuart and Barbara, of course. Barbara had lost a lot of weight and was leaning heavily on her stick. Geoffrey. Would he be there if it weren't for the music? A few others from the village whose names she'd forgotten. Two men she didn't recognise at all. They seemed to know each other, gravitated together.

She heard the older one, grandad age or older, say, 'How's she been? Looks much better than I expected. Finally has some certainty, perhaps?'

'I've been impressed. Coping well,' the other replied.

Eileen went over and took the hand of the grandad when she saw him.

'Roy. Thank you,' she said. She turned to the younger. 'Ian.'

He clasped her hand, and she let him.

Wonder who they are, Sharon thought. She meant to ask someone but forgot.

Sharon recognised the humanist woman, she lived a few doors down from their old house. She was the only person who spoke. 'Many of you will not have known Alice, Eileen's daughter, who was lost so many years ago, but no doubt you are here for Eileen, to help her finally find closure from her terrible ordeal. We will never know what happened. But at least we now know that Alice's remains are safely at rest…' She continued for a while, though it looked as if Eileen was no longer listening.

No wake. Sharon supposed Eileen was never really sociable, wouldn't have been comfortable. A few people drifted down to the pub. Sharon found herself in a corner next to Geoffrey.

'That wasn't too bad,' he said. 'When my dad died, my mother insisted on a proper, church funeral. I thought, he's dead, he can't be upset by it. But I hated it. On the day, I was nearly late. I'd stopped for a beer, dreading the service. You'll say I'm exaggerating but the priest was awful.'

'Oh, yeah?'

He put on a pompous face. '"Mrs Johns, we condole your loss, but we rejoice. Charles has gone to a better place and is at peace. The sense of loss we have when a loved one dies is a primitive reaction, dating back centuries to the age of ignorance and superstition. Our Saviour showed us to a way of life that negates grief at the demise of a loved one and replaces it with joy at their accession into heaven."'

He was right, Sharon couldn't believe anyone would actually say such things. She sipped her wine.

'I was incensed. Primal ignorance and superstition replaced by more ignorance and superstition. Instructions to suppress natural grief, the implication that it was wrong.' He sighed. 'But the congregation appeared content with such rubbish. Mother seemed uplifted. While I stood there, next to her, seething.'

Sharon could believe that.

'The only good bit was that sunshine was streaming through a stained-glass window, colouring the dust motes. It reminded me of walking one time with Dad in Derbyshire, in fields stippled with wildflowers. We found a skylark's nest, hidden in a deep rut in the track. I've not seen one since.' Geoffrey rubbed his eyes then continued. 'It was my dad's interest in birds that got me into it. I still use the binoculars he gave me as a child.'

Some days later Sharon wandered past the burial place. The pot of wildflowers was embedded in the little mound of earth over Alice's grave. Eileen had already made it look cared-for. Daisies, wood anemone and celandine. Suddenly Sharon was imagining the end of Lizzie's life. She just stood there, tears trickling down her face.

# FORTY-FOUR
## SHARON IS SHOCKED WHEN GEOFFREY IS SUSPENDED

JJ Lock came into the parish office. He looked anxious. He was after Geoffrey. Sharon told him he hadn't been there and wasn't expected. JJ stood at the hatch, brow furrowed, hesitating. Sharon got up. 'Can I help at all? Can I take a message?'

He looked at her for a moment and replied, 'It's a bit awkward. Personal. Though I know he talks to you. Probably okay.'

Sharon picked up her bag. 'I need to get some milk. If you're going to the school, I could walk along with you?'

He nodded. When they were out of earshot of the Zumba ladies he said quietly, 'I'm worried about him. There was a scene at school. This thug of a parent, Karl Steadman. Turned up and started yelling at the secretary – Burton, the head, was in a meeting. The door was open so everyone heard. The cleaner, half a dozen kids, teachers, God knows who else.'

'He was slagging off Geoffrey? What on earth for?'

JJ nodded, hesitated, swallowed, looked away. 'Gee caught Steadman's lad, Ryan, selling pills. Gee grabbed him and took them. Don't know what they were, yet, but the boy was suspended. Even if they turn out to be sugar it's not good.'

'And they probably weren't sugar.'

'No. But Ryan's dad went ballistic when he heard. He's accused Gee of interfering with Ryan. Told everyone Gee's gay.

Equates that with paedophile. And now Gee's not allowed on the school premises for the duration.'

They'd stopped on the pavement. Sharon stared at him, open-mouthed. 'But...'

'I'd said to him, over and over, he should come out properly. Keeping it quiet could make him vulnerable. And now it has. Mr Burton had to suspend him, I suppose, with the physical contact... But now I can't find our man.'

'At Liam's restaurant?'

'No. I've already tried there. No joy. And I couldn't really talk to Liam, he was busy and there were too many people about.'

Sharon considered. 'He might be on the footpath that goes past Sawyer's farm. There's a kestrel's nest at the back of the green barn. He likes to watch the birds there.'

JJ looked helplessly at her and shrugged. Obviously had no idea where she was talking about.

'Tell you what, I'm off in an hour, I can go look?'

He seemed reluctant.

'Or I can take you?'

He smiled.

She looked at his feet: Italian shoes. 'You won't want to wear those. Muddy. Come back to the office at five.' He nodded. She left him and went to get the milk.

They found Geoffrey by the barn.

'Told you so!' Sharon crowed, then saw Geoffrey's face.

'Hi,' he said, miserably. 'What're you two doing here? Disturbing the peace.'

He was in no mood to talk. And after they'd made the effort... Ah, well. He seemed alright. He had his bike with him and said he'd be going home soon, so Sharon left JJ with him. JJ didn't stay for long, she learnt later, though Geoffrey hung around there for hours before pushing his bike back to the road at dusk.

· · ·

239

There were witnesses to Geoffrey's confiscation of the pills, no molestation reported, so he was soon back at work. Sharon heard he had to sit through a long lecture from Mr Burton about openness and honesty that she was sure he could have done without. The boy was also back, after a warning, since he probably didn't sell anything and the tablets proved to be anti-histamines. Did he think he'd get away with selling fake drugs?

Geoffrey was quieter than usual. He told Sharon, with a hollow laugh, 'Liam's bringing me little treats home from work as if I was sick. A shot glass of colourless essence of tomato, served iced, "to boost my faded appetite". Have you ever tasted that? It's stunning. A tiny almond cake topped with sugar violets. Yesterday, a blueberry tart decorated with a lattice of caramel.'

Sounded lovely.

'I'm grateful my mother doesn't seem to have heard the story.'


Geoffrey gradually relaxed. Mr Steadman, apparently, did not. Some days later Geoffrey was called back to Burton's office to be read a very unpleasant letter. The head talked about contacting the police.

Geoffrey told Sharon, 'I didn't think that necessary. Steadman'll calm down. I don't think the threats are real. Though I asked for a copy, just in case.'

Later, Geoffrey said, he saw Steadman loitering at the school gates, long after the kids had gone home. 'I thought it was odd and kept an eye out. I spotted him again a couple of times, in the distance. I thought I'd maybe not have noticed except for what'd happened. He's probably often been around. Doesn't do to get too paranoid.'

Then there was the summer break, and it went quiet. Until, that is, Geoffrey landed up in hospital.

# FORTY-FIVE
## GEOFFREY IS ATTACKED

Geoffrey was trying to work out what had happened, knew he was confused. He muddled between dreams and thoughts.

That hurts. I can't lie on my back, where my head's sore. How'd my head get bashed? Why can't I remember not to lie on my back?

He woke from a dream about Liam. Strange scenes with him as a rock star. Liam's a chef, he reminded himself. An image of his man swam to the surface, him coming home late from Lampeter's. Short, lean, almost wiry. Cropped, fair hair in gelled spikes. Leaning over to kiss him.

Geoffrey rolled on his side and fell back to dreaming.

The view shifted to Liam at work, as if he were on TV. Him, swaddled in chef's whites, calling instructions peppered with four-letter words. Geoffrey thought, that's not right, he's not crude, he'd be telling jokes.

Liam was making desserts. His long, cool fingers made the lightest, crumbliest pastry. He was careful, gentle, precise. Then he was presenting his signature raspberry soufflé.

A voice said, 'As airy as willow-seed down, the flavour gorgeously intense.' The scene shifted to the commentator, who looked like Sting, as he continued. 'He doesn't favour the fashion for square towers of food, stacked piles of vegetables and meat.' His hands outlined rectangles. Then he made circles. 'His plates carry rounded mounds, perched together like Cotswold hills, with sauce trickling down the valleys.' There was a close-up of lamb shank with minted mashed potatoes and chilli-broccoli.

'Hey, teach?'

Geoffrey woke. For a moment he thought he was at home, wondered why Liam had come back so early. Of course, he recalled, he was in hospital, and this was a visit. How had Liam managed to get away from work? He beamed. 'I was just dreaming about you.'

'Nothing too raunchy, I hope. Put your blood pressure up, start your head bleeding again. That won't do.'

Geoffrey made a face at him.

'Just came to check up on you. Can't stop long, food to cook.' He leant over and kissed Geoffrey softly on the lips.

'You shouldn't…' Geoffrey looked left and right, but nobody seemed to be taking any notice.

'Hah! You're powerless to stop me here, teach!'

Geoffrey hoped he was teasing, wasn't planning anything outrageous.

'How's it going?' Liam grabbed a chair and sat, one hand on Geoffrey's arm.

'Well… Don't know, really. Brain feels strange. Something wrong with my eyes. Don't remember beyond walking on the road in the dark and being very wet. Thinking how being a teacher somehow connected. It was after my dad died.'

'Your eyes look fine. You're not making much sense, but I suppose I shouldn't expect you to. What was after your dad died?'

'Thoughts keep jumping about.'

'Yeah, well. Under the circs…'

'Deciding to teach. When I learnt how useless my mother was. My head hurts. Tell you another time.'

Liam was looking anxiously at him. Geoffrey didn't have the energy to explain. His eyes closed again.

. . .

A couple of days later the fog had lifted, and his memory was returning. He was dressed and lying propped up on his bed when Liam arrived. Liam kissed him. Geoffrey said quietly, 'You taste good enough to eat.'

Liam smiled. 'I'm not on the menu till you get home.'

A sigh. 'I'm making a bit more sense, I think. I hope. Though still can't see properly. They've checked my eyes. They're fine. I told you that, did I? The notion keeps popping up that my cracked head is linked to me teaching. Can't work out why I think that.'

'If you're less confused now, I'll ask. I'm curious, what was that about your mother being pathetic and that's why you became a teacher?'

Geoffrey was hesitant. 'You might regret that question.'

'I'll doze off if you get too boring. Though it would be good to hear you droning on. Back to normal.'

Geoffrey made a feeble attempt at punching Liam's arm. 'You asked for it, so I'll tell you the story. We've neither of us talked much about our pasts, have we? Anyway. I'd no idea, until after my dad died, quite how useless my mother was. I was in Oxford then. She'd phone me: a bulb had gone in the kitchen, there's a letter from the solicitor, the central heating – I'd had it installed – was set too high. When I visited of a weekend, National Express and then the 85 bus, the list of things she needed sorting would be enormous.'

'So not much joy in visiting, then.'

'No. Well. One time the kitchen light bulb went. I discovered she'd avoided the kitchen in the dark, prepared a snack on a tray in daylight and kept it on the sideboard for her supper. I hadn't imagined she wouldn't know how to change a bulb. I tried to show her, got her on a chair below the light fitting, but she couldn't put the bulb in properly. She seemed convinced that when she gripped it, to push and turn it into place, the glass would shatter.'

'So what did you do?' Liam was being unusually patient, letting him moan about his mother.

'Thought about changing the fittings to screw-in. Table lamps for when the main light went. Though that wouldn't do in the bathroom. I talked to her neighbour, Mrs Price, saying how mother seemed unable to do anything for herself and was too scared to try. Paying by cheque, even tuning the radio, I couldn't be there that often and every day there was something she couldn't do or didn't understand. She'd phone in tears and eventually I'd discover it was just that the rates bill had arrived. Mrs Price, kind soul, agreed to help and, for a while, went round each morning. But not much encouragement from mother. She'd say, "It's alright, Geoffrey will be here, he'll sort it out." Dad must have done everything for her.'

'Sounds wearing.'

'I trailed over almost every weekend. I found a schoolboy to mow the lawn for a bit of pocket money and did the other work in the garden myself. I liked it out there. Bit of exercise. Peace and quiet from her mithering. I wondered if that was how my father had felt.'

'How long was it before you moved back?'

'Best part of two years. I finished my thesis, got it done before the grant ran out, fortunately. Then I had to decide what next. Didn't want to do more research. Intensely competitive. Didn't suit me. I knew it'd be easier all round if I moved nearer mother. I'd enjoyed the teaching I'd done. Had no trouble getting onto teacher training. There it was. Decision made. Though I couldn't live with her. Inane conversation, drab food, religion. Plus, I needed my privacy.'

Liam grinned. 'So there you were, teaching biology and living in a cottage, five miles away from her, with no bus route. Just waiting for me to turn up. Do you realise I didn't know she lived so close until we'd been together for, what, a year?'

Geoffrey smiled. 'That's one reason I never got a car, once I moved back. Not just the carbon waste.' He tentatively touched the back of his scalp.

'And teaching suits you. You like the class projects, they let you investigate things. Youngsters always curious about life. The kids must like your directness – they put up with it at any rate.'

'Mock me behind my back, of course. I can live with that; there are things I'm passionate about and I'm not going to stop talking about them.'

'No, well, you wouldn't be you if you didn't go on and on. And on. When was it you got into the parish council stuff?'

'2010. Not long before we met. Labour government ousted, David Cameron prime minister. Decided to put my money where my mouth was. There was no one queueing up for the PC, so there it was again. Done.'

'Still don't know how you bear it. All those interminable meetings. Going round in circles. I couldn't be doing with it.'

'You're not free in the evenings anyway. Would be impossible, even if you wanted to. Sorry, I haven't asked. Have you been busy?'

Liam was just telling him about a customer who tried to avoid paying the whole bill because his floozy didn't like the pepper sauce, when Geoffrey sensed something had changed. He was learning. He turned all the way over to his left, and there was Eileen. She'd arrived like a ghost.

Liam knew who she was, and greeted her cheerfully. 'Hi! We haven't met properly before. I'm Liam. Thank goodness you're here so I can leave this wreck and get back to work.'

Eileen gave a timid smile. It was amazing how well she was coping with everything. He remembered her, numb, at Alice's funeral. Not that long ago, really.

Liam squeezed Geoffrey's hand and dashed off.

# FORTY-SIX
# SHARON VISITS GEOFFREY IN HOSPITAL

When Sharon first went to see Geoffrey on the ward, he was confused and kept falling asleep. He had just the thump to the back of his head and some bruises on his arms. But it was serious: he couldn't see.

His vision came back. What a relief.

'But there's something not quite right about it yet,' he said on her second visit. He didn't elaborate. The great purple areas on his upper arms were now turning to yellow. He said, 'Maybe I fought back.'

'Good,' she said, 'I hope you did. Though I bet you didn't hurt the bastard as badly as he deserved.'

There was a pause. He seemed to be thinking. 'Am I making sense now?' he asked.

She smiled and nodded. 'As much as you ever do.'

'I hope I was coherent when the police came.'

She sat up.

'Two uniformed officers, one tall, one short, like Laurel and Hardy,' he told her.

She shrugged. Who were they?

'I wasn't impressed by their attitude. They seemed to think it was a hit-and-run. Weren't really interested. Maybe they thought there was little chance of finding the culprit, so no point in bothering.'

Sharon pursed her lips.

'The small one said, "Of course, since you weren't wearing your helmet..." Implying the damage was my fault. I didn't have the energy to argue. But Eileen was here.'

Sharon knew it was Eileen who found him and stayed with him until a car came. What was she doing out there in the middle of that horrible night?

'She'd brought me a book: Jennifer Owen's *The Ecology of a Garden*. It's in Leicestershire, so local. Over a fifteen-year period. I can't seem to concentrate well enough yet, but I'm looking forward to reading it. She'd just handed it to me, hadn't said a word. But when she heard that about me not wearing a helmet, she stood up straight, getting their attention. She said, "Always wears a helmet. Teacher." And that seemed to get them thinking straight.'

Well done Eileen, Sharon thought.

'By then I'd recovered enough memory to know I was walking, pushing the bike. I told them this, said I hadn't heard a car before I was knocked out. I didn't think there was a car.'

Just as well there was one came later, Sharon thought, the man who called the ambulance.

'Little turns to Large with, "The doctor said it was odd that he'd just got a big whack on the back of the head, that it seemed strange for a vehicle impact. Perhaps it wasn't a car that hit him?" They left, saying they'd be back.'

Must have been Steadman, Sharon thought, but I'll bet his wife says he was curled up in front of the telly with her.

'I'm learning about cortical blindness,' Geoffrey said. 'That's what it's called. The visual cortex is at the back of the brain, where I was hit. That's why I don't see properly. My eyes are fine.'

Sharon was doing her best to follow his explanation. Cortex, she thought, the grey bit on the brain's surface.

'I actually read about it, years ago. Oliver Sacks' stories about sight loss due to brain damage.'

She'd heard of Sacks. 'Him that wrote *Awakenings*, right?'

'Mmm. I can see now. See pretty well, I think. And I'm grateful I don't have the really weird thing Sacks described, where you can see but not understand what you see.'

That sounded horrible.

'Though the tests show my vision is damaged more significantly than I'm aware. It seems that I can't see anything low on the left. But that isn't obvious to me because my brain's working to cover up for the damaged bit.'

You've completely lost me now, she thought.

'I get to see a woman to train me to work safely, to "manage the loss".'

'That's good.' Sharon thought he would be depressed but instead he was just fascinated. Weird bloke.

'The neurologist's suggested I read old articles about brain trauma from the First World War. He's dug some out for me.' He gestured towards a small pile of photocopied sheets. 'Written in lovely archaic language, they are. Some of the case reports are really bizarre. You couldn't make it up,' he said.


When he was back home, Sharon cadged a lift and called in on him there. She noticed that there was no evidence of Liam in the spartan sitting room. For when his mother visits, she guessed. She must have visited, him being poorly. Who took her there?

Geoffrey was rather gloomy. 'Despite the training, I'm not doing very well,' he confessed. 'Liam suggested I go with him to the restaurant, to help relearn how to do things. Peel vegetables, take down bookings, pour wine.'

'How'd that go?'

'Not good. Even knowing the layout fairly well, I kept bumping into things.'

'It'll get better with practice?'

'Don't know. Hope so. But I feel frustrated and irritable – I was warned I might be short-tempered, perhaps emotionally unstable, for a while. I am.'

Sharon moved herself back in her seat, in mock fear.

He ignored that. 'On Friday I peeled a pile of potatoes, even though there's a machine to do that, only to find that I'd missed altogether a stack placed on my left, though I've been taught to move my head and check.' It all seemed too much for him. 'I've had to give it a break.'

'Can't rush things.' She thought she sounded pathetic.

'I've told Liam I want to go and see Eileen. I haven't thanked her properly yet. He's said he'll find time to drive me, but he's worried about leaving me there.'

Sharon wondered what he meant.

Then he added, 'I said, "Don't worry, I'll get a taxi home. I won't use the trip to practice stumbling into things." He wasn't amused. He's having difficulty understanding what's happened to me – so am I, come to that. I don't suppose my teasing helps but I can't be serious about it the whole time. Got to laugh.'

## FORTY-SEVEN
## SHARON HEARS GEOFFREY'S ACCOUNT

The village pub was an ordinary place, pictures of local horses on the walls, a nice atmosphere. Sharon and Geoffrey were sitting by the bar, drinking beer.

'You haven't told me exactly what happened that night,' she said, 'though you might not want to talk about it...'

He smiled, 'You know me, like to talk.' He thought a bit. 'It was stormy and wet.'

She nodded.

'I'd been into school for one of those meetings. About the next Ofsted inspection, this one was.'

Sharon grimaced.

'Some of us had come in here for a while afterwards, to recover. I set off for home eventually. A mile down the road, found I had a puncture. Late, dark, rain pouring down. I was on a lane, no streetlight, so I decided just to push the bike, not even try to repair it.'

Sharon cocked her head, waiting.

'I took my helmet off, pulled my hood over my head, trudged along, whistling to try and cheer myself up. A tune from *Dirty Dancing*, it was. You'll know it.' He sang, rather loudly, 'La la, time of my li-ife, da da, never felt this way before... Never been so wet.'

Sharon took a sip of her Abbot Ale, avoiding looking at the man along the bar, who'd turned towards them, frowning at the racket.

'Heavy cloud, very dark, only the front light to see where the road was. Water soaking through my jeans, socks so wet I could hear my feet squelching.'

She shivered, picturing the black, sodden night. She knew the next bit. 'Bastard hit you,' she said, and she winced.

'Then there's a gap. Next thing I know I'm coming round. It was different from waking from sleep. I remember thinking, something's wrong. It felt very strange.'

Strange surely didn't say it. Awful. Petrifying.

'I didn't know where I was or even how I was, at first – I couldn't feel my body.'

Hard to imagine that.

'I could hear my heartbeat, pounding fast. I seemed to be lying, twisted, mostly on my front. I remember my right hand twitched and I realised I could move it.'

Sharon didn't move a muscle, listening.

'I could feel gravel against my face, and taste mud and blood. Bits of me started to hurt. My left hip hurt a lot. Turned out my bike, the handlebar, was under it. I moved my hand up to feel the back of my head – my scalp stung – my fingers came away sticky. I could smell the blood.' He was lost in the account, sitting all hunched up. 'All I could see was flashes.' He glanced up and saw the look on her face. His back uncurled and he laughed, more at himself than her. Pulling a face and taking a gulp of beer, he said, 'I guessed my eyes were shut, and I tried to open them but the picture didn't change. Like fireworks in slow motion. A swirling purple, orange and yellow sparkly pattern.' A short laugh. 'I kept thinking it was raining too hard for fireworks.'

He was laughing about it but that didn't make it sound any less awful.

'I blink.' He blinked. 'And now I'm certain I can open my eyes. But I can't see anything around me. It wasn't like it was just night, not that I knew whether it was day or night.

'I managed to roll myself off the bike, but I couldn't get up. Couldn't work out how. I must have drifted off again.'

Sharon had heard about what followed. She relaxed a little.

'Next time I surface, I'm very cold. There's this small hand holding mine. Warm, squeezing my fingers. And a little voice, light and soft, singing.' He sang quietly, 'Somewhere, over the rainbow, way up high, there's a land that I heard of once in a lullaby…'

Sharon hadn't heard the bit about Eileen singing. Sweet.

'She sang and hummed and sang and held my hand for what seemed like a lifetime. She must have been sitting in the wet on the road. I'm very tired but I try to pay attention. It felt important to listen to her. Then I hear a car. She abandons me and I hear her call out, hear the brakes squeal as it stops. I remember seeing, faintly, some proper light.'

They sat quietly for a bit.

He said, 'I must go and see Eileen, to thank her.'

# FORTY-EIGHT
## GEOFFREY IS HELPED BY EILEEN

Geoffrey walked down Eileen's front path, trying to make Liam smile by parodying the hunchbacked gait of Richard III. Liam stood by his car, groaning as he watched. Eileen must have seen them arrive. She opened the door, smiling, stepped forward and waved Liam away. As he straightened, Geoffrey thought Liam looked relieved to go.

Eileen said, 'Tea?' and led him indoors to her sitting room, watched him sit. Geoffrey hadn't entered the house before. He gazed around. The cluttered room was oddly pretty. The sofa didn't match the armchairs, each a different style and covered with a different floral print. The floor was a patchwork of old rugs. He made a mental note to be careful not to trip when he got up. On the mantelpiece sat a row of little vases, various shapes, each containing different seed-heads. He didn't recognise all of them. Either side of the chimney breast were fitted shelves, crammed with books. Three glass blocks perched on the middle bar of the sash window. Prisms, he realised. She must have put them there to catch the evening light, to make rainbows.

While Eileen was in the kitchen, Geoffrey gathered his thoughts. He was uncertain what to say, they'd never had a proper conversation before. When she visited him in hospital, she mostly just sat quiet.

She returned with a tray of tea things.

'I wanted to thank you.' He paused and looked at her as she stood pouring the tea. 'For what you did on the road that night.'

She put the pot down, turned slowly to look at him and gave a small nod. She looked away, out of the window, saying nothing.

He continued anyway. 'I don't remember much, but I do remember your being there. You gave me something to hold onto. More than just your hand, I mean.' He was feeling embarrassed, struggling to talk against her silence. He was unsure she was even listening.

But she looked down at her hand. That was encouraging.

'In the hospital, too. Your visits. I looked forward to them. You never said much. You're not talking now. But it was good to have your company. I felt... Supported. Hopeful.'

She turned and gazed at him, gave another small nod.

He was feeling rather desperate. It must be possible for them to talk. He tried a question. 'In the ward, I remember you hummed a tune. What was the song?'

She thought. 'Old folksong,' she replied, and she left the room.

Where's she gone? He fidgeted.

On her return, Eileen handed him a small, battered book, open at a page entitled 'Farewell he'.

He read out loud, 'It's fare you well cold winter and fare you well cold frost. Nothing I've gained but my true love I've lost...'

She hummed the tune.

He laughed. 'Steeleye Span, 1975, "All Around my Hat". Or very nearly. It's the song their hit was based on, isn't it? Willow, around the hat, for sorrow, as in "weeping willow". I looked it up at the time. Maddy Prior, brilliant voice.'

She said, 'Alice liked it. Would have liked the Maddy version.'

He placed the book gently on the table and stood, stepped forward and, hesitantly, put his arms round her. He thought she might shrink away, but she didn't. He hugged her. Felt her little, bony, old body. Releasing her, he kept his hands on her shoulders, fearing she might lose her balance. She seemed so frail.

'Tea,' she said softly.

They drank out of mis-matched Victorian cups with saucers and ate ginger nuts. He talked about the problem with his vision, how weak he still felt, how he needed to get fitter.

'We could walk,' she suggested.

'I'd like that. If you stood on my blind side, on the left, I'd know what was there.'

Another nod. She might need more explanation, he thought, but she seemed to at least partly understand. She got up and held out her right hand to take his left and they walked out the back together, into her piebald garden. It was like at the front: patches of this and that – tired rhubarb, bolted onions, a mass of Japanese anemones. Those darkening purple heads on long stems were verbena flowers, he thought. He could smell the fennel as he brushed past it.

'Practice,' she said.

'Come back next week,' she told him when he departed.

Liam dropped Geoffrey off the same time on the following Saturday and drove away. Geoffrey stood at the gate, looking at Eileen's plot. Rounded stones, sea shells and bits of sea glass in addition to the scallop shells Liam had donated. Where did she find sea shells? Had she ever been to the seaside? She always seemed to be in the village. A clump of daisies, flowering in the wan sunlight; the remains of a huge thistle. The gate opened with a click and he walked up the path, catching his foot on a raised paver. Blue brick, with that Victorian criss-cross pattern. He was quietly cursing at himself as she opened the door. He saw she was expecting him. He'd got that right.

This time, with the tea, there were home-made scones and home-made strawberry jam, although it was morning.

'Freda, next door,' Eileen said when he complimented her on the jam. 'Over ninety now but never stops helping. Never gives up trying to make a Christian of me.' She laughed, a high-toned chuckle.

Geoffrey couldn't remember hearing her laugh before. Or that much speech in one go. 'Can we walk?' he asked, draining his cup and brushing away the last of the crumbs. 'I'm still not very good. I may stumble.'

Eileen nodded and replied, 'Tell me. Your problem. So I can help.'

He was thinking how to explain. Several people had asked but he'd struggled to make it clear, and he imagined Eileen had little education. Except she had all those books. 'My eyes are fine,' he started, 'but a bit of my brain that I need for vision doesn't work. So, on the left, low down, I've a blind spot.'

'A dark patch,' she said.

'Well, no. And that's part of the problem. But it's difficult to describe. It's called "cortical blindness", but there's no black hole in what I see.'

Her forehead was furrowed.

He tried again. 'The blow to my head has knocked out a part of my visual cortex, so the signals sent from my eyes can't be processed there.'

She nodded.

He was surprised she'd followed thus far – 'visual cortex', he thought as he said it, will she know what that is? Encouraged, he continued. 'I've no image of what is situated low on my left, but I see the world as if I have.'

She looked very puzzled now.

'Let me think,' he concentrated. 'You know how your eyes move about when you look? Little, abrupt movements, then brief pauses?'

She nodded.

'Each time the eyes are stationary, that's when you focus, and it's as if a snapshot's taken. All the images of each area you look at are processed by the brain into what we perceive as a smooth, continuous scene. No holes. No gaps.'

She was sitting listening to him carefully, watching him, her head tipped slightly to one side.

'The brain joins the dots, so we have a complete panorama. Which is great. Works well. Except it creates a problem for me because my brain fills in the section it can't actually process. It seems to me as if I'm seeing normally, but I'm not. Something can come up from behind into that bottom, left-hand quadrant, a cat, say. If I don't hear it, I don't know anything's there. I can't see it, but I can't see that I can't see it.'

She was staring at him. Her mouth worked but no words came. She got on her feet and gestured for him to stand, then crept round behind him, towards his left side. He kept his head still.

Crouching, she had to step almost in front of him before he said, 'There. I can see you there.'

She took his left hand in her right and brought him out of the house, into the street. He'd forgotten about the little steps she made. Every few paces she skipped in front, swung round to smile at him, then returned to his side.

'Bollard,' she might say. 'Tilted paving stone.' 'Oops!' with a laugh, when she failed to spot a hazard in time.

This must look ridiculous, he knew, but she wasn't a bit bothered. He turned his head round to look at her properly. She was completely used to people thinking her behaviour peculiar, he realised. Well, if she didn't care, nor would he.

He'd not seen her this happy. Before, even when she smiled, there was a haunted look about her. People talked about closure, perhaps that's why she was better. Not that he'd ever really understood what 'closure' meant. But her cheerfulness was infectious. Soon, between them, they had a system. He could feel his confidence build, his stride lengthen. She started to hum. He recognised the tune: 'Bridge over Troubled Water'. He recalled the words and sang as she hummed:

'When you're weary, feeling small.
When tears are in your eyes, I will dry them all;
I'm on your side.'


They didn't say much to each other when they roamed the autumn footpaths together. None of the idle banter he'd had with Sharon... he hadn't been out with Sharon for ages, she was busy with her course work. The silence was comfortable, companionable. Muddy patches and tree roots continued to catch him out. She kept to his left as he gradually became used to his brain's deceptions.

One cold December day, they stopped to watch a fox traverse a rime-whitened field, leaving a grey-green track behind it.
 He said, 'Broad daylight. Where's he going? Where's he been?'
 'I always wonder how Alice came to be here,' Eileen said quietly.
 Startled, he stopped and stared at her. He realised this path led to the new pond. 'You think about her all the time,' he said.
 She nodded, looking sideways at him calmly.
 He couldn't think what to say. But it didn't seem to matter.
 She took his hand and they continued on their way.
 He tried to imagine what it was like for her. He said, 'If Liam… was badly hurt. Or died… I'd be devastated.'
 He could tell she was listening.
 'But if we had a child and that happened… I think I'd go mad.'
 She gave him a sharp look. 'I did.'
 'Yes.' He wanted to hug her but didn't dare.

They walked on Christmas day. Liam was working and Geoffrey was due at his mother's for dinner.
 'I'm really grateful you could come out today. She's likely to drive me nuts. But with a bit of exercise first, I'm hoping I'll cope.'
 She gave him her familiar quizzical look.
 'You know she's very religious?' he explained.
 She smiled and patted his arm.
 He hesitated. 'I'm not even sure if she knows I'm gay.'
 A nod.
 'Can you believe, we've never talked about it? Can't see how we ever would. But that's crazy in this day and age.'
 'Talk to me then,' she said.

He was stunned.

'Tell me all about Liam. I'd like to know more about him. Does he have brothers or sisters?'

To Geoffrey's amazement, out it all poured. Later, when he arrived at his mother's cottage, he found himself relaxed and sunny, telling her funny stories about the schoolkids as if she were a friend.

Being often with Eileen had him thinking of her, her past, and how she'd changed since Alice's remains were found. He hadn't expected they would talk so much. Other people had noticed the changes, too.

Sharon had commented, 'Eileen seems more peaceful. Looks better. Neater. I saw her wearing a lovely scarf with blobs of pink and purple on it. I even had a proper conversation with her the other day, outside the library. She was taking pots of flowers for Maggie and Barbara.'

Geoffrey hadn't seen Maggie in a while. He gathered Stuart wasn't able to take her out much, with Barbara being so ill. The man looked exhausted. What would happen to Maggie? Might he have to put her in a care home if…when…?

Then something else surfaced that Sharon had said, way back. What was it? About Maggie maybe knowing Alice's bones would be there by the stream. Was she perhaps there when Alice died? Who took Maggie out for walks in those days? He had no idea.

# FORTY-NINE
# STUART'S LIFE FALLS APART
## 2018

The backache that started a couple of years earlier became worse and was eventually found to be due to a return of Barbara's breast cancer. Both she and Stuart were devastated. She'd been discharged from hospital follow-up in 1977, five years after her treatment. They both thought she was cured. To be told that it was not uncommon for recurrence to declare itself decades later made her feel they'd not been honest. Though she couldn't blame the doctors she was seeing now, they were all new, and very sympathetic. Stuart was glad she hadn't lived all these years knowing about this possibility.

Her health slowly deteriorated, and now Barbara had become too weak to manage the stairs. Stuart made a bedroom for her on the ground floor, next to the kitchen, removing the dining table and chairs. He got a man in to install an en suite. He put her spider plant on the windowsill, and her paperweight with the dandelion clock inside, where any sunlight would catch it. Their wedding photograph went on the dresser, with the one of her with new-born Maggie in her arms, a smile of total delight and love on her face. A third picture was also of Maggie, aged five, when she finally managed to walk. He paused to look at that one. He remembered that Barbara, out of the shot, was holding her hand. Maggie stood on the hearth mat, wearing a pink gingham dress with smocking across the top, and an immense toothy grin.

As he finished preparing the room for her, doing his best to make it nice, he was fighting the impulse to throw something. He picked up the paperweight, tossed it from hand to hand, frowning at the window he'd just polished, imagining the sound as it shattered. Then he made himself put it down again. Cruel, what was happening to her. Unfair. 'Must keep calm,' he said out loud, clenching and unclenching his fists.

Stuart often sat with his wife. He'd discovered J B Priestley's stories, originally written as radio plays, were perfect for reading out loud. He read them to her as she lay quietly suffering, floating in and out of consciousness.

And he talked to her. 'Geoffrey came to the council meeting in quite a rage. His mother had asked him to sort out a problem with her chimney. The man was supposed to come when Geoffrey was there, but he arrived unannounced, made a mess as he poked about doing his assessment, and said he'd get back to her with the quote, which he thought would be around three thousand. She was horrified – she's no idea of what such things cost – and told him to go away, he was trying to steal her savings, and she knew better.'

Barbara moved a bit, trying to sit up. Stuart stood, helped her lean forwards, re-arranged her pillows. With his arm under her shoulder as he'd been taught, he supported her upper body while she pushed herself backwards with her heels. She looked exhausted for a few moments, then nodded for him to continue.

He smiled at her. 'Geoffrey had spent quite a bit of time asking around, and the chimney chap came strongly recommended, but she wasn't going to have him in her house again. Geoffrey wouldn't be able to pretend his bill was a few hundred anyway. But that wasn't what had really upset him. He phoned the man to apologise and was told what his mother had actually said. Which was something like, "You godless, ignorant people think you can prey on old ladies, make money out of us to finance your gilded mosques and your violence, help raise your terrorist sons. Go back home and take your stinking food, and your bejewelled relatives on benefit." The man has lived his whole life here. He isn't even a Moslem.'

Barbara smiled wanly. 'Poor man… What's wrong with her chimney?' but she was asleep before Stuart could reply.

He struggled to find food she could manage. Fruit yoghurts were good for a while but the flavours, one by one, became unpleasant to her. Scrambled egg was alright, but then she vomited one time after eating it and the smell of eggs became nauseating. She could drink – cranberry juice then elderflower cordial, now cold, sweet mint tea.

When she had a better spell, they often talked about Maggie. Barbara worried about her even though Stuart had coped with their daughter on his own in the past, and she went to a day centre now, with others there to help look after her.

'I know it was me determined to keep her at home. Not have her moved to residential care. They warned us…' She drifted off.

Stuart sighed. They'd talked about this so many times. He knew he'd put Maggie in a home after Barbara was gone. After all, he was seventy now. But he wasn't going to tell her what he envisaged.


One day, in an alert interlude when she was quiet and sad, her voice soft, she said, 'You know, I blame myself for how she is.'

'No, no. We've been through this…'

She put her hand on his to stop him. 'I want to tell you. I've never really told you why. There were things that happened when I was a girl, that damaged me and, I think, made Maggie how she is.'

He was suddenly chilled. She looked for her beaker and he held it for her as she drank.

'We had a gardener, for the garden at the big house in Gerrard's Cross.'

'That was a lovely place.' She didn't seem to hear him. She was aeons away, in her past.

'He was a short, wiry man. Strong – he did all the heavy work in the garden and the outside of the house: clearing leaves from the gutters, shovelling snow, chopping wood.' She paused to rest. 'There was always dirt under his nails,' she added dreamily.

Stuart scarcely wanted to ask, but she seemed to need to tell him something important, so he prompted her. 'Something happened?'

She started slightly. 'Oh, yes. Well, I was on my own a lot, as you know. When I was little, I would trail after him for company. I would show him my toys and I'd chat to him, though he didn't talk much to me. I wanted him to be my friend so, as I got older, I tried to be helpful. With the weeding, tying up the plants, little things. I must have been eight or nine when he started to take an interest.'

Stuart couldn't look at her. His hands fumbled with a fold of her duvet cover.

'He began to fondle me, stroke my hair. I was so young, I had no idea there was anything wrong with that. Then one day when we were weeding it started to rain heavily so we went in the shed to shelter. He sat me on a large, upturned pot and said we'd play a game. While we waited for the shower to go through.' Her voice had become husky, and she had to stop for a while and take more sips of water.

Stuart was silent, a sick feeling in his stomach.

She resumed. 'He unzipped his trousers and brought out his... He stroked it. I hadn't seen one before. I wasn't shocked – I didn't know to be shocked. He smiled at me. He stroked it and it swelled up, popped up like a jack-in-the-box. I remember the round end was mauve and slightly shiny, like a baby turnip. He said it needed to be protected from light and would I help? He held my head with one hand and told me to open my mouth and put my tongue out... I was young. I didn't know anything. I let him. You'll know what he did.'

Stuart took out his handkerchief to mop his brow.

She sighed, continued. 'After that he did it lots of times. He called it our 'rain game', though it didn't need a rain shower after the first time. He always took it out of my mouth before he... was finished. I don't recall what he did with... His handkerchief, perhaps.'

Stuart felt powerfully nauseated. Keep calm, he told himself, it's not her you're angry with. His palm hurt where his nails were digging in. 'My poor love.' His voice was a croak. He thought, can't I do better than that? But nothing came to mind that didn't seem completely inadequate. She paused long enough for him to think to ask, forcing himself to speak quietly, 'You said you were damaged. You mean psychologically? You must have been, though I'd never have guessed at something as terrible as this. You're always so sensible, so sane.' He remembered, though, how she hated to have her head touched, how she'd never enjoyed having her hair washed at the hairdressers.

'It wasn't so much that that did the damage. It was what came later. Physical damage. Inside. I must have been nearly eleven when he... He went further...' She stopped and didn't elaborate.

She didn't need to.

'Then I did the eleven plus and got into grammar school. I learnt a lot in the first year there, from the other girls. I learnt that it was wrong, and I told my mother and it stopped; she had the gardener sacked.'

'Didn't she contact the police?'

Barbara paused. 'No, she didn't. When I told her, she said, "Don't tell your father. He'd be angry, and we don't want that. No one must know." She never spoke about it again. I thought it was my fault.' She was exhausted.

Stuart smoothed her hand.

She roused herself to say, with resignation, 'It was a very long time before I understood I was not to blame.'

He watched the small twitches and shivers of her face as she drifted off.

. . .

When she was no longer able to make love to him, after Maggie was diagnosed, he'd not tried to persuade her. Thinking back, perhaps he'd felt guilty, too, about how Maggie was. He was lucky to have married Barbara, lucky to have had sex with a woman at all. Fat lump that he was. And she was kind to him. She found other ways to pleasure him. She'd always been so loving towards him.

He'd known about her lonely childhood and her severe, distant father. Now he saw a terrible glimpse of another, hidden part of her. She probably wouldn't tell him anymore, and he'd not ask. When she woke, would she even remember what she'd said?

These days, Stuart thought, she could no longer see the things around her properly, but he still put a vase of flowers or a pretty shell from their holiday collection, next to her bed. The shells normally lived in the garden, by the bird bath. He remembered he gave some of the nice ones to Alice, all those years ago.

It was a still, foggy Wednesday when she asked him about Alice. He was seated beside her, reading an article in the *Radio Times*. She moved slightly, attracting his attention. He looked up to find her grey eyes focussed on him.

She said, her voice little more than a whisper, 'Stuart, did Maggie know Alice's body would be there?'

He stared at her. 'What?'

'It was as if she knew, wasn't it? She was so upset that morning when she saw the digger working on the stream bank. But how could she have known? If she was there, you must have been there too, since I wasn't. She was always with one of us in those days.' Barbara closed her eyes; she was breathless with the effort she'd made.

Stuart gazed at her, his mouth working, a long-buried memory stirred up by her words. 'Let me make you a drink,' he said, and left the room. In the kitchen he stood, facing the window, his fingers pinching the waistband of his sagging trousers, working along the seam of the fabric. An image surfaced of Alice's limp body, floating upwards from the bottom of a deep pool. He staggered, catching hold of the edge of the sink to support himself. He saw, reflected in the window glass, his contorted face, violet blotches across his pale forehead and cheeks. A cold sweat trickled down his chest, he had a pounding pain in his head. He pushed the image away, filled the kettle, but he had to stop.

His mental picture of Alice came into sharp focus. There was water nearby, she was lying on grass with wildflowers in it, lots of buttercups. Her cotton dress was wet and plastered to her legs. She was all streaked with thin mud, the ribbons in her hair stuck down.

Stuart retched, leant over the sink, heaving. His mind went blank, but then the scene returned and expanded to include little, stocky Maggie, her eyes wide with fear, one fist stuffed in her mouth, drool spilling down her front.

He collapsed onto a chair, his head in his hands. The story, which he must have hidden for years even from himself, unfolded, fragment by awful fragment. He saw willow branches waving in the breeze, downy willow seed floating away. He could smell the meadow, hear the birds chattering. How could he have known this, and not known it? For all these years. Decades. It was the time Barbara was diagnosed, had her breast cut off, wasn't it? He'd suppressed the memory? How could that happen? He couldn't think that possible.

Barbara had asked. Could he tell her? He didn't want to tell her, any more than he had when it all happened. But she'd been so honest with him. How could he refuse? And she was... Dying. She was dying.

Stuart shuddered. He was cold and sweating, hands numb. Pushing himself upright, he turned and walked slowly back to Barbara's bedside. She was unconscious again. He sat down and took her hand in both of his.

Her fingers were moving slightly, as if she was dreaming.

He began, 'I remember we had walked down to the stream,

me, Maggie and Alice. It was a beautiful, warm, sunny afternoon. We sat in the grass and the girls played with the wildflowers. I fell asleep.' He was sobbing quietly as he spoke.

She didn't react. He could tell her what happened, if she stayed asleep.

'When I woke, Alice was dead. Her lovely, little body just limp. Her face all crumpled and dark. Maybe she had one of those heart conditions that children can have? Anyway…' He was silent, struggling with his thoughts. Even though he was sure Barbara was unconscious, he couldn't bring himself to tell the whole truth. 'I must have panicked…' There was a longer pause. He could only just hear his own voice. 'I thought I'd be blamed.'

Barbara sighed in her sleep.

'You had enough grief, going through the chemotherapy.'

Her breaths were so shallow.

'I… I pushed her body into a hole in the bank of the stream.'

Was she still breathing?

'I must have pushed away the memory too.' His tears had made Barbara's hand wet. He dabbed at it carefully with his shirt-sleeve, then gripped hard so that she gasped. She stirred but didn't surface.

Stuart bowed his head, to rest it on the edge of the bed, crying soundlessly. He asked himself, what am I going to do? Now I've remembered, what am I going to do? But he couldn't think about it now. Barbara needed all his time and energy.

# FIFTY
## STUART GRIEVES

After the funeral, Stuart didn't know what to do with himself. He wasn't even able to eat much, though his neighbours tried to encourage him. He fed the donated casseroles to Maggie. People's sympathy didn't help. 'I'm sorry for your loss.' What was he supposed to say?

Geoffrey dropped by, asked how he was getting on.

'I don't know,' Stuart said. 'It doesn't feel real.' He took a sip of the beer Geoffrey had brought. It was going straight to his head. Perhaps that was why he blurted out, 'I'm hallucinating. Seeing her. I woke in the night and was certain it was morning and she was handing me a cup of coffee. All I could think was that we normally have tea in the morning. Then, when I woke up properly, of course she wasn't there. I'm going mad.'

'You're not,' replied Geoffrey, touching his arm. 'My mother had that – seeing him – after my dad died. It's really common. You're not going mad. It's just that you miss her.'

Stuart couldn't help himself. He started to cry. He saw Geoffrey look away, embarrassed, but he couldn't stop. 'I didn't deserve her,' he spluttered. 'She was really good to me. I'd have been such a miserable clod without her.'

'Hey, now. Don't...'

'If it weren't for her...' Maggie, next door, was making

unhappy noises; she must have heard him. He blew his nose.

'Sorry. Thanks. But I'd better go and sort Maggie out.'

No one had offered any help with Maggie. He'd have welcomed some relief from her.

He went into the council office when Maggie was at the day centre, but he couldn't concentrate. He normally looked forward to council activities. Over the years, it had been a good way for him to leave Maggie behind; he'd never stopped being ashamed of her, had he? Was that why he'd become parish councillor in the first place? It was not long after Alice… Oh, God.

Eileen came to the house. He wasn't expecting that. Standing in the doorway, he stared down at her, unable to speak, a spasm of pain grabbing his gut, his eyes blurring. Eileen just silently patted his hand and went away again. He shut the front door and leant on the back of it. His knees gave way and he slid down into a heap on the mat. He couldn't bear to think about Eileen.

Every day, every night, memories of the awful day when Alice died. What he'd told Barbara and all he hadn't.

He shuffled into the sitting room. Maggie was in her big, padded chair, tearing the village newsletter into strips and dropping them around her feet. She stopped the shredding and gazed up at him.

He said, 'You remember that day.'

Her face was blank.

'It was all your fault,' he said angrily.

Her mouth puckered and the grizzling started. Her nostrils filled with snot. Sometimes he simply hated his daughter. He'd been able to hide it from his wife. But now Babs wasn't here…? He knew Maggie would become properly mardy if he didn't comfort her. But he just wanted to smack her. He roughly wiped her nose with a bunch of tissues. She wouldn't even blow when he told her to. 'If I confessed and was put away, at least I'd not have to wipe up your messes.'

Maggie picked up the pages and started ripping again. 'I can't cope with you without Babs. I just can't. And you'll have to go in a home one day. I could have a heart attack tomorrow. Just die. Wouldn't have to feel guilty then.'

Perhaps I should just get it over with, he thought, do away with myself. He shivered. He knew he couldn't cut his wrists or step in front of a train. But he might take pills. There were all those of Barbara's, left over. Maybe tablets and whisky? That might do it. 'What if I got it wrong, though, just made a fool of myself?' And if he were to succeed, who would find his body? Somehow, even hating her as he did now, he couldn't have it be Maggie.

The kind look on Eileen's face when she stood on his step. He pushed the thought away. He muttered, 'Can't confess now. Far too late. What good would it do?' He couldn't imagine walking into a police station. Saying out loud, 'I was there when Alice Mallory died. I want to tell someone about it. Want to explain.' He just couldn't see himself doing that.

But he couldn't get it out of his head either. Waking or sleeping. However it was he'd managed to cover over the recollection, it wouldn't work any longer. 'I have to make myself forget it all, like I did before,' he told his daughter. He could hear his voice was high and strained. He groaned, 'But how?'

Geoffrey dropped in again, bringing a small hamper, saying, 'I thought you mightn't be looking after yourself properly, so I got Liam to put together some tempting treats. Most of it will keep a while, but that little goat's cheese on the top will run away if it's not eaten soon.'

Maggie wouldn't eat smelly cheese.

Stuart took Geoffrey's hand, shook it once, but then didn't let it go. 'I'm going mad.'

Geoffrey squeezed his hand then extracted his fingers and patted Stuart's shoulder. They moved into the house to sit in the armchairs Stuart and Barbara used to occupy when they watched television, before she was ill.

'Have you been able to sleep?' Geoffrey asked.

'Not really. Not properly.' He was afraid to fall asleep; the dreams were terrible.

'Got outside at all?'

'I take Maggie. I've always walked with Maggie.' Though the walks had been short since the funeral.

'You must be missing your wife all the time.'

'Yes. Yes, I do. But that's not the worst of it.' Stuart paused, wondering why he'd said that.

Geoffrey looked at him. 'Maggie alright?'

'About the same. I'm not even certain she knows Barbara's gone. No knowing what she understands.'

Geoffrey said, 'She recognises people, I think? My guess would be that she knows her mother's not here. You'd be able to judge, of course, better than anyone.'

'Mmm,' Stuart conceded. 'She's certainly grim at the moment.' Stopping himself picking at a nail, he glanced up to see Geoffrey had turned in his seat and was looking at him.

Geoffrey went on, 'I've seen Sharon talk to her, and she understands things like, do you want a drink? And I know you can sometimes see a reason why she's upset. If she's wet, for example.'

'Or... The other. Yes.'

Geoffrey directed his gaze outside, through the window. He said, 'Though, looking to make sense of her behaviour, you maybe find a cause that isn't one. I heard she was in a terrible state, that day Alice's remains were found. Almost as if she knew they were there, by the stream.'

Stuart shuddered, watching himself squeeze the fingertips of his left hand with his right, until he noticed he was hurting himself. How could Geoffrey know that? Stuart glanced briefly at him. 'What do you mean?'

Geoffrey shrugged, his face a mask. 'That day the men with the digger found the bones, you were up there with Maggie. She got very upset. You brought her into the office. Sharon looked after her. Maggie was in a state *before* they started excavating.'

'Sharon told you.'

Geoffrey nodded.

'You're right.' In the long silence that followed, Stuart heard a passing motorbike backfire. He said, 'Maggie remembered. All these years.' He lifted his head and looked out of the window, into the distance. He realised he had admitted he was there.

Geoffrey hadn't moved.

Stuart swallowed. 'When Barbara was going... She asked me about it. And I remembered. Since it happened, I must have suppressed the memory. But now I can't get it out of my head.'

Geoffrey gazed at him as if hypnotised.

Stuart could feel his face twitching. He said, 'Alice was at our gate that Saturday afternoon, the day she disappeared. I saw her come up. She was following a kitten.'

'So that's how she came to leave Eileen's garden,' Geoffrey said, almost to himself. He had shifted back in his chair.

'I was just setting off on a little walk with Maggie, so Alice came with us. Alice played with Maggie, like she always did. Among the flowers on the bank. She was always charming with Maggie.

'It was warm in the sun. I was worn out – Barbara was having her chemotherapy then – I fell asleep. I shouldn't have. When I woke, Alice was dead.'

Geoffrey whispered something.

'She'd drowned... I think Maggie may have pushed her.'

Tears welled in Geoffrey's eyes. His knuckles were white where he gripped the armrests.

Stuart felt cold. Sweat was beading his forehead, trickling down his temple and the side of his nose. 'I must have panicked.'

The silence expanded to fill the room.

'I hid her body in the bank, under the water.'

'That's why even the dogs didn't find her,' Geoffrey said in a strangely matter-of-fact voice. Then he gathered himself and looked directly at Stuart. He said, 'You have to go to the police.'

They both sat, looking down at their empty hands.

'I've no choice, now.' Stuart heard his own voice, sounding hollow and desolate.

Geoffrey said, 'Eileen...' and shook his head helplessly.

Stuart stood. He said, 'Well, I've told you now.' He wiped his face with his big, crumpled handkerchief. 'I'll make us some tea.'

# FIFTY-ONE
# ALICE FOLLOWS A KITTEN
## 1972

Hot. Alice pushes away her fringe from where it's stuck to her face. She's playing in the back garden with her stuffed rabbit, Henry, giving him a lesson about bees. He knows about the slugs and snails now.

'Bees are very important. They go to all the flowers to bring them food so that they can make seeds. Henry! Pay attention! Bees are very important. They make honey. You like honey.' There's a blackbird at the back of the flowerbed, throwing leaves about. She knows it's a blackbird, Mummy told her it's the black one with a bright yellow beak.

A speckled grey and white kitten steps through the hedge, scaring the bird, which flies off, calling loudly, to land and bounce on the clothesline.

Alice drops Henry and gets to her feet, moving carefully towards the cat. 'Here, kitty. Here, little one. Come here,' she calls softly. The kitten pauses and gazes at her. Its tail curls and flicks. It turns away up the garden to the path beside the house, past the dustbin. Alice follows.

'Naughty kitty. Don't go. I'll get some milk for you.' The cat slips under the side gate, Alice following, out through the front garden onto the pavement. It runs across the road. Alice checks there's no traffic, like Mummy taught her before she crosses too.

The kitten doesn't look back. It goes down the road, along the lane, round the next corner and then all the way along the back street. Alice wants to stroke the pretty creature, feel its silky fur. She skips along behind it, nearly catches up with it several times, but never quite reaches it. They meet no one until the far end of the village, at Maggie's house. The kitten stops, looks up at the big friendly man, Maggie's dad, then disappears out of sight under the hedge.

## FIFTY-TWO
## STUART TAKES ALICE ON A WALK WITH MAGGIE

Stuart left the house quietly with Maggie, not wanting to disturb Barbara, who had fallen asleep on the bed. The chemotherapy was really taking it out of her. They met Alice at the gate.

'Hello there,' Stuart greeted her. 'What are you doing here, out on your own?'

'There's a kitten,' she said, pointing to the privet, looking disappointed.

Maybe Eileen allowed Alice out alone now that she was seven. Maggie wasn't safe anywhere on her own, but that was different. 'We're just going for a walk. Do you want to come too?'

Maggie beamed and gurgled, waving her fat arms in encouragement.

They went across the road and down the footpath towards the stream, to the open stretch, where there were wildflowers. Stuart stopped and slumped awkwardly down onto the grassy bank. He was weary. Worrying about Barbara, caring for his daughter, trying to keep the business together. Maggie, never one to walk far, collapsed onto her bottom beside him.

Alice picked buttercups and brought them to Maggie. 'Do you like butter?' she asked solemnly as she held a flower under

Maggie's chin to see the yellow glow. She laughed each time, then ran and threw the blossom in the water, watched it float away.

She brought a buttercup to Stuart, chanting, 'Do you like butter?' She peered under his chin to look, seemed dissatisfied.

Perhaps my stubble makes it difficult to see, he thought.

Her head leant on his chest as she craned sideways. 'I don't think you do!' she accused. She looked puzzled and cross. 'I've seen you eat bread and butter. Don't you like it?' she asked, twisting her head round to look up at him, bright and innocent.

'Of course I do,' he replied and he started to tickle her. She laughed into his face, giggled and squirmed to escape. She scrambled away, picked a grass head, rushed back with a big grin to poke the soft fluff of vegetation up his nose. He grabbed her to tickle her again, taking her little body in both his hands and running his fingers up her ribcage and down to her hips, then back again. She screamed in delight.

Stuart realised he had an erection. He rolled away, appalled at himself. This had never happened before. He couldn't believe it was happening. He was sweating profusely. He tried to ignore it, waited for it to subside. But it didn't.

Alice was laughing, had wriggled away, was fussing with Maggie again. Stuart thought, I'm thirty years old and I've not had proper sex in seven years. They can't see if I just... He put a hand down the front of his trousers and grasped his penis. With his back to the girls, he worked frantically, his eyes tightly shut. Moments later he was taking deep breaths, wiping his hand on the grass, appalled, ecstatic, shamed, relieved and exhausted. He lay still, feeling the sun on the side of his face and his ear. He relaxed. He fell asleep.

Stuart was deeply unconscious when the sounds roused him.

Alice was calling, 'Maggie, no. Maggie. Oh…' Or something like that.

There was a scream and a splash.

'What game are they playing?' flitted through his dreams as he slowly came to.

He woke gradually. He rolled over, moved to stand, but when he went to put his weight on it, his right leg was completely numb, and he fell. He struggled up onto one elbow, his attention drawn to Maggie. She was mewling, arms thrashing, in a state. Why was that? He vaguely wondered what had happened. What was the sound that woke him? He looked about. Alice had been with them. But he couldn't see her. He dragged himself towards Maggie, at the water's edge. Willow down drifted through the air and landed on the grass, floated in the stream. Sunlight flashed off the down-spotted surface. He squinted. Was that Alice in the water? His heart missed a beat. It couldn't be her.

But it was. Alice was floating, face down. The current caught the hem of her dress so that it billowed then collapsed. One of her hands was on the surface, clutching a torn willow branch.

Stuart heaved himself up, lumbered into the water. She wasn't struggling at all. In the age before he got to her, he knew he was too late. He dragged her limp body onto the bank. His clumsy attempts to rouse her, have her breathe again, proved useless. He sat, sodden, cradling her little body, paralysed, sobbing. Maggie was making strange, wild sounds, which rose higher and louder. He looked at her. 'What did you do?'

I shouldn't have… I'd never have fallen asleep if I hadn't… Bile filled his mouth. He coughed and spat. If only I'd been able to get to her sooner. He shivered, head pounding, his fingertips tingling and numb.

Maggie must have pushed Alice in. Why would she do that?

What am I going to do? A crushing pain pierced his temples.

Stuart lifted himself, laid Alice down, moved away a little. Her small face was grey and creased, weed and mud stuck to it. He stumbled to his feet. Suddenly angry, he prodded her with a foot. He was shaking, one leg trembling so badly he nearly collapsed again. He wanted to run, but Maggie was there. He wailed, 'This can't… How? I can't…' He thought, I can't go home and inflict this on Barbara, not with the cancer and everything. I just can't.

Abruptly enraged, he picked up Alice's body and threw it, with a strength he didn't know he had, back into the middle of the stream. Maggie screamed. He stood, tears running down his face, watching the current swirl under Alice's thin skirt. A dragonfly paused over a floating strand of hair. He realised she would not sink, she would not disappear out of sight.

There was no one watching. No one had seen them. He waded effortfully back out into the water and picked her body up again, looking about.

From the centre of the stream, he saw a screen of willow branches lift in the breeze to reveal a cavity under the tree, in amongst the roots. Reeds either side. He ploughed over to it, folded Alice's flaccid limbs and carefully tucked her into the space. He pushed her body deep into the hollow, submerging it. Breathing heavily, he stood, assessing, then clambered back up the muddy bank to the path. Nothing could be seen from there apart from a swirl of brown water marking where he had been, and that was already settling. There was a thick bush above the spot. The willow branches flowed smoothly around it, their leaves showing white where they were caught by the wind.

Maggie was quiet now. She sat staring down at the grass between her sprawled legs. Her hair was matted to her forehead in damp curls. Mucus, bits of grass and soil were smeared across her reddened face. She hiccoughed.

He squatted down beside her. 'There now, Maggie. There now.'

Her expression was blank, but the small noises she made, and the way she twisted her body to and fro, told him she was utterly miserable. Like she got when she was ill. He took out his wet handkerchief and cleaned her, struggling to unfurl her fingers, tightly balled into fists. He knelt by Maggie in a stupor, he'd no idea how long, eventually roused by the sound of a car passing on the distant road.

'I should pull her out again,' he said to Maggie, now dozing. 'I should go to the police.' But then he thought of what he would have to say, imagined the sentences unfurling.

'My daughter, who doesn't understand much of anything, pushed Alice into the brook and she drowned.'

'And where were you, sir, when this happened?'

'Well, I was there, but I was asleep.'

'You were with two young girls, by a watercourse, and you fell asleep?'

'I feel so guilty. I woke up but couldn't get to her in time. I fell over, my leg had gone dead.'

'No one else around? No one to help you? No witnesses? So we only have your word for it. As I understand it, your daughter can't talk. Can't defend herself. Convenient, that, if it was you who drowned Alice. After whatever else you did.'

Stuart knew he couldn't blame Maggie anyway. Whatever she might have done, she couldn't have meant to. She hadn't the capacity to be malicious. And it was his fault for not being there to intervene.

They wouldn't believe him anyway.

He thought of what this would do to Barbara, depending on him, already devastated by the cancer. Her whole world centred on Maggie. She couldn't bear this. And telling anyone wouldn't bring Alice back. Nothing could do that. Best to just keep quiet. No one had seen them. No one knew that Alice went with them. He saw Eileen in his mind's eye, then dismissed the image with a sob.

Stuart struggled to his feet, waking Maggie as he did so. The stream had settled. All appeared peaceful. Holding one hand, he persuaded Maggie to stand. She was unsteady for a bit, then found her clumsy rhythm and they made their way back. His wet clothes rubbed between his thighs, stuck to his legs. They would attract attention. He thought he'd say he fell in the brook, make himself look even more of a lummox than usual. But he didn't have to, there was nobody to notice the mess he was in. He checked all around as they trudged, he could hardly believe it.

He kept thinking he should go back and pull the body out. Just leave it in the water to be found later. No one had seen them. No one knew they'd been there. There was nothing to connect him. But someone could appear at any time. So he didn't go back.

By the time they re-entered the village, Stuart had put together a story for Barbara. He was dozing in the sunshine and woke after a bad dream feeling guilty – because something bad could have happened to Maggie, while he slept. He shouldn't have let himself fall asleep. Then he was scrambling up to make sure she was alright and found he had a dead leg. And he'd ended up in the water, like an idiot.

In the event, he didn't have to tell the tale. Barbara was out when they reached the house, she'd probably taken a stroll herself. She'd told him it could ease the nausea. His mind vacant, he removed his wet clothes, put them with others to run in the machine, rinsed his shoes and left them in the outhouse to dry. When his wife got home, he mumbled something about going down with a cold and took himself off to bed, where he fell instantly unconscious.

# FIFTY-THREE
## SHARON MEETS ADAM
### 2018

Sharon met Adam at the small ceremony at the estate, to mark the completion of the first house, its opening as a show home. The pocket park would soon be lovely, the silver birch trees were growing well. She thought of them as Alice's. Would the spot always be tinged, for her, with sadness? Though not like it must be for Eileen. She'd heard that Eileen had been seen up there. It didn't bear thinking about.

She was surprised that Jack brought his wife and son to the site that day. Remembering what Jack had said about the plans, in the early days, perhaps the boss wasn't the only one taking a personal interest. Jack introduced his family. Adam had his father's muscular build, moved with a confidence that made her tingle.

He said, his eyes smiling, 'I've heard about you. You work in the parish council office, don't you?'

'And you're a trainee astronaut, I suppose.' She grinned at him.

'No. I'm a famous rock star. You didn't recognise me?'

For a split second she thought he was serious, then spotted the twinkle in his eye.

The action began and they turned to face forwards. She couldn't wipe the smile off her face and, when she snuck a look sideways, nor could he. Though when the speech was done and the ribbon cut, he went off with his parents.

Sharon took a look at the show house when the rush had died down. Adam appeared at her elbow. So was he interested in the décor?

He must have read her mind. 'Dad said these were unusually well planned and executed. I thought I'd check it out for myself.'

'You in the same business, then?'

'Me? No...'

He really didn't want to say what he did. Wonder why not. Nothing to lose by asking. 'So, what *do* you do?'

He looked away. 'I'm at uni,' he said. 'Nottingham.'

'At uni' was vague. But he probably didn't mean he was a cleaner, he'd be a student of some kind. He surely wasn't ashamed of that. If he was an undergrad, though, that'd make him younger than her. She shrugged and turned away.

'Fancy a coffee?'

Turning back, she looked him over and he blushed. Sweet! 'Maybe. But you have to answer my question properly.' She gazed archly at him. But then he looked really crestfallen, and she had to relent. She grinned. 'You know what I do for a living, it's only fair you tell me yours.'

'I'm a postdoc.' He was looking at his feet.

Research fellow, she knew about them. Janice's brother was one. She'd talked about how clever he was, how much study it took. Sharon was less impressed when she met him, he seemed a bit of a drip. But that would make Adam over twenty-three. She perked up. 'Oh yes?' She circled one hand, demanding more information, smiling at him.

He groaned. 'Well if I must, but you won't like it. I'm studying male contraceptive drugs. Chemistry degree before, now sponsored by Astra Zeneca.'

She laughed at him. 'Can't see anything wrong with that. Useful, I'd say. Particularly when the world's full to overflowing.' A sudden image of Geoffrey brought her to a halt. 'Remind me, does that involve teaching?'

'Some. Tutorials and the odd lecture.'

She cocked her head at him. Just 'cos Geoffrey droned on at every opportunity didn't mean this one would.

'Coffee, then?' he asked.

'Okay,' she said. 'But the only caff in the village belongs to the church, the coffee's instant, and I wouldn't be seen dead in there.'

'Wistow do?'

The place at Wistow did a magic apple, almond and apricot cake. 'That'd do nicely.'

He had an original Beetle. Must have a sense of humour, Sharon thought, feeling encouraged. As he held the door for her to get in, she was glad she was wearing skinny jeans and her best trainers.

Over the coffee, they found plenty to talk about. She told him about her OU course. He laughingly told her how, alongside the physiology and pharmacology he was studying, he was learning psychology.

'You'll probably know how some blokes hate the idea of the snip. Seem to confuse it with castration, think it'll affect their virility. But it's even worse with a male contraceptive pill. Much of it irrational, but that just makes it more difficult. Women put up with quite bad side effects with the first versions of their pill. But then they had a powerful incentive – it's them that get pregnant.'

Sharon nodded.

'I keep dreaming up mad marketing slogans.

"*Already got two kids and fancy a motorbike?*"

"*If she doesn't get pregnant, you could use your money to learn to fly a helicopter.*"

"*Want that delicious, bareback ride, without the risk of getting caught out?*"'

Sharon grabbed his arm, spluttering; there were people at the nearby tables. And they'd only just met. Though she supposed, if this was his day-to-day work, he was used to chatting so boldly.

'Sorry. Forgot.' He was blushing again. 'Better change the

subject.' But he seemed too embarrassed to think of anything to say.

Sharon said, 'Your dad must have told you about the hold-up with building the estate, when the little girl's remains were found?' Probably not a good topic, either, but having been up there, her head was full of it all again.

'Yes. I'd never seen the old lady, her mother, until last week. I'd borrowed Dad's car and came to pick him up, saw her wandering down the village main street. Knew it was her, from Dad's description. Talking to herself. Counting. Can't imagine how anyone recovers from such a...' He shook himself, picked up his phone. 'Fancy a film?' he said.

Moving on, then. 'Maybe. What's on?'

# FIFTY-FOUR
# GEOFFREY INTRODUCES LIAM TO HIS MOTHER

'Mother, this is Liam.'
Geoffrey hadn't imagined that Stuart's appalling confession would make him want to be honest with his mother, but it had. And, when he thought about it, what could she possibly do or say that would be so awful? Though he found he was very nervous.

'How do you do?' she said, proffering a hand. Her tone wasn't the disapproving, over-polite one she often adopted.

Liam brought out a bouquet of flowers from behind his back. Posh ones, from M&S, Geoffrey noticed. He wasn't expecting that. Liam must have hidden them in the boot as he drove them both over. 'Geoffrey said you like roses, Mrs Johns. I hope the colour's alright. He couldn't tell me the colour scheme of your sitting room.'

So that was what that strange conversation was about.

'No,' she said smiling. 'He's not one for noticing such things.'

'He just about manages to co-ordinate his clothes,' Liam punched him gently on the arm.

Geoffrey did not like being treated like a child but bit his tongue.

Mrs Johns led them into her sitting room. He saw Liam's eyes skim the dull, old furniture and furnishings. Geoffrey thought, any colour flower would do against this sea of brown. Perhaps that was why he hadn't been able to describe the room, it was too dreadful. It wasn't true that he was indifferent to how things looked. He daren't catch Liam's eye. He was waiting for his mother to bring out her sweet sherry, knew it would be ready in the kitchen, on a small tray, in that horrible cut-glass decanter, with a prim bowl of raisins and raw peanuts. He was hoping Liam wouldn't say what he thought when he tasted the sherry. But then things took an unexpected turn.

Liam said, 'I know Geoffrey told you we'd just drop in, early evening, for a short while. But I was really hoping I could persuade you to do me a favour.' He'd taken her by the elbow, steered her towards the window. 'What a lovely array of flowers out there. I am impressed. Of course, Geoffrey must have got his talent with plants from you. I should have known.'

Was his mother simpering? Good grief. Of course, Liam knew it was Geoffrey who looked after the garden.

Liam kept his back firmly towards Geoffrey.

'Lampeters – that's my restaurant, you know – has been asked to do the wedding breakfast for,' he dropped his voice so that Geoffrey couldn't hear the names.

'Oh!' she replied. 'That's wonderful! What a feather in your cap!'

She was clearly very impressed. What names had he picked for this outrageous lie?

'It's all very hush-hush. They don't want any press coverage. Nothing. It's already a nightmare. But I wondered if you could help. I need a very discreet, discerning person to try the menu. Could I possibly drag you away right now? You and Geoffrey both, of course. Though he'll eat anything, I can't rely on his assessment.'

She coloured with pleasure. He'd never seen her do that before. She said, 'Well, I've a chop ready for my dinner, but I suppose I could keep it in the 'fridge and have it tomorrow. If it would help.'

Liam gave Geoffrey a wicked glance. 'That's wonderful. Thank you so much. Let me put these roses in a vase and we can be off. Incidentally, that's a lovely outfit, perfect for eating out.'

Outrageous! Liam wasn't even going to have to suffer the sherry. He had charmed her perfectly. Had her eating out of his hand – literally. Geoffrey couldn't help but smile. All these years… Rather belatedly, he registered Liam's comment about his mother's outfit, and looked properly at her. Not the tweed skirt, twin set and pearls she usually wore for visitors. The pearls were there, it was true, but they looked rather different against a pale blue sheath dress, probably linen, with a matching jacket which had silver piping and mother-of-pearl buttons. He'd not seen it before. New shoes as well, perhaps. And she'd had her hair done.

She said, 'I presume yours is the expensive kitchen equipment at the cottage. I didn't think it could be Geoffrey's. Does he ever cook for you? Can he cook?'

Liam just smiled.

'You must have worked so hard to help him recover from the blow to his head. Thank you. It would have been such a worry for me if you hadn't been there.'

So, she'd known for ages. Geoffrey was stunned. Flabbergasted, as his father used to say.

# FIFTY-FIVE
## EILEEN

There's a knock at her door. That'll be Geoffrey, come for tea. She can ask him about the table.

He has helped so much in the last year. Would she have gone to the pond on the estate if it hadn't been for him? He was right, though, it helped to visit. It was his idea to bury something of Alice's there. Eileen chose Pippa, the little polar bear. Threadbare, tufts of stuffing poking through the thinnest patches, only one eye remaining. Geoffrey dug a hole. He found a rock from somewhere, to go on top. Eileen likes to think of the worms wriggling through the old bear.

Geoffrey gives her a hug and asks, 'What have you been up to?'

'I went for a wander in the sunshine. Not many birds to see, they'll be moulting now that the youngsters have fledged and can fend for themselves.'

Geoffrey nods as he hangs his jacket on a hook in the hall.

'Those tiny zip-lock bags were under the hedge behind the church again.'

Geoffrey pauses, sniffing the air.

Eileen says, 'Yes, you're right. I smelt it the minute I came home. I wasn't sure it was real until I found the smoking wood. If something strange happens, I always worry I might be getting ill again.'

He looks concerned.

She puts her hand on his arm to reassure him. 'It's alright, nothing too dreadful, though the smell is lingering. Let me show you.'

She leads him upstairs, hesitating, as she always does, outside the room that used to be Alice's, where she keeps her sewing things. The smell is stronger inside, the black scorch mark the first thing to see.

She points to the new magnifier, on its little stand, which she's moved to a shelf, where the sun can no longer shine through it.

'To help me thread the needle,' she says, waving at the sewing machine on the pine table. 'But I didn't think...' She strokes the honey-coloured waxed wood next to the burn. 'I'm fond of this table. It's older than me. My great aunt gave it to my mother as a wedding present.'

'It's right in the middle, you can't easily hide it under your boxes and baskets.' Geoffrey is looking at the big glass jar half full of buttons. 'That looks like an old-fashioned sweetie jar, with all the colours inside.'

Eileen smiles. 'It was a sweet jar.' She pauses, 'I thought, maybe, turn the table round?'

'Don't you use the drawer, then?'

'Not often.'

He glances at her. Perhaps he notices the catch in her voice.

She can feel a tear coming.

He finds a tissue for her to dab her face. 'Is there something you want to talk about?' he asks.

She sighs and replies, 'Let me show you.'

The opened drawer reveals scraps, bits and pieces. She hands him a postcard of the beach huts at Southwold. She says, 'I kept this for Alice, she loved the bright, simple colours... I've never seen the sea.' She passes him a card, showing the lavender fields of Norfolk. 'My last birthday card from Ena. I've not been there, either.' A bundle of letters, tied with a ribbon, is put to one side. 'Letters that people sent when I was in hospital, after Alice...'

'Went missing.'

'Yes.' She pauses for a while. 'I didn't read them until months later. I read them again today. Freda said she was praying for me. Barbara told me Maggie was miserable, she must have thought she was missing Alice.' Eileen hopes Barbara never knew that her husband hid Alice's body.

Geoffrey sighs and runs his fingers through his hair.

'There are all sorts of mementos I'd forgotten about.' She points. 'Buckles from a pair of shoes, a favourite when I was small.' Eileen brings out a crumpled slip of paper. 'This is a bus ticket.' She turns it over. 'That's an old phone number.'

'Five digits.' Geoffrey seems to know to hold it carefully. 'That's a long time ago.'

'Alice's father was called Callum.' She smiles at the thought of him. 'He was a stand-in bus conductor for a while, on my route to work. He never knew he had a daughter. At first, I would wonder should I try to contact him. But then, after, I thought, he has been spared all that grief.'

Geoffrey folds her in his arms and hugs her, his chin resting on the top of her head.

Muffled in his embrace, Eileen says, 'You're the first person to hear his name.'

Geoffrey releases her and stands back, gazing, his hands on her shoulders.

He does that, she thinks, when he imagines I might fall over. She smiles.

'I suppose I do want to be able to open the drawer,' she says.

He grins. 'We'll have to get it repaired properly, then. Have the burnt bit cut out and matching old wood grafted in. It'll need a specialist carpenter. Shall I see who I can find? I remember Sharon mentioning someone.'

'Thank you.' She squeezes his hand, then tidies the bits away, tucking the bus ticket under a pin-box. It holds a tiny bird's skull, cushioned with cotton wool. A present from Geoffrey.

She had got to know him, with his talk and his gentle enquiries, as they walked together. He cared. And gave her someone to care about, that was it.

'Tea?' she says. 'And I have a gift for you. Nothing to do with the table.'

Geoffrey follows her downstairs.

In the sitting room, she turns to face him. 'The last thing Alice said to me was that she wouldn't come to the shop with me, she was busy teaching her stuffed rabbit, Henry, about slugs and snails.' She hands him a small cardboard box.

Geoffrey swallows hard.

'Open it,' Eileen tells him. 'It won't bite.'

He does as she says. Inside is a glassy thing, the size and shape of a beach pebble. He lifts it out. Embedded inside is a small snail's shell.

'Oh… It's a grove snail, *Cepaea nemoralis*. Look at the colours! What a beauty. Pink, yellow, tiny stripes of white, streaks of dark brown.'

'From my garden,' she says.

'Really? But how did you…?'

'Liam. A customer of his embeds things in resin. Liam thought you would like it.'

There are tears in his eyes. 'Like it?' but there, his words fail him.

'Not like you to be speechless,' she says, smiling.

Made in United States
Cleveland, OH
12 March 2025